Peter Fleming has been teaching and writing professionally his entire adult life. Beginning with journalism and short stories at Brock and McMaster Universities, he moved into professional free-lance journalism and writing book and restaurant reviews for local Hamilton publications, as well as joining the creative team at Multi Media Techniques, a boutique advertising agency. Recently retired from teaching, Peter is a regular contributor of essays, stories and memoirs to *The Hamilton Spectator's* on-line community platform. He lives in Hamilton Ontario.

I very much feel the need to thank Tom Hogue, editor and risk taker, encourager and the voice of reason – a friend and a brother – without whom these stories would not exist. Long may you run, Tom.

This book is dedicated to my mother, Olive Isobel Fleming, and to the memory of a good man, my father, Joseph Eric Fleming.

Peter Fleming

An Irish Tale and Other Stories

Copyright © Peter Fleming (2017)

The right of Peter Fleming to be identified as author of this work has been asserted by him in accordance with section 77 and 78 of the Copyright, Designs and Patents Act 1988.

All rights reserved. No part of this publication may be reproduced, stored in a retrieval system, or transmitted in any form or by any means, electronic, mechanical, photocopying, recording, or otherwise, without the prior permission of the publishers.

Any person who commits any unauthorized act in relation to this publication may be liable to criminal prosecution and civil claims for damages.

A CIP catalogue record for this title is available from the British Library.

ISBN 9781786129277 (Paperback)
ISBN 9781786129284 (Hardback)
ISBN 9781786129291 (eBook)

www.austinmacauley.com

First Published (2017)
Austin Macauley Publishers Ltd.
25 Canada Square
Canary Wharf
London
E14 5LQ

"I am the boy
That can enjoy
Invisibility."

Ulysses

I

Not long after my father's death I wrote an account of the events leading up to it, an account which in due course appeared in print under the title "Long Ride Up." My sister Shona sent it via email link to our relatives in both Canada and Ireland, and that was how it came about that I received a surprise message one day from my uncle Conrad – my father's younger brother – who wanted to know what more I could add to the sorry tale, and which of the many recordings of Beethoven's Violin Concerto in D – which I'd referenced in the story – I would recommend, since he'd never had his brother's ear for classical music but was eager to learn. I was glad to oblige him with a recommendation – I now possessed two interpretations, to choose between – and to ask in turn what he could tell me about my father as a boy, bout *his* father (or rather their father) and what their lives had been like during the mythical time before I was born. What Ireland had been like. What the *world* had been like. Thus began an exchange of historical findings, field notes and love letters, and I must admit it was a gratifying thing – this computerised 21st century proximity to the closest living blood-relative of a man who, it was only now beginning to sink in, I would never see or converse with again.

Uncle Conrad and I were as close as nephew and uncle can get, I suppose, who are separated by an obstacle the size of the Atlantic Ocean. Growing up I'd been back and forth to Ireland many times, and to each visit a handful of fleeting recollections of my good-natured uncle and his nervous, flighty wife were attached – though when I reached an age to make my own decisions the number of trips tailed off considerably, to my parents' disappointment. Less frequent were my uncle's visits to Canada, thought he came often enough, on holiday, and it was always a pleasure to see him. I recall on one of these visits I took both him and my dad to The Gate of India for lunch. Indian cuisine was newly arrived in Canada, though it had been popular in Ireland for a while, and my uncle was a big fan, although my father – whose default position always seemed to be mistrust and even contempt for untried experiences – was less enthusiastic. Even so, he soon changed his tune and the afternoon turned into a grand feast of beef, shrimp and lamb curries, naan, tandoori chicken and basmati rice, all washed down with several bottles of chilled white wine – a feast which, sadly, put both my uncle and my dad into matching coma-like states for the next three days. A terrific time was had by all.

My father and uncle didn't much resemble each other – Conrad was taller and trimmer – though they both possessed the same thick, wavy hair I inherited, as well as the Crowley weak eyesight. My uncle spoke in the same lyrical northern accent which decades of living in Canada had failed to erase from my father's tongue, although in my uncle's mouth it seemed to come more naturally, as though my father were consciously deploying his accent to further an argument in court. In his emails my uncle reminisced about growing up in Belfast with a fierce, older brother who, from time to time, was called upon to fight off the tougher bullies at Methody Grammar school on his behalf, or of their gruff, uncommunicative father – my grandfather, from whom my uncle had inherited his height – an officer of the Royal Ulster Constabulary who never seemed to have a word for his children which wasn't a reprimand, or a criticism. The familiarity of that revelation saddened me a little. While growing up my own father had had little patience for the kinds of spontaneous displays of affection which, the passing of time would reveal, were more the rule than the exception I'd ever dared imagine. Most fathers liked their children, and enjoyed their company! That came as a surprise to me.

And what about the war? I wondered aloud via cyberspace one time. Both my father and uncle were of an age when they might have fought in it, yet mysteriously, neither of them had. I knew Ireland was not sealed off from the larger events of the world – my mother told tales of the times when, as a little girl, she and her siblings had been whisked away to the countryside to avoid Nazi aggression against Belfast's shipyards. And more personally, up in our nana's attic on Orby Road, my sister and I had discovered a cache of long-forgotten treasures from the Great War – the First World War – more than forty years earlier. There were bits of ancient uniforms, field fatigues and olive-green jackets of some rough, thick material, decorated with swatches and rank insignia long since faded, even rows of medals, though we couldn't have identified them as such. There were also old boots, packs of playing cards, tins with no labels and helmets of a sort, flatter and not as sporting as those the dashing soldiers wore on *The Rat Patrol*, on television. Strangest of all, there was a box covered in grime, within which we found a half-dozen canvas and rubber gas-masks of all sizes, some small enough to fit even a child, though disfigured with ancient layers of filth and some other unspeakable hideousness, that clung to them like ectoplasm on a malevolent spirit. Shona and I knew better than to try them on for size, and today I find myself wondering whose eyes had stared out from behind those monstrous, thickly-goggled masks, and what might there have been for them to see? Just toys now, however – youthful distractions for the amusement of a more privileged age.

"What are they, Winter?" Shona asked, in a timid whisper.

"They're old."

My name is Winston Crowley, named after a British national hero and an Irish nut, though I can claim kinship to neither. How Winston got "shortened" to Winter is a mystery to me, unless it was meant to cast aspersions on my chilly personality. But chilliness ran in the family, it seems to me. My father and uncle – and countless other young men of their age and nationality – didn't take up arms against the Nazis (my uncle explained via email) for reasons I might have deduced unaided – as proud Irishmen and nationalists during their late teenage years, they operated under the dictum that the enemy of my enemy is my friend, and even though it was far from the accepted attitude, especially in Ulster, which after all is a province of Great Britain, there was a certain satisfaction at the thought of the Germans taking the British down a peg or two. This hardly made these young nationalists Nazi sympathisers – not at all. Remember, these were only boys – teenagers who felt unjustly brought to heel by the British oppressor. And exactly what, and who, the Nazis were destined to become during the months leading up to the war, was as yet unknown to the people of Northern Ireland, or the world in general. My father may not yet even have been familiar with the term 'Nazi,' and if he were, it as yet held none of the horrifying implications it would become associated with as time rolled by. No, these were Germans, first and foremost – Germans who were out to give the British their comeuppance – not Nazis, and where else in the world but Germany was there to be found a more cultured people, of a more noble nature, with a more deserving claim to the laurels of a lasting civilization? This was the land of Beethoven and Hayden after all – of Schiller, Wagner, Goethe, Nietzsche, Heidegger, Spinoza and Immanuel Kant. From their vantage-point in Northern Ireland, this younger generation of which my father and uncle were a part were in no position to see for themselves what the wire services were refusing to broadcast, the growing unrest and anti-Semitism in Germany, the fast solidification of absolute power under one blood-red banner, the nationalist propaganda and evolving brutality in controlling the civilian population. Who was this Adolf Hitler after all, but a hot tempered little scoundrel with a ridiculous moustache, who'd already served time in prison and would again before long, when his fellow Germans came to their senses.

I see that, already, only a few hundred words in, I've broken my cardinal rule and said something which might be construed as badmouthing my old man, who is no longer alive to plead his case, and here I mean not his political views – which in hindsight are easily enough understood – but his lack of human warmth, or whatever combination of characteristics goes into predisposing a man to spontaneously love his children. On this front too – as on the battlefield – I would (on my father's behalf) plead extenuating circumstances. All that he knew of fatherhood he had learned, after all, from his own father, and god knows my grandfather Crowley had been a cold, aloof man – sour of visage under almost every circumstance, and gruff towards one and all – so much so I often wondered if gruffness were a quality inherent in the Irish Presbyterian nature. I remember at a family reunion my uncle Ken telling me the story of an old aunt and uncle of his acquaintance, who, when in the middle of a church service the old man was felled by a stroke, and literally lay dying at the foot of the pew, his wife hissed down scornfully at him, "Get up, Bertie! For the love o' God man, get up! You're making an unseemly spectacle! Bertie, *get up!* It's an embarrassment!" In stitches though I was over my uncle's mimicry, I couldn't help wondering if he hadn't put his finger on a universal truth about the Irish temperament. "Those old Irish gals," he chuckled, shaking his head in wonder at the conclusion of his story. "By God, they could take the starch out of a man!" Aye. That they could. And maybe not just the old gals. My father caught himself on and, from time to time, made large showings of his affection for his family, but it was an effort – this you could tell. Yet as aloof as he appeared in hindsight, it certainly seems now he neither meant nor did any harm, when it came to this business of bringing up children – unless an unusual talent for the telling of tales both tall and true can be construed as evidence of child abuse, which, frankly, I seriously doubt.

    Not that the bringing up of my youthful self was without its problems. My early approach to life—and life's approach to me-- was perhaps a little unorthodox. I somehow managed to elude the Presbyterian curse of the gruffness, probably by feinting stage-left on my mother's side, who were a more cheerful lot, and I was a pretty popular kid, excelling in many areas – music, mathematics, table tennis, gymnastics (I was a whirling dervish on the uneven bars) painting and, eventually, creative writing. Butter wouldn't melt in the mouths of most of my little playmates, but I'd also been befriended by Sir Allen Macnab's three designated Bad Boys (I'll call them Wynken, Blynken and Nod since, unlike myself, they've since grown up to become respectable citizens) and it would be safe to say that between the four of us we raised a little hell. We smoked tobacco.

We evolved sassy tongues. We drank strong drink – often as not a vile concoction blended from the contents of Blynken's father's liquor cabinet. We shoplifted plastic trinkets, candy bars and bubble-gum, before graduating to larger things – the legendary Nod was known to stroll into the Woolco Department Store at James and Fennel Avenue in Hamilton, pushing before him an empty shopping cart, filling the cart with clothing and the latest records by the hundreds, then strolling right back out again without so much as a how's yer granny? It was in this manner that he was later able to feed his addiction to amphetamines and model airplane glue, while the worst I'd done was drink – a habit bad enough which one Saturday afternoon brought the wrath of my father, himself a heavy drinker in those days, down on my head in a most original and, dare I say, Presbyterian way.

I'd discovered I liked drinking at age fifteen – the otherworldly euphoria it brought was a welcome change from my otherwise restless, manic day-to-day adolescent state. It was a pleasant – and by virtue of that a welcome – state to be in, this euphoria, when not up-ended by the pious, hypocritical moralizing of the grown-ups, as though your very moral foundation could be stove in, as effortlessly as alcohol could stove in your liver, or, as I would soon discover, your judgement and common sense. My personal worldly woes – and I need hardly mention that, at that age, a fifteen year old girl loomed large on that sad list – seemed more manageable, not nearly as threatening as in the sober light of day. Acquiring alcohol was no great accomplishment – the cupboard beneath the sink in our family kitchen was stocked with a bewildering variety of bottles, and ancient guzzlers of Baby Duck could be appealed to at the entrance to our local LCBO, if approached in the proper light. My dad by his nature was an outgoing, sociable man, and preferred to do his best drinking at a favourite pub, or better still surrounded by his fellow countrymen at the Irish Canadian Club of Hamilton, of which he was a founding member and where he'd held office for decades. I on the other hand preferred the company of my own thoughts, and so it was while teetering down the stairs from my bedroom that my father, passing on his way up, snapped to red-alert as though by distant gunfire and, eyeing me strangely, dragged me back upstairs by the wrist, to my room, where he quickly discovered the half-empty twelve-ounce 'Mickey' of vodka I'd been tippling away at for the past hour. Such was my naiveté that it hadn't occurred to me alcohol has an unmistakable odour – one my father would have been intimately familiar with.

Oh, Jesus Christ in heaven, saints preserve us! thought I, breaking out in a cold sweat, for my father had threatened to throttle me for less grievous infractions than this. Oh, Jesus Christ Almighty, spare my mortal soul this day, for I have sinned! Yet instead of unleashing the sharper edge of his caustic tongue, my father did something so unexpected it didn't compute at all at first. He sank to my bed with a sigh, both aggrieved and grievously sorrowful, then, clasping his hands between his knees, he slumped forward, his head bowed low and quietly began to cry. As I say, that did not compute at all – this mysterious man whose only purpose for being in my life was to act as a cautionate warning and a scold, was for the first time in my memory visibly upset, and, oddly, I think I felt even worse about that than if he'd pulled his belt from his trousers and given me the hiding he must surely have thought I deserved.

"Son," my dad finally said, raising his streaming eyes to meet my own. "My father--my own father – your grandfather, James – was not a communicative man. In many ways he was… a cold and distant fellow. Growing up I felt I hardly knew him. And when he died – well – you know. It was too late. Too late for us to get to know each other. Too late to change things. To make things better. When your mother and I began having children of our own, first Shona and then you and finally Ben, I made a vow. I vowed I would do a better job by you than my own father had done by us. I vowed I would be a better man, for your sakes but also for my own. I know this may sound silly now, son, but things between a father and a son – are difficult – but they're also important. So very important! Too important not to be taken with the utmost seriousness – while there's time."

I stood there watching him for a while, bewildered and wondering what his intentions were for that goddamn vodka.

"Tell me about him," I finally said. "I was always curious to know more about him, since I hardly remember him at all. What sort of man would you say your father was?"

II

Disembarking at Belfast International Airport, at Aldergrove, the first thing I saw was a construction site which had been boarded off by a high plywood wall. Every inch of the wall was plastered over by rows of identical posters – Marc Bolan, posed on the iconic front cover of his band's latest best-selling album, T. Rex's *The Slider*. Those of a certain age may remember the picture I'm talking about – an ethereal, stylized depiction of this mysterious man-child, against a backdrop of dappled sunshine, slender as a reed, pale as a wraith – turned out in a black wizard's cloak and an enormous top-hat that seemed to droop under the weight of its own portentousness, even as the copious entangled locks of Bolan's cork-screwed hair spilled out from under it, framing the heavy-lidded, delicately-featured young rock-star, his Cupid's bow of a pout as undecipherable as any modern-day Merlin's, but guaranteed to bring fresh masturbatory urgency to the dreams of teenage girls from the misty mountaintops of northern Wales to the tropical sun-drenched shores of southern Italy, and every nation between.

Though not Canadian girls, I thought, the first of many differences great and small I would notice that distinguished Ireland from North America in the year 1975. I'd seen the album kicking around somewhere back home – after all I recognised it now – but I didn't own it, and neither did almost any other teenager living on Canadian soil. Unlike so many of their illustrious predecessors, and as white-hot as they were in Great Britain, and on the continent, T. Rex had made hardly the slightest dent in the markets of the New World – venues which had sold out for concerts by The Who, the Rolling Stones, and especially the Beatles, went half-empty, or worse yet shows were cancelled altogether, such was the indifference to T. Rex's weird blend of power-metal and their goblin-like preoccupation with things ancient, fanciful and occult. God knows why – if ever a boy had been born to be a rock-star it was Marc Bolan – who looked the part so well he might have been clipped from a fan magazine – but T. Rex had been the first major British non-starter in North America since this entire ditsy business of British blues had begun to infest the airwaves, ten years earlier, with the so-called British invasion.

"Who's this young buffoon supposed to be?" my father snorted derisively, as he approached to help me with my luggage. "A bloody warlock?"

I slung my gym-bag – bulging with jeans, tee-shirts and fresh underwear – over my shoulder, and we turned to make the brief walk into Aldergrove's busy little terminal.

"Yes," I said.

"Yes, what, son?"

I smiled at him. "Yes, he's meant to be a bloody warlock."

"Surely you don't–" my father began, then caught himself on. I was here, after all, at his behest, for a special reason. In only a few short days I would be turning twenty – my childhood put behind forever – and my dad had taken it into his head before I moved on to university in September, to take one last stab at mending the rift that had grown between us over the years, in the form of an extended tour through Ireland – just the two of us. So to begin it by slagging a musician who, for all my old man knew, I worshipped as a god, would hardly be a promising beginning. He needn't have worried. I liked T. Rex well enough but I was not likely to take offence at the besmirching of Mr. Marc Abracadabra Bolan's – or *any* rock star's – sacred name. Yet there it was, wasn't it? The old man didn't get it, so without a moment's hesitation he pissed on it from a great height, and operating under the tenet (and in this how much was I being my father's son?) that the enemy of my enemy is my friend, I found myself suppressing the urge to defend this band and its curly-haired prime-mover, even though I couldn't have named more than three songs from their entire output, and not a single tune from *The Slider*.

"Are you hungry, son?"

I smiled and shrugged. "I could eat," I said.

"Aye. Good! I could eat too. We have a grand adventure in front of us, son, a grand adventure! Come, let's get you squared away with the authorities – you'll hardly recognize the place after all these years! Then we'll drive back to town and find a quiet place where we can have a pint, and eat a sandwich or two."

He tentatively put a hand on my shoulder. I smiled over, resisting the urge to pull away. The old scoundrel was full of surprises, and so too was Belfast.

The Belfast of 1975 was not the Belfast I remembered from 1969, which was the last year I'd been there, any more than it was the Belfast of 2015. All the famous landmarks had remained unchanged though – the Lough and the river Lagan still flowed through the Harland and Wolff shipyards, the little shops and markets off the Antrim and Newtownards Roads still bustled with fabric and apparel outlets – the manufacture of linen being an enormous factor in Belfast's industrial base – hardware emporiums abounded, movie theatres and ancient, picturesque pubs with lead-tiled roofs and sawdust on the floors – to sop up the vomit at night, I supposed. There were bookstores, record shops and fish markets aplenty – the markets always with a pleasantly briny smell about them, from that morning's catch a quarter-mile away in the rolling waters of the Atlantic. The old city hall hadn't changed much either, squatting as enduringly in the centre of town as though carved from a mountain-range, while pretty girls in their summer dresses skipped between the flowing traffic, and the double-deckers competed for turning-lanes with canvas-topped lorries, heavy with barrels of Guinness. Horns honked and seagulls cried, wheeling through the air on the lookout for a dropped chip or a bit of battered fish. It felt great to be back – a great time to be here – twenty years old (almost) and bursting with imagination, with rough, animal vitality and good health – walking through the familiar streets, smiling at those pretty lasses, and receiving their smiles in return. Yet some things were obviously different, too. The down town core of the city had been broken up into slices, as of a pie, by what were diplomatically being called 'peace lines,' tall frost-wire fences topped by razor-wire, with a heavily guarded gate every fifty feet or so, through which in order to pass you were obliged to be searched and frisked by a grim-faced cadre of British soldiers, clothed in battle fatigues from head to toe, with SA80 semi-automatic carbines – weapon of choice for the blood-thirsty everywhere – slung over their shoulders. Besides the double-deckers and the delivery trucks – and the unceasing parade of passing Porsches, Audis, BMWs, Mercedes-Benz (Benzes?) even the odd

DeLorean, fresh off the assembly line, and Rolls Royce, for Belfast was a well-heeled little town – there were also truck-loads of newly recruited British soldiers being brought in from the military bases, a few of them with looks in their eyes like they'd been air-dropped into the Syrian foothills. The city may have been flourishing financially, but these were tough times – the Troubles had reached their peak on 'Bloody Friday' in 1972, when the provisional IRA detonated twenty-two bombs right here on the same streets I was skipping along, winking at the lassies, killing eleven people, and the retaliations and counter-retaliations were showing little sign of slowing down. The Europa Hotel, where in a few weeks' time I would meet Michael Palin of Monty Python fame, was a favourite target for nationalist extremists, and was currently so well fenced-in and sentried-off you might have mistaken it for the confines of a prison, or the National Treasury. Little black dots in the sky were all there was to be seen of the military helicopters, bobbing well above the reach of surface-to-air missiles, hovering way up yonder day and night, keeping a close observance on the goings-on far, far below.

While preparing for our 'grand adventure' we lived at my grandmother's house, which I also remembered well from earlier visits – and held reunions there which included both the Crowley and the Adams contingency of the family. Boatloads of cousins came to call – strangers whose uncanny resemblance to me was enough to give me the heebie-jeebies. Over roast lamb and baked potatoes, I found myself wondering – for the umpteenth time – how completely different my life would have been except for that one decision on my father's part, to come to Canada. Or would it? Who could say? Would an Irish upbringing have robbed me of my headstrong ways? Would it – as was the case with my cousins – have turned me into a devout Christian, singing piously away at the hymns of our forefathers, from the pews on a Sunday morning? Bobbing and weaving my way through the old prayers, even while my city was being accosted and disfigured by hostile alien forces? Would I have become one of those mousy little people, in their suits and ties, their hair fluffed and quaffed after the best conservative tradition, all rosy-cheeked smiles and rainbows for their fellow parishioners, or would I have become a casualty of war – wound up a captive rotting to dust in Belfast's notorious Maze prison, where political dissidents like Bobby Sands were held, and where they sometimes starved themselves to death in protest. But no. As capricious fate would have it, unpredictable as a feather on a summer breeze, I had been destined to write about them, not join their ranks, and certainly not the ranks of the true believers either, who, upon hearing of the latest outrage out on the Shankill Road, would mutter a pious 'God help them!' to heaven, rather than do anything about it. I was surprised – even a little charmed – to observe that such a good Christian son was my father he went outside to smoke his cigarettes, in his mother's back yard, hiding amongst the drying laundry and the petunias, so as to shield from her – even after all these years – this pernicious habit of which she would have disapproved. That the old woman was only pretending to be deceived – she was no doddering fool, after all – didn't bring the deception to an end, which I suppose, in their different ways, they were both in need of preserving. Maybe this too was a little understood characteristic of the Irish Presbyterian way – this willingness to collude with your fellows in avoiding and even ignoring unpleasant truths. Even when they're looking you in the eye – like human failings which both the observer and the instigator, for different reasons, has no stomach for acknowledging.

"You know she knows you smoke, right?" I said, striking a match to light first my own cigarette, then my father's.

The old man sighed. "Aye," he said. "At least I assume so. But you know son – well, no. No, I don't suppose you do."

Was that a note of accusation in his voice, mixed in with the defensiveness?

"Would it have been better for you, Dad, do you think, if I'd kept it from you that I'd taken up smoking?"

"It would have been better for me," the old man said, puffing away, "and also for your mother if you'd never taken up smoking in the first place. It's a filthy habit. son. A disgusting habit."

"Well," I laughed. "Then maybe you should have set a better example."

"Don't blame me for your bad habits, Winter!"

Can you actually feel the blood turning cold in your veins? It seemed at that moment, as I flicked my cigarette over the high-fence that separated my grandmother's property from a public soccer pitch, that you could.

"I'm tired. I – it suddenly feels very late," I told my dad wearily. "Jet-lag, I suppose. I'm going to bed."

The next morning I went for a leg-stretch, out through the broad busy avenues of east Belfast, registering as always a faint surprise at the thousands of signs that this was a happy, prosperous land – at least this stretch of it was – until I reached University Avenue – a good thirty minutes from my grandmother's – where I bore south with the intention of revisiting the campus of The Queen's University. University Avenue was bursting with prosperity, and also with evidence of the proximity of a vigorous youth culture. There were fashionable little coffee shops, boutiques and clothing stores lined with racks of bohemian rags; from the open windows of the restaurants the latest pop tunes could be heard – including something by T. Rex which I assumed was from the aforementioned *The Slider*. Youthful buskers of every persuasion, early though it still was, were already beginning to ply their trade. Boys and girls on acoustic guitars, penny-whistles, traditional Irish drums and even the odd harp or two played the old folk songs, or belted out heartfelt renditions of Bob Dylan's latest critique of this acquisitive, fallen world. On several of the broad sidewalks, the nearer I got to the university, large sections had been cordoned off by rope to create concrete canvasses for Queen's more talented art students, who were bent in fierce concentration over their reproductions of famous paintings in multi-coloured chalk. One ambitious young gaffer was even recreating a big section of Michelangelo's fresco on the Sistine chapel, including the ultra-famous *Creation of Man*. The talent on display here was especially noteworthy, since the chalk drawings were created in the open air, unsheltered, and although it was a sunny morning now, Ireland was not known throughout the world for staying sunny too long.

"What when it rains?" I asked the artist, scanning the sky above for omens good or bad.

"Then the chalk runs and I go on to do something else."

"Ah," I laughed. "I see. A sort of existential exercise, then?"

He looked up at me quizzically. "Is it the south yer from?"

"Aye," I told him, then took my leave. I had been conversing with him (and everyone I spoke to on University Avenue) employing an Irish accent, which, while imminently passable in Canadian circles, would not easily fool the more discerning ears all around until I'd had a few more days to iron out a thousand small nuances of rhythm and exact pronunciation, Irish being a hard accent to wrap your gob around. Even after all these years, my mother could spot a fake accent a mile away – regardless how persuasive it might have sounded to me – and with the real thing and nothing else she could pinpoint not only if you were Northern or Southern Irish, but which county you'd been born in, where you went to school, what your father did for a living, and what crockery your ancient granny preferred to serve the afternoon tea. In my father's presence, I dropped this innocent ruse, for fear he'd find something foolish about it, but otherwise I kept it up, in order to spare myself the botheration of having to explain, again and again, what a Canadian boy was doing in Northern Ireland. Not employing the accent, I should add, was also helpful when dealing with the British soldiers at the peace lines, many of whom seemed like they were only looking for some excuse to dragoon you.

I strolled around the university campus, enjoying the fragrant air and listening to the lyrical Irish chatter of the students, boys and girls without a care in the world, as was I, at the beginning of their own great adventures, brimming with intellectual curiosity and enthusiasm for learning. Eventually, I made my way to the Queen's University's bookstore, which even to my untrained eye seemed unusually cluttered with young 'literary' types, and where, I was informed, I'd just missed the opportunity to shake hands with one of Northern Ireland's foremost new poets, Seamus Heaney, who only the moment before had been here in the company of a voluptuous publicist (who I now pictured blowing the Great Poet in a dorm somewhere) signing copies of his latest book. I bought a copy of the book, made the more expensive by the autograph, only ultimately, years later, to misplace it, which is a pity as Seamus Heaney would go on to win the Nobel Prize in Literature. But such is life. The bookstore was filled, as I say, with young *aesthetes* in ragged jeans, berets and loosely-knit baggy Aran sweaters, silk scarves thrown pretentiously around their necks, some even puffing thoughtfully (and ridiculously) on briar pipes or rapier-thin cigarillos, while blathering incessantly about the virtues of Singe, O'Casey, Dylan Thomas and, yes, even the old grandpapa himself, William Butler Yeats. One or two of them caught me on, and attempted to draw me into their conversations, but I had no stomach either then or now for talk of a literary nature, not even after a few stiff drinks, so I smiled and begged off, not willing either to test my accent on them. Instead I meandered further back into the book-lined rooms until I'd arrived at the Queen's Bookstore's vinyl record collection, where to my surprise I discovered (in the import bin, and the more expensive for it) a copy of Neil Young's most recent offering, *Harvest*, which I bought. The irony wasn't lost on me that I'd travelled a quarter way around the world to buy an expensive, imported record by a fellow Canadian, which to boot had been recorded in Nashville. As you can see however, it makes a good story, and I've been dining out on it ever since.

Jet-lag I suppose. Walking back up University Avenue, I found I once again was thinking about my father. That morning we had greeted each other in the tried-and-true Presbyterian manner, both colluding to agree that nothing unpleasant had occurred in the garden the night before, regarding cigarettes, nor at Aldergrove over a young buffoon made up like a bloody warlock, and because we agreed it had never happened, it was erased from reality, the waves of discord quelled in accordance with my father's wishes, so he could continue apace in the secure knowledge all was right with the world. This business of being Colm Crowley's son could be pretty bloody exhausting. And in any case, who would want to live like that? The world around us is the real deal, after all – it didn't look with trepidation to my old man for authentication. It exists in three indifferent dimensions, at least five more scrolled tightly up where they can't be seen, but without which the whole enigmatic enterprise would collapse in a mighty cataclysm. The only thing remotely supernatural about it allows for energy in the form of particles passing through a field of bosons to acquire mass, generating the requisite gravity, as if by magic, to bend space/time into the form it presents today. All without the moral support or approval of Colm Crowley. This is well understood, and there was no point hiding from it in a church, no matter how sublime that edifice might be – the universe is as it is – not the invention of some Michelangelo, with his muscular, scantily-draped God bequeathing life from on high. It was lunacy run amok, but in my father's eyes the greater lunacy lay in the *not* believing, so I accommodated him as best I could, pretending things were other than the way I knew them to be.

While walking up University Avenue, thinking these glum thoughts, I came upon a pub – a big, venerable pile of bricks, all brass-plating and stained-glass windows – so I turned in to buy a pot of tea and look at their lunch menu. Thinking all the while the same question Leopold Bloom had put to himself, when he wondered, in *Ulysses,* if there was any possible way to cross from one side of Dublin to the other, without passing a pub? Bloom doubted it seriously, and I doubted it too, up here in Belfast. I ordered a pint of Harp instead of the tea, and found myself admiring the elaborately carved woodwork along the curved panelling of the bar. The place was well named, 'The Empire', for the woodwork depicted every known British trope and cliché – knights of yore on horseback, brandishing long trailing coloured banners, like royal insignia, and jousting poles; damsels-in-distress in flowing robes and pointed hats, bosoms heaving; fire-breathing dragons; rampant lions and unicorns, insignia both royal and common of vintage, all in a grand parade of pageantry and splendour. *The grand parade*, the thought popped into my head, from a recently-released Genesis album, *of lifeless packaging.* It was while studying the artistry of an armrest, which had been carved into the likeness of a lion's fierce, shaggy head, complete with sceptre and crown, that I was treated by the barman to an instance of the famous Irish wit. "You can stare at him all day, if you want," the barman said, as much to a couple of regulars as to me. "But that's all he does. He just sits there!" Ah – funny! I thought. He just sits there doing nothing. I pulled a fiver from my pocket and, smiling at the barman, tossed it beside my untouched beer, then wheeled to go.

"Wait man, you have change comin'!"

"Keep it."

"Ah, *c'mon man* – it was only a cod! On the house!"

But I was already out the door.

III

By noon of our first day on the road we'd passed through Newry, where my dad took it into his head to cut west across the bottom end of county Down, as far south as you could get and still be in Ulster, in order to stop in on some relatives on his mother's side, but there was no-one home. Even so, my dad wanted to walk around the perimeter of the house – taking a wee stroll down memory lane, I could see by the look in his eyes, the old farm-house obviously newly renovated – my father lost in wistful memory.

"We stayed here once or twice, your uncle Conrad, your aunt Esther and myself," he explained, pushing back the hair that had been tousled by a raging North Atlantic wind. "When we were children. I don't remember why. It was before the war. Perhaps I never knew why."

"When would this have been?" I asked him, lighting a cigarette. "When had they all first lived here?"

"At first? Oh – starting in 1920-21. Perhaps a bit later. Landry, they were called. He was the son of my great-granduncle's daughter, Megan. A beautiful young girl Megan was reputed to be. So said my father from her pictures. When your sister Shona was young my father used to say she resembled Megan. A real Irish rose. In any event his name was Ken–"

"The old great-granduncle you mean? Like uncle Ken?"

"Well, no, son," my old man chuckled. "Sure your uncle Ken is kin on your mother's side. The Adams side. So no, but in any event, he married a country girl named Martha Griffin who had come from good, plain county Antrim stock, even though old Landry was originally from south of the border, in the Republic, not a stone's throw from where we stand right now, really, no great distance. Aye, Megan was reputed to be a true Irish Rose. When they bought the place it was still a working farm – a sheep farm. Also, they raised pigs. I remember one time when I was out here as a boy, and they were preparing the pigs for market, old Ken Landry took his shovel and knocked a gouge into the snout of a pig struggling to escape the gate that set my head to reeling, to observe; to see such violence at such a young age! It was a great shock. The pig knew it was off to meet its maker, you see – a great, slow-moving waddler it was, sure enough – but old Ken taught it the error of its ways. I thought that bloody pig had been sent for, it gushed and squealed so brightly. It was bloody terrifyin,' begum! But it lived to make it to market. And of course after that I never saw it again."

"Yet you don't remember how you all came to be here in the first place?"

"No, I don't," my father admitted. "Like I say, it was before the war and we were all just children."

"Might it have been on account of the Troubles?"

"The Troubles!" my father exclaimed. "Ach sure no. At least I don't think so. There's been no end to the bloody Troubles here in Ulster since before or after the war, and besides we were still on the Ulster side of the border. The Troubles?" My father hunched against the wind to light a cigarette, then straightened up with a look as though perplexed, as though thinking of something for the first time. "No," he continued. "It wouldn't have been on account of the Troubles."

"Your father was an officer in the Royal Ulster Constabulary."

"Yes, that's true, son."

"He couldn't have been too popular with the IRA."

"All this was before the time the IRA was a force to be reckoned with, Winter."

"But you know what I mean? It was guerrilla warfare."

My father smiled, pushing his thinning hair back off his brow.

"Aye," he admitted. "I know what you mean."

We stopped to eat in a little tavern just above Drogheda, in county Louth, having crossed without incident over the border from Ulster into the Republic of Ireland unobserved, except by a flock of sheep who had more important things on their minds. We'd been on the road for the better part of five hours by then – having done a warm-up lap around the little ringlet of towns including Bangor to Donaghadee, where my Aunt Kathleen lived, and as far south as Portaferry before heading back up through Newtownards and Holywood, then setting our sights on a course forever southwards – with little to show for it on the map I'd brought to document the journey. Had we stuck to the main freeway, we'd have been in Dublin by now, but we weren't here to set any land-speed records, and stuck to the hedgerow-lined smaller country roads, which twisted and turned over the hills and dales of Ireland's rural topography – regularly presenting blind turns where head-on collisions with oncoming traffic seemed only a matter of time. With my father behind the wheel of my aunt Esther's Volkswagen Golf – my father had intended to rent a car, but his sister wouldn't hear of it – I found my left leg had gone numb from incessant hard pumping on imaginary brakes, while my dad sped on, cheerfully pointing out small landmarks of geographical or historical interest.

"Let's stop here and eat," he said, pulling into the dusty environs of the tavern. "You go ahead and reconnoitre, while I see what's to be done about parking the car."

"Good," said I, hopping out and limping through the welcoming doors of the King Edward Arms. I thought it odd that a pub would have such a posh pedigree, here in the Republic, but we were only barely across the border, in territory where allegiances, I supposed, were still mixed, and in any case that was to be the least of the surprises.

As is often the case with Irish pubs, this one was boxy and spacious, reminiscent of a pre-regulation size gymnasium, with wooden panelling through and through, the walls cluttered with ancient black and white photographs, the aroma of sawdust and beer filling the air, and the mirrored wall behind the barman glittering with a vast assortment of colourful bottles. The barman himself was muscular enough to be a prize boxer in that smelly gym, and in this vast space, where we two appeared to be the sole inhabitants, he was busying himself with the pouring of half-pints of Guinness beer into full pint glasses.

"And for you, sir?" he looked up, smiling from this inane preoccupation. "Something to drink?"

"A pot of tea, eventually," I told him, smiling. "My father and I are here for our lunch. Do you mind if I ask you, what on earth are you doing?"

The barman had already poured at least thirty uncompleted pints of the dark, frosty brew, heavy glasses sweating shoulder to shoulder on the top of the bar, and even though it was just the two of us – and I'd just ordered tea! – he'd shown no sign of slowing down.

"It's Sunday."

"And?"

He glanced up from the task at hand to look at the clock hung on the wall behind my back. "Give us three minutes," he said, smiling. "And all will be explained."

Even as he said this a bell started chiming out the hour from the steeple of the chapel, across the road; a clean, clear twelve clangs that echoed out over the last bridging point before the River Boyne let out into the Irish Sea, announcing the noon hour, and along with its final echoes the two side-doors of the chapel were flung open both to north and south, and a twin procession of town-folk began streaming forth, some of the older men in morning coats and black derby hats, the younger men in their tweedy Sunday best, womenfolk and children in tow as they made their way towards the road. I watched in charmed astonishment – farmers they looked like, for the most part, though well scrubbed and polished for the service, their children in different states of restless boisterousness – the men turned out in their caps and vests, gold pocket-watches slung elegantly from vest pockets, looking strangely like a tableau from an earlier era – an Edwardian *daguerreotype* of contented simple village life – the women chattering about the price of eggs and milk, while their husbands – with stalks of straw between their teeth – ran out the odds on that week's Gold Cup Race, down in Dublin town. When they reached the road the twin procession divided yet again, with the women turning either up or down the road with children in hand, for to be getting home to start the noon-hour meal, while the men proceeded across the road and through the welcoming doors of the King Edward Arms, where the barman was already topping up the pints he'd started before. Three minutes the barman had allowed, for the great mystery to be dispelled, but ninety seconds was all it took, and when my father walked into the place – looking like he was bearing witness to a miracle of biblical proportion – it was shoulder to shoulder, standing room only, with as cheerful a crowd of contented Irishmen as ever graced a fine summer's day, raising their glasses, lighting cigarettes and pipes, and rolling up their sleeves preparatory to a game of darts or two.

"Well, son," my father exclaimed, astounded, "if I'd known you were preparing a welcoming committee, it'd have worn a better hat!"

"Ach sure, it was nothing," I laughed. "The opportunity arose, and who was I to say no?"

Of course tea was now out of the question – Guinness for the Crowley boys! – though the younger of the two found himself hoping his stomach would forgive him the rude awakening of an unpleasant surprise. It was now also that yet another surprise – though hardly an unexpected one – was revealed. Because we had passed over the border between Ulster and the Republic, our British currency – though not disdained – was no longer to be accepted at face value, but only at the value of its Irish equivalent. Of course my father had foreseen this eventuality, and during the course of our preparations we had both bulked up with Irish pounds – or 'punts' as they were called, appropriately enough, since a good drop-kicking was all I felt they deserved, as it became more apparent just how less valuable they were, and how much more expensive everything was in the south. "Cheer up, son!" my dad cried, while I gloomily did a mental calculation and reckoned as best I could, between beers, just how much this part of our little jaunt would cost us, as compared to the British north. "It's only money!"

An hour and several pints later, the Prince Edward Arms was again deserted, as dramatically as it had filled, the men-folk unwilling to risk incurring the wrath of their wives and mothers, were they to show up late for lunch, and were as quickly out the door as they had entered it, leaving my father and I to drain the last of our glasses then go for a stroll about the village. "Drogheda," my father told me, lighting a cigarette, "was twice besieged during the time of Cromwell and the Irish Confederate wars. Aye. It's hard to believe, son, but a great massacre of Irish Royalist defenders took place right here, where we're standing, their officers summarily executed, every tenth man of the soldiers killed, literally decimated! And the remainder shipped off to a penal colony in Barbados. Strange times, strange times."

"It's a violent and bloody land," I said. "This land we love so well, and call our home."

"It's a land of wilful men with strong ideals, is what it is, son: men who aren't afraid to fight and even die for what they believe."

"I think for my own part, I prefer the Ireland of the poets over the Ireland of the warriors."

"You and me both, Winter, you and me both, though too often are the times a poet must be a warrior as well."

"Aye."

"In St. Peter's Church, just down the way there, son, the severed head of Saint Oliver Plunkett was put on display, after he'd been executed in London in 1681. I'd be interested in seeing if it's still there – rumour has it is. Will you come with, and have a look to see?"

"Ah – no," said I, on the advice of the contents of my belly. "I'll meet you back at the car, in an hour shall we say?"

"A half-hour would be enough time, son."

"Very well then."

Not much later we were back on the coastal road, swerving and dipping through the hills and dales, still in dreaded anticipation of the head-on crunch that seemed but a matter of time in the coming, with nothing but the wind, the hedgerows and the sheep to keep us company – though I dare say we weren't terrible company for each other either. Ireland! Was it any wonder the poets sang so lyrically of her? That the warriors fought so fearlessly on her behalf? At times like these I could easily regret my father's decision, made so long ago, and under circumstances beyond my understanding, to abandon all this bountiful goodness and stake a claim instead in the frozen canyons of the New World – a world whose only claim to his affection was an ancient aunt who had moved there with her husband for unknown reasons, many years before. As the little road dipped and then came up, every now and then we caught a clear view of the Atlantic, bottle-green and foamy in its restless swelling – its tidal machinations – like a great primitive goddess as ferocious as she was beautiful – and I thought how very like the ocean's tidal pull were the forces that determined our paths through this beautiful, ferocious thing called life. There were times when I could even fancy I caught a glimpse of the God whom my father worshipped without doubt or hesitation, smiling out from between the crashing waves, ruefully shaking his head as though mocking my high seriousness, even as the wind howled all around and the sea birds shrieked their baleful poetry. What were the shrivelled dimensions and the mass-imparting fields of cold, hard science when compared to a God who could cause a star to spin on its axis, and the moon to eclipse the sun? Mere parlour games for *dilettantes*, played while stupidly hesitating before the beckoning gates of heaven. Where had I been, after all, when Michelangelo's muscular God had created the heavens and the earth? Absent without official leave, that's where, absent without permission and futilely seeking out the random comings and goings of sub-atomic particles, as they rushed from nowhere to nowhere through the wrong end of an electron microscope.

IV

She came as though in a dream, bathed in emerald and gold, standing somehow both naked and clothed in a gossamer gown of finest manufacture, a damsel in distress from days of yore, a warrior priestess, an enigma – she came as though from some distant land, her banded arms laden with heavenly fruit, her eyes deep wells overflowing with radiant kindness, and unadorned lust. What is it you call yourself? , she asked and I told her my name. And would you suffer your sadness gladly, Winter, she then said, as though it were a blessing, or would you have me lift it from you? Her blonde hair seemed to float around her face, yet fell no further, as though she were suspended in water, her throat long and graceful – her presence alone enough to fill me with rapture. I asked where she had come from? Do you fear, she laughed, I am a plaything sent from afar, by a devil to corrupt your immortal soul? What if I were to show you my true intentions from the shadow-lands of things unseen? Or are you so timid you build temples of dreams to cower within? No devil can undo that which God has done. You are safe, here in my arms, if only you invite me in. Still I hesitated. What was her name? I asked her. What was her name? What was her name? What –

A rapping at my hotel door startled me awake. God damn it, I laughed weakly to myself – what *was* her name?

"Dad?"

"Aye," my father replied. "It's well after nine, Winter, were you planning on having breakfast any time shortly? You must have needed the rest, son. Just now I heard you cry out in your sleep. Were you having a nightmare?"

"A nightmare? No no," I laughed, my erection tangled awkwardly amongst the sheets. "Just the opposite."

"Well then, what do you say, son? Here we are in Dublin's fair city, and opportunity knocks."

"So it does. Give me ten minutes."

"Good."

On the morning we'd arrived (a Monday) in the great capital of the Republic of Ireland, there had been jugglers and buskers in St. Stephen's Green, a large-scale promotional push for the movie *The Rocky Horror Picture Show*, including muscular men (with Irish accents) dressed in silly costumes roaming the streets; the rock band Queen – on the strength of their recently released *A Night at the Opera* – were gearing up to put on a mega-concert in Phoenix Park; an international bicycle race was entering its second day; a big boxing match was scheduled, and rumour had it the deputy Prime Minister of Canada was preparing to chopper in from Buckingham Palace, to preside over a charitable event in support of childhood cancer. All that didn't even include regularly scheduled special events like the Gold Cup, horse racing being a normal part of the fabric of city life. This was a busy place, even on a Monday, this cultured little town.

"Dublin town was founded during the time of the Vikings, did you know that, Winter?"

I did, I told my dad.

"There's enough Viking and Roman bones in these hills to build a ladder to the moon."

I said, sipping tea, "That would be some ladder. A cathedral maybe, would be a better use of the material. Or a hospital."

"It's strange to think, isn't it?"

"Aye. Tell me more about the family, the Landrys and the Crowleys."

"Well, sure the Landrys began their lives in this fair country not so far removed from where we sit right now, and not long after the Norman conquest. That's how far back family legend has it, though with our dim lights we can see but a short way into the past. And of course the Crowleys didn't always reside in the north either."

"Really?"

"Sure you knew that, son."

"No – no, I don't believe I did."

"Both families were itinerant landowners across the way, in county Kildare, in the case of the Landrys, and in the case of the Crowleys further afield in Cavan. Of course in those days if you owned land that made you a farmer – with the few exceptions of them that could make a living at forestry – but farming was the ticket, and that meant the raising of sheep, of pigs, of chickens for their meat and for eggs, and of course, cattle. The sheep was the line of least resistance, you could say, as they needed only to be turned out for the grazing in the hills."

I nodded my head thoughtfully. God knows Ireland had a lot of sheep. You couldn't throw a dart blindfolded anywhere from county Kerry to the Antrim coast without maiming a sheep.

"I remember my own grandfather telling stories of his father's father – he was named James too – who in a great leap of faith bought a herd of calves – well, just eight but it was a great leap of faith, nonetheless. He tended to those calves day and night, watched over them like they were his own children. If any one of them so much as sneezed funny, or belched, day or night it was off straight away to the county vet, for to be seeking advice for what to do, and picking up a bloody prescription. Those calves had the old man in rare form, so they did, so I'm told, so much so his regular work felt the effects of his neglect – nevertheless he kept at them wee cows day and night, petting them, seeing they were warm, well-fed and well tucked in for beddy-byes. For all I know he sang them to sleep with lullabies. And every Sunday, in strict accordance to his Baptist upbringing, it was off to church to be praying to the great God almighty to keep an eye out over them bloody calves, and keep them from harm's way."

"Our family were Baptists back then?"

"Tried and true, son, tried and true. They only became Presbyterians after moving to county Down. So maybe they bet on the wrong pony, because – wouldn't you know it? – one of them wee fellahs comes down sick with the hoof and mouth disease – only the one cow to get sick with it in all of county Kildare! – and the loss of that cow wiped out the entire profit margin. But it gets worse. The whole bloody lot of them cows were soon ordered destroyed by the authorities, as a precaution, and that pretty much brought the old man down in bankruptcy."

"Was this before or after the famine?"

"The great famine is it, son? *An Gorta Mor,* the Irish call it. Ooch it was after, after! No man alive during my lifetime lived to see that, sure, though some came close. But Crowleys and Landrys there would have been at the time, of that there's no doubt, although the great famine didn't really feature strongly in the ways of things for our kinsfolk. In Ireland in those days – and in these days too – there were only two types of people, those who owned the land, and those who worked the land. Which is a polite way of saying Protestants and Catholics, I suppose you could say. Anyway, when along came the famine the owners hunkered down, and weathered the storm, while the workers – well, the workers either starved to death, or made arrangements to get the hell out of bloody Ireland!"

"Aye. And what was it caused you and Mom to make the same abnormal arrangements, if I may be so bold as to ask?"

"Now that's a good question, son, and not an easy one to answer. No, not easy, not at all at all."

Not long after lunch I found myself strolling down Sandymount Strand – my father had wanted to see Christ Church Cathedral and the action in Mountjoy Square, so he'd dropped me off with the promise to reconnoitre at three. It was very much after the manner of a pilgrim that I pulled myself, cursing and muttering, through the same briny, low-tide muck that James Joyce had described Stephen Dedalus pulling himself through, in the 'Proteus' episode of *Ulysses*. We'd driven the remaining few hours, after leaving Drogheda, with only a brief stop at Warrenpoint to enjoy the sunset – a celestial phenomenon that could last hours in Ireland at certain latitudes.

"See that castle over there, son?"

"Aye."

"That's known as Narrow Water Castle, and was built in 1840. Not long ago, a British convoy was ambushed there by the provisional IRA. Eighteen soldiers were killed, the greatest loss of British life attributed to the Troubles. But it's a lovely view, isn't it?" My old man and his lists of British slaughtered! Still, he knew his history. I'd been introduced to the works of James Joyce via my learned dad's bookshelves, where I'd found the Penguin Edition of *Dubliners*, the Chekhovian precision of which – and the keenly drawn understatement – had opened my eyes to the possibility that Irish literature didn't have to be all limericks and plays about drunken lechers. Next came the poems and *A Portrait of the Artist as a Young Man*, which I thought as close to a perfect portrait of Edwardian Society as there was to tell, either British or Irish, as well as a painful snapshot of the life of a public schoolboy. Not unlike young Stephen, I'd had my run-ins with Irish public schools, when I attended Orangefield Grammar school back in the sixties, although unlike Stephen when I found the experience not to my liking, I did something about it, being politely asked to leave the place and never come back after threatening to decapitate four young bullies with an eight-inch Bowie knife, because that's the way we roll in Canada. Like James Joyce, I survived to write down and publish the tale, though I could never hope to hold a candle to the Master, the one and only Joyce, whose portrait was no less true than my own, but told with a compelling intensity of feeling I could never hope to equal. Indeed, I've often worried over the years if my early discovery of the works of Joyce – and especially of *Ulysses* – hadn't done some irreparable harm to my own prose style. *Ulysses* had impressed me through and through, and I suspect it took me a couple of decades to get over it.

Up on the blustery ramparts of the Martello Tower – the Meccan omphalos of the Joycean Universe, where Stephen Dedalus had first stepped forward to greet the dawning of the greatest day in world literature – I came upon a pretty young Australian girl named Rebecca McNamara, whose tomboyish blonde hair and chatty, frank manner reminded me of someone I couldn't quite put my finger on. The wind whipping in off Dublin Bay also whipped her short locks all around her face, as she smiled and, very optimistically, tried to light a cigarette.

"So, have you read the Great Book?" she asked me. As soon as I'd heard her accent I dropped any pretence of sounding Irish. In fact, I'd dropped it even before that, having discovered it was less tedious to explain my Canadianness to anyone who asked, than the fact that I was recently arrived from Northern Ireland. The further south we travelled, the more obvious it got there truly was a great divide here – perhaps not as dramatic as the divide between east and west Germany, but no less real for all that. The Irish of the Republic of Ireland, as far as I could see, were genuinely curious to know what the hell was going on up there, as in, what were we thinking? Sociable, affable and laid back as they were to a man, this business of the Troubles had them genuinely perplexed, and I was the last person to be explaining the ways of the one sort of Irishman to the other. So I dropped the accent – it wasn't useful any more, and besides, this sexy young Kiwi was even further removed from home than I was.

"Every other one, but," I said, not quite accurately. I lit a cigarette and gave it to her, then lit another for myself.

"What's your name?" she asked me.

I told her, and asked if she'd been down on Upper Gardiner Street that morning, since our hotel was there and she looked familiar.

"Just in off the boat this minute, mate!" she laughed, pulling an orange from her pocket. "Fresh from Oz," she added, handing it to me. "I have family expecting me in Cork, in a day or two, but I couldn't resist the temptation to come out here, to see where the great man had set his bleedin' book."

I laughed. "Yes," I said. "A lot of people seem to have had the same idea." The Martello Tower had long since been converted into the James Joyce Tower and Museum, a tourist attraction for literary nerds all over the world, and no less hopping now than any other day of the summer season. It was early days in June just yet, my own birthday was on the 10th, and by Bloomsday – the 16th and the day the events depicted in *Ulysses* take place – this tower would be swamped, as would all the rest of Dublin. When I'd pointed this out to my father, he had insisted that, whatever else we were doing, we should forthwith drop it and drive directly back up (or down? or over?) to Dublin, so that I could be present for the blessed occasion, but I just laughed and reassured him it wouldn't be necessary. That I may have been a literary nerd, but not *that* big a literary nerd. Also, the place would be a literary nut-house.

"You American, mate?" Becky asked me, looking up with a mischievous smile.

"Canadian," I said. "Though that's not really true. I was born in Ireland and raised in Canada. I'm here on a trip around the country with my old man."

"Huh, funny coincidence," she said, taking a final puff then flicking her cigarette out into the sea. "I was born here too, then raised in Oz."

Next (I'm ashamed to admit) I said the single most stupid thing I've ever said to any girl. "Well then," I said. "We're neither of us in Kansas anymore," I said. Yes, you read that right. Guess you could say I was a little tongue-tied.

"Too true, Winston!" Becky laughed, instead of punching me in the nose, as she should have. "Well, I'm off. Thanks for the light. Mind yourself, you don't get trampled under-foot by Fergus's horses out there," she added, nodding towards the sea. Somewhere in Joyce – I couldn't remember where – I remembered with maximum amazement that the Master had likened the crashing Atlantic waves to "Fergus's Brazen Cars" suggesting chariots pulled by horses.

By three o'clock we were back on the road again, my father and I, and leaving Dublin behind – we'd spent two full days there, seeing all we'd wanted to see: all the Joyce landmarks, the Yeats landmarks, the pubs – establishments where the locals had once spit at the mention of Joyce's name, but where the proprietors now hung his likeness with pride; the Book of Kells in the library at Trinity College; the Anna Livia monument; the Custom House, St. Patrick's Cathedral, the University of Dublin, where Joyce had gone to school, and much more. A constant carnival atmosphere seemed to be the fall-back position of all Dublin's citizens, during the summer months – all year around for all I knew! – and in two short days I'd marinated in enough boisterous public revelry to last me a year back in Canada. Yet even so, I didn't want to go. Rebecca Judith McNamara, her full name had turned out to be, Rebecca Judith McNamara, with the full lips, the large eyes, the firm young breasts, the tomboyish mop of wind-swept hair, the wide hips and long, lovely legs beckoning to hold me back, and to hold me down. I found myself thinking I'd be more than willing to abort the rest of this unlikely mission altogether, even if only on the off-chance I might run into her once again.

V

I'd allowed five weeks for this victory lap around the coastal waters of Ireland with my father, and had harboured misgivings about the wisdom of the enterprise from the beginning. Having spent the whole previous year slogging away at part-time work, after school, during the summer and on weekends, pumping gas and doing odd jobs at the Motel California in Ancestor, with a steely work-ethic and raw determination to spare I had scraped together more than enough money not only to pay my tuition, but the residential fees at Brock University – experiences which found their way into my stories, *Welcome to the Motel Pandemonium* and *Entangled*, respectively – so as at last to be out of my childhood home, once and for all, and never again have to live under the confining command of my father. Now he wanted me to put all that in jeopardy, for no better reason than to bask in scenery, beautiful though it was, I'd seen before, on the off-chance there was something to be salvaged of this mythological bond between a father and a son.

"I'll pay for everything," the old man assured me. "It won't cost you a penny of your university money!"

Well yes, I thought. Damn right he would, that went without saying. Even so, I would be beholden to him, and would have lost five weeks' gainful employment. Then I remembered the Saturday afternoon, so long ago, when my father had caught me with the vodka and had sat down and made his tearful confession. That like his own father before him, he had been a cold and distant man, and when he died it would be too late to change things, to make things better. My father wasn't a bad man, he wasn't an evil man, I understood that, even in the heat of adolescence: he was merely an impossible man, or maybe, had found himself in an impossible situation. He expected perfection of himself – or the illusion of perfection – and expected no less from everyone around him. That expectation had been drilled into him as inexorably as his accent, but it was a perfection based on a self-image deeply mired in false information, which for me – even if he didn't see it himself – went a way towards defining everything he had chosen to escape by moving to Canada. A fresh start in a new land, free from the shackles of history, of custom and family tradition – indeed, free from family! – to live untethered from a father's criticisms, and even smoke cigarettes in his own house if that's what he had a mind to do. Maybe that wasn't the final deciding factor, but intuitively I felt certain it played a role.

We continued south until we came to Bray, where, after a brief debate, we decided not to stop but pass through the village, not around it, in case there should be some local excitement – an unannounced concert by Van Morrison was my fond hope: in my father's case the prospect of a bridge being exploded by the IRA – chatting and exchanging stories, all the while, of what we'd seen and heard and experienced in Dublin. I rolled out quite the soliloquy on the subject of the Martello Tower, of all things James Joyce, choosing however – I don't know why – to pass over mention of the guardian angel who had haunted my dreams, and who now haunted my waking life as well, having shown me (as she had promised) her true intentions from the shadow-lands of things unseen. There was no good reason for me not to have mentioned Becky, except that the mental image I had conjured of her was so intense, too fragile to share, as though putting it into words would have shattered it in an instant. But that isn't to say she was ever too far from my mind. As we pressed onwards down the eastern seaboard I found myself dreaming of a fantasy life with her, in the Billabong Territory of Western Australia, where Becky McNamara and I ran naked as feral wombats amongst the shadows of the baobab trees, subsisting on bananas and coconut fronds, toasted nut-brown from stem to stern by the forgiving rays of the Australian sun, on the lookout for crocodiles or worse, our attention to the chirping conversations of the parakeets and lorikeets only interrupted from time to time by the urgent need for regular, thirty- forty- fifty-minute long demonstrations of extravagant, steaming-hot copulation – displays so operatic (and noisy) in their intensity that the very vampire bats, gliding lazily overhead in the dusky twilight of the evening, in search of field-mice or perhaps a plump, juicy koala for dinner, would come screeching to a halt and tumble out of the sky in admiration and awe.

"I must say," my father said, "the ancient Irish were ever a very practical lot when it came to the naming of these wee coastal villages."

"How do you mean?" I asked him.

"A 'bray' in Gaelic just means a hill."

I laughed. "Then all these wee coastal towns should be called Bray."

"In medieval times, Bray was right on the southern border of a strip of the coast known as The Pale, which was ruled by the British directly from Dublin Castle, but they knew they were surrounded on all sides by Gaelic warlords and chieftains who didn't much care for the cut of their jibs, or their ungodly British ways, and made their lives right lively, so that to live beyond the Pale meant to live in the land of the Gaelic chieftains, who would as soon eat yeas as pass the time of day."

"Huh," I said. "Beyond the Pale."

"Cromwell liked to stop here, on his way to Wexford from Dublin, or so the story goes."

"So I guess the good folk living within the Pale had something going for them, after all, if it attracted the likes of Cromwell."

"They have a film studio here," my father laughed, "though I doubt that figured into Cromwell's reasoning. They made that picture with yer man, what's this his name was now? Richard Burton! The Spy Who Came in from the Cold. Did you see that movie?"

"No," I laughed. "I did not."

"Me neither."

This was a mountainous part of Ireland – not that there's so many parts that aren't – and particularly pretty was how the mountains and the turbulent waters conjoined, the shadows of the mountains rippling across the water, while the reflected sunlight off the water shimmered upon the mountains, like the assembled spirits at a ghostly convocation. Bray was so close to Dublin, that its outer reaches were still in county Dublin, and as Dublin had grown and expanded over the years, Bray had become little more than its suburb, but you couldn't have asked for a more charming suburb to live in. On and on we rolled, my aunt Esther's little VW Golf humming away like a contented bumble-bee, with the sun sometimes retreating into hiding, above the shadows of the enormous architecture of the clouds, followed by a light dash of rain just to make sure we were still paying attention. My father had turned on the radio, then further stupefied me by asking what I wanted to hear – a sure sign of the depths of his desire not to wreck the mood we'd established since before even Dublin – though I suspect if I'd found a thrash-metal station, he'd have left me at the kerb, and driven away. Instead he found what appeared to be a classical station, although after listening to it for a while I came to the conclusion their real speciality were the works of Henry Purcell, Bach, Antonio Vivaldi and the great G. F. Handel.

"It's not classical, after all," I said. "It's Baroque."

My father looked over with keen interest. "Oh?" he said. "And does that make such a big difference?"

"Well," I laughed. "It makes a difference of fifty-odd years, which is no mean difference if you were alive at the time."

"You know, son," my father now decided to tell me, "you really are an extraordinarily clever lad. I mean that now! Your mother tells me your grades in school are the best – despite all the part-time work – and that you won awards in mathematics and music. I've seen your work around the house," – by my work he meant my oil paintings – "and I gather you've even taken up the guitar! Those are sterling accomplishments, for a boy your–"

"My paintings are terrible," I muttered, sinking deeper into the leather upholstery of the passenger seat. "And as for my musicianship–"

"But you're still only just young, Winter! And proficiency in these things requires time."

I said nothing, and my silence hung in the air between us like a distant alarm. I didn't like being flattered, or complimented. Such things are distractions from the task at hand, nothing more. I didn't like it from strangers, and I sure didn't like it now. If his generous words were a cynical ploy to earn my affection, or gratitude, my father would have done better to have deployed them when I was six, or eight, or ten, and still naïve enough to be duped – and if genuine? I think I would have needed to respect his opinion on a whole lot of matters, much more than I did, before I could respect his opinion of me. But in a very concrete sense, I can say that my father's *not* being there, with flattering words, when I was a kid, did me an enormous service. What do we work so hard for as children – all children – except the approbation and praise of our parents? Our fathers especially, I would say, in the case of young boys. And at what point do we cease our pursuit of our childish endeavours – no matter what the field – and consider our ambitions fulfilled, except when that approbation and praise has been duly rendered? In this manner, a sort of minimum threshold of required effort-to-congratulations is established, between parents and their children, which for a child to work beyond can only bring a sort of approbation of diminishing returns. So why bother? On the other hand, my father's utter disinterest in even my best efforts guaranteed that no such threshold would ever be established, and how good I got at any one skill, or skill-set, was left entirely up to me, with whatever devices I had to bring to the challenge. To speak of children 'succeeding' or 'failing' is a deceptive paradigm, and a false analogy for something as dynamic as the growth and development of a boy. There are only degrees of success. And with nothing to show me at what point I had reached the threshold, and had succeeded sufficiently, I proceeded to begin to succeed spectacularly.

"We may be in for rain," I suggested tentatively.

"Aye. But we've been here a week now, and the weather's been better than normal."

"Aye. It's been grand. No complaints."

As we continued south of Bray, the prediction was fulfilled, first in the form of a light scattering, but accelerating quickly into a weird, monsoon-like primordial deluge, such as I had never seen before. Neither had my father, judging from the worried look in his eye. "By gum," he said, "this is quite the downpour! I don't think I can drive through it son – the washer-blades can't work fast enough to keep the windows clear!"

"At the top of the next hill, just pull well over," I suggested. "And we'll wait it out."

"Good."

With the coming of this mighty downpour, I'd noticed, the near-constant gusting of the Atlantic wind had subsided to nothing, as though bowing to a superior force of nature, so the lashing rain fell vertically from the sky. 'Raining staircase-rods' was how my mother described such weather and as we awaited its passing, unable to see a thing through the streaming windows, I began forming mental pictures of cars trapped at lower altitudes being lifted in the building rush of run-off, washed away out into the path of Fergus's mighty horses. With no exaggeration I can tell you I've never before or since seen such a deluge. And so we sat there, my father and I, smoking and chatting, listening to the music of Johann Sebastian Bach and Friedrich Handel, dreaming of cars floating out to sea and koalas carried away in the talons of ravenous vampires, and waited out the storm.

Half an hour later, as abruptly as it had begun, the deluge ceased and the sun split the clouds, revealing yet another celestial phenomenon which I can say, without exaggeration, I'd never seen the likes of before. "Jesus H. Christ!" I cried, struggling with my seat-belt. "Just look at that rainbow!"

"The Lord's name, son," my father reprimanded me, though I was too astonished to care. "Take care with your language."

Naturally, I'd seen rainbows in Canada – Niagara Falls painted some pretty impressive rainbows – and many more in Ireland. The combination of sun and rain, mixed with the wind that carried evaporated seawater inland, had very much made Ireland the land of the rainbows, and rainbows featured heavily in her mythology, especially as the magical place, at the end of which you could find a leprechaun's pot of gold. In all of *Ulysses* I can think of not a single mention of a rainbow – although I must surely be mistaken – which seems odd if true, so intrinsically entwined is every other aspect of the weather in Joyce's great book. But here – after that monsoon-like display of vigorous raining – here was a rainbow worthy of Joyce's powers. Shimmering between the ultra-violet and the infra-red, it spanned from the mountains to the north, and over the Atlantic in an enormous curve, with every colour in between glowing so bright you couldn't see the clouds through it. I'd climbed out of the car and stood – grateful for the stretch – in the sopping long grass beside a hedgerow, slack-jawed as the village idiot, gawping at this spectacle, and it didn't take long to realize I wasn't the only one for from this elevated point I could see another car or two, also pulled over, their passengers out and pointing excitedly, cameras clicking away. My father joined me, and rested a hand on my shoulder. "Now there's a sight," he said, "you don't see every day."

"Aye."

"In ancient times, rainbows were considered a sign of God's blessing."

"I know, Dad." Everyone knew it, I thought uncharitably.

Even as we stood there, heads thrown back, I became aware that far above the first rainbow a second was quickly coming into being, fainter than its more glorious counterpart, but with a whimsical mystery all its own, clearly visible one moment, and then the next almost gone. As the air dried out, the heavenly vision began to fade until finally – though Wagnerian enough, still – it came to resemble any other rainbow you might happen upon on a spring morning, and we decided it was time to push on. So we loosed the main-sails, trimmed the quarter-afts, raised anchor and once again were southward sailing, pitching and yawing along the coastal roads, passing through Arkley, where we deemed it still too early to stop for a bite, and numerous other small villages – fishing villages for the most part – their ports cluttered with colourful boats, seemingly tangled in spider-webs of netting and rigging – each with its story to tell – each with its hidden dramas and wonders – until at last we reached Arklow – not to be confused with Arkley – where even though neither of us were particularly famished, my father wanted to explore a bit, this being (he had been told) one of the many homes to the fabled Poor Clares, less widely known as the Order of St. Clare, and originally the Order of Poor Ladies, the Clarisses, the Minoresses, and the Franciscan Clarist Order, the second Order of St. Francis. What my father's interest in nuns might have been I had no idea – my own knowledge of such women was confined to what I'd learned from 70s porn movies, where they had been portrayed as a wild and randy bunch, when behind closed doors. So we parked the car in Arklow town – a town no less charming than any other, despite the rumoured infestation by an Order of St. Francis – nestled scenically between the mountains and the sea – and got out to make enquiries, and stretch our backs. As was often the way, we parted company, my father and I, with the agreement to meet back at the car by some designated hour, with my father walking south, trailing a thin reed of cigarette smoke behind him, while I set out to poke around amongst the many little shops and stores that lined the busy streets.

It didn't take much looking to find that least resistible of landmarks, a bookstore, which I entered to the sounds of a creaking latch, and a warm welcome from its proprietress, a Mrs. O'Fallon, whose girth and buxomness after its motherly fashion threatened to start the bookshelves tumbling domino-style, each time she made a sudden turn. A black cat purred and rubbed itself against her beefy ankles, looking me over in frank hostility and suspicion, as though it suspected I was here to steal its saucer of milk.

"Good day to you, young sir!"

"Good day, Mrs...?"

"O'Fallon. And is it something specific you might be looking for, or are you only in for a wee peek around?"

I smiled, and the cat seemed to take that as a bad omen. "Just browsing for now, Mrs. O'Fallon. Although I'll let you know if there's anything that catches my eye, or comes to mind."

"I was just about to pour meself a wee cup of tay. Can I interest you in one?"

I looked down for advice from the tabby, licking its claws on the matted rug. "Thank you very much, but no thanks," I replied. Then added, "I'll just be looking around, now."

"You do that," Mrs. O'Fallon said cheerfully. "Is it the United States of America you're over from? Sure that's a long way to come, in search of a book!"

I made deference to the cleverness of her quip, in the form of a smile and chuckle, thinking all the while, oh damn it! What were you thinking, Winter? You should have switched-on the Irish accent! "I'm from Canada," I said. "On holiday with my dad."

"I see, I see," she answered, nodding thoughtfully. "I see. Then I'll let you get on with your browsing in peace, and welcome to our funny wee corner of the world, young sir!"

"Thanks!" I laughed, then turned my attention to the shelves.

I emerged from the shop twenty minutes later with a paperback edition of *The History of Irish Poetry*, and an ancient, hardbound copy of Dante's *The Divine Comedy*, illustrated by Dore, which to my untrained eye looked like it might be worth a few quid, then noticed almost immediately, up the street, a busy little shop with a sign across its frontage announcing: *Chemists: William Landry and Sons, proprietors since 1954.* I need hardly tell you, I ditched the books in the car and proceeded forthwith, in all due haste, to be investigating this Mr. William Landry, and the latest startling turn of events.

"Aye," a pretty, dark-haired teenager told me, after I'd asked. "My father and brothers have been running this shop since forever." From the way she said it, I deduced that 'forever' was a bit too long to suit her temperament. "And rumour has it we have kin who was Crowleys, also, though most of them moved to the north, and I don't recall ever meeting one before now. You should stick around. Me da will be back within the hour.

I'm sure it would give him great pleasure to shake the hand of such a distant relative."

I told her I surely would stick around, and with me own wee da in tow to boot, then started further up the street, starting to feel a trifle peckish. It was only then I remembered about the Poor Clares, whose story I had meant to investigate at the bookstore, but had forgotten to, and had forgotten again while within the Chemists, William Landry and Sons, proprietors since 1954. So when I intercepted a soccer-ball that had gotten away from a group of boys, playing in a park, I asked them if there was such a thing as a Priory anywhere hereabouts.

"A nunnery is it, you're talking about, mister?"

"A nunnery, yes. Is there any about?"

"No nunneries here, mister. Hey, Gordon!" he cried to a friend over his muddy shoulder. "Sure there's no nunneries in Arklow, is there?"

"Don't be daft, man! Come on, and bring us the ball!"

Then turning back to me:

"No nunneries in Arklow, mister. Nor anywhere nearby. There you have it, mister."

"Are you sure?"

The boy gave me a look, as though to say he'd expended his allotted time for talking to eejits, then trotted off to rejoin his mates.

Not too much later, over a lunch of fish and chips, my father's washed down with a pint of ale, and mine with a pint of milk, I updated him on these most recent intelligences, that there appeared to be no Poor Clares haunting the highways and byways of Arklow, nor any other town in its environs, and that some distant cousin or other, one William Landry, appeared to be plying the trade of a chemist – what we in Canada would have called a pharmacist – not ten minutes down the road. The news of the absence of Poor Clares seemed especially distressing to him.

"The more's the pity," he sighed. "I've either been misinformed, or have misremembered what I'd been told. The latter, as likely as not. Ach well. There's Poor Clares in Galway, this I know from many sources."

"I wouldn't discount there being any here just yet," I said. "There's a Post Office down the way, where we can find out for certain. The kids I spoke to were just boys – thundering dunderheads probably not even twelve years old, with their ears full of wax. They probably wouldn't know a Priory from a whorehouse at twenty–"

My father got a chuckle at that, though I could see he disapproved.

"Let's check at the Post Office," I said. "Just to be certain."

"No need. There are seven monasteries of the Colettine Observance here in Ireland, the oldest being the one on Nun's Island on Lough Lene. The Poor Clares were the second Franciscan order to be–"

"Nun's Island?" I echoed my father, incredulously.

"Aye," he said. "In Galway. Nun's Island. What's funny about it?"

"Not funny exactly, just – I don't know." To my vulgar ear Nun's Island sounded a bit too much like some weird fancy Walt Disney might have dreamed up, to stick in a movie to frighten the bejeebers out of small children, like the Fantasy Carnival in *Pinocchio*, where naughty boys where transformed into braying donkeys. *Welcome to Nun's Island!* A spooky Bella Lugosi-like voice intoned over loudspeakers in my noggin. *Nun's Island, where all your worst nightmares will come true!*

Of course, I breathed not a word of this to my father, who had pressed forward on the subject of the Poor Clares, as though he were giving serious consideration to joining their numbers. "They were organized after the manner of the Friars Minor – which was to say the first order – and founded by St. Clare of Assisi, and Saint Francis of Assisi, on Palm Sunday of the year 1212, and as of now there are over twenty thousand Poor Clare nuns in 75 countries all over the world."

"Huh," I said, or rather tried it out, experimentally, as my eyes glazed over. "Imagine that."

"The Irish contingency moved to Dublin in 1629, under a single mother superior, and were the first and only monastic community in all of Ireland for more than a century, although war forced them to move to Galway in 1642, where they remain – and in other places in Ireland – to this very day. Just," he added, clearly vexed, "just not here in Arklow!"

"Can I ask you something, Dad?"

"Certainly, son – anything at all – just ask away."

"Why on earth are you telling me about the Poor Clares?"

He looked at me a bit perplexed, for a moment, then smiled.

"Why, because it's an important aspect of Irish history son, that's why – surely as important as Oliver Cromwell, and the wars. And it's interesting! Come, have you finished with them chips? Let's be on our way – there'll be plenty of the Poor Clares to be seen, once we're swung down around by Galway."

"Wait a minute!" I as good as cried out. "What about the Landrys? These may be relatives you've never even met before – surely you want to at least shake hands, and give them a hail fellow, well met?"

"No, son. That doesn't matter. This trip is all about you, not me."

"But this might be a once in a lifetime opportunity!"

"It *is* a once in a lifetime opportunity," my father said. "And I don't intend to spoil it by muddying the waters with ancient relations I don't even know."

Well! Incredulity doesn't seem a strong enough word. It seemed my father had attached an importance to this trip beyond anything I could imagine, and I didn't know what to make of it, except to say I began to resent the burden of responsibility that now seemed to fall to me, to see to it henceforth that all should be well between us, this suddenly vulnerable-looking old man and myself.

"I would enjoy this trip more, if I thought you were worrying about its outcome less," I told him.

"Enjoy it anyway," my dad said, pulling his wallet out to pay for lunch. "It's a magical place, son! And sure that's the whole idea."

Soon afterwards we were on the road again, but a small shadow had fallen between us. Just how desperate, I wondered, was my father for my absolution? And more even than that, did I have the power to bequeath it? The thought irritated the outer extremities of my consciousness, the extremities, that is to say, not already being nibbled at by Becky McNamara, in her post-coital bliss. And as time went by – in keeping with the natural ebb and flow of human nature – I found myself wondering if my father might not have some other, more ulterior motive for not wanting to have anything to do with the Landrys, and that if he had been so completely mistaken about the Poor Clares, what else had he been mistaken about – or perhaps lied about from an error of omission – over the course not just of this trip, but of our lives?

VI

At some point between Arklow and Wexford, as a mathematical certainly, we had completed exactly one quarter of our odyssey, my father and I, as I could plainly see from the large, detailed map of Ireland I had brought from Belfast, on which I had been tracing our route and dating the towns and villages where we had stayed each night. You might think from reading what I've said so far that it was a pretty eventful thing – and certainly it was eventful enough – but I've left plenty out as well, for want of sufficient interest or because certain things didn't conform to the great narrative arc – the rainbow-like curve from beginning to middle and end – that I envisioned my tale must inevitably take. There were walks down streets both broad and narrow, both busy and lonely, quiet moments over a glass of Bushmills, admiring the moon and stars, swims in the black ocean by starlight, leprechauns to be cross-examined (though more about that later) shops to be poked into, historical tourist attractions to be seen, castles, venerable houses, famous battlefields, as well as the natural wonders of the geography itself. We witnessed a uniformed brass marching band, evidently serenading an enormous walrus, grunting and braying hoarsely in a harbour, and had many a talk with village and townspeople who, upon hearing I was from Canada, couldn't seem to stand me enough free drinks, such was the nature of their friendly, courteous way in the company of strangers. As time passed, things settled back down to the way they had been before, between me and my dad – the cheerful dialogue between us restored, with him reminiscing about his own childhood, our relations, distant both in time and space, or near, and of course the topographical and historical features of this most fabled land. If he didn't want to say hello to a cousin, twelve-times removed, what was that to me? I had plenty of cousins of my own, over here, whom I could take or leave, and who no doubt felt the same way towards me, the Spy Who Had Come in From the Cold. We spent the night in Wexford, but then pushed off directly the next morning for our real destination, nearby Clonmel, home to the legendary Clonmel Crystal works, the birthplace of one of the world's most highly-esteemed and acclaimed manufacturers of fine glassware – everything from tureens to champagne flutes, salad bowls, whisky glasses, flower vases, chandeliers, candelabra, you name it, and everything in between. My mother had a grand collection of this fancy clutter – her pride and joy, worth thousands. When it was brought out on special occasions, to festoon her glittering dining room table, under the candle-light, I dare say her blood pressure went up discernibly for anxiety, and her smile grew a little strained around the corners.

From the factory exterior, you could as easily imagine them manufacturing hob-nails, or iron-plate rivets in there. We were greeted at the tourist-gate by a representative – a youngish matron, stylish yet growing elegantly snaggletooth – who clearly wasn't here on the strength of her enthusiasm for industrial joiners. On the contrary, she appeared so refined she might have been cut from crystal herself, and spoke the King's English in such a clipped and proper manner she made Princess Margaret sound like Germaine Greer. "If we can just walk this way," she aspirated breathlessly, "we can meet our docents, who will begin our tour at the glass-blowing stations, on the first floor west wings. And may I say, on behalf of management and staff," she added, with but a feeble effort at sounding welcoming, "welcome to the home of Clonmel Crystal, the world's finest crystal! Your experience will conclude with a visit to our gift-shop, where, as an exclusive courtesy to our guests, the glassware may be purchased at a significant discount."

The glass-blowing stations were just that – thirty-odd large brick kilns, set up in stations separated by perhaps twenty feet, all housed in an enormous room with large, paned windows on either side, thrown open to create a cross-breeze against the temperature of the place, although even with industrial-sized fans blowing at full capacity, to help the breeze along, the temperature was considerable. Not that the glass-blowers, their apprentices, and secondary assistants seemed to mind. Slick with perspiration, and stripped down to their sleeveless under-vests and caps, they busied themselves with a concentration to be admired, capturing a glowing blob of the golden melted crystal from the kilns on a metal tube, which they then started blowing into and spinning in the air, while the blob expanded like a party-favour until at last it had acquired the desired size and shape. By that point it had cooled off in any case, made no longer amenable to the glass-blower's art. Repeated up and down the two long isles, it was an extraordinary thing to watch, all those glowing bubbles slowly cooling into crystal. On occasion the glass-blower would adjudge the *objet d'art*-in-progress blown insufficiently in compliance with his standard of perfection, and then back into the kiln it would go, for a remedial reheating, in order to rework the glowing ball again and again, until it looked just the way the glass-blower expected it to, all the while fielding questions from the apprentices, or barking orders at the assistants. It would be a cheap dig on my part to liken this hot, noisy environment to something out of Dante, as boys and men alike clearly enjoyed, and took fierce pride in, their work, and besides, the company provided them with a complimentary chilled bottle of Harp at lunch, with which to replenish their precious bodily fluids.

One of our guides was a young man named Dennis, around my age or a little older, who turned out to be a Trinity student working on his Master's degree in British philosophers, and at the Clonmel works only to make a quick quid during the summer months in furtherance of his education. Dennis seemed to take a liking to me – though I would have preferred the attentions of his docent partner, who was a knock-out – and had begun hanging back, the better to add a running commentary *sotto voce* in my ear, along with the scripted twaddle.

"Don't mind old Mrs. Russell," Dennis began, referring to the representative who'd greeted us at the gate. "She imagines she has friends in high places, and fancies she was born with a better pot to piss in than the rest of us."

I laughed.

"I was beginning to get that impression."

"You a Canadian, man?" Dennis next asked me.

"Congratulations."

"On what?"

"On being the first person not to have taken me for Yankee-born."

Now it was Dennis's turn to laugh. "Ooch, I can tell a Yankee a mile away," he said. "Vulgarians, the lot of 'em!"

"I couldn't vouch for that."

"You don't need to! They're terrible, those boys. So what brings you to our little neck of the woods, man?"

I told him and Dennis nodded his head, as though deeply satisfied with the quality of my answer, a harmless affectation he'd doubtlessly picked up from some favourite professor at Trinity.

Next came the cutting and polishing room, considerably cooler though a little more crowded, in a space as vast as the glass-blowing room had been, but instead of kilns the stations were large metal tables on which lathes were bolted and into which the blown crystal could be fixed and spun. The process was akin to that used to manufacture baseball bats, though compared to a Louisville Slugger, the delicacy, fineness of detail and precision required was considerable, so much so I wondered how the crystal cutters, hunched over in fierce concentration, could stay sufficiently focussed over the course of an entire shift?

"They aren't made to try," Dennis explained. "There's two teams per eight hour shift, each team doing the cutting for thirty minutes, then with thirty minutes between, so they can catch their breaths, perform their necessaries, give it a good shake, then have a wee puff."

"Jesus!" I laughed, shaking my head. "Clonmel should have its picture in the dictionary, as an illustration of the word Magnanimous."

Dennis smiled and shrugged. "Well, it's in their best interest too, sure. Those must be a hellish thirty minutes. I can't imagine it. In that amount of time, each cutter can rough-cut maybe five pieces of crystal. That's a hundred quid plus at current market value. And if you bugger one of them up – which is always a possibility, given the limitations of human stamina – it's back to the kilns with that lot. As you can imagine there's considerable pressure to keep that sort of thing to a minimum. Any cutter with a track-record of cutting less than flawless crystal, every bleedin' time, would soon find himself up before the president of the whole damn shebang, trying to justify his continued existence on the cutting-room floor. And there's always three or four of those boy-oh's out there. You can tell them by the puddle of cold sweat on the ground beneath their feet. No no!" Dennis concluded with a laugh. "I couldn't do it, not even under those circumstances. I'd be a grease-stain of nervous anxiety before my first day was out. C'mon, Winter, the official tour is almost over, then after I'll introduce you to young Jimmy."

"Young Jimmy?"

"Oh aye," Dennis laughed. "Young Jimmy. He's a fellah well worth meeting!"

When the tour was finished we were rejoined by my father, who after his roguish manner had stayed closer up with Dennis's sexier young counterpart, at the head of the tour group, and, well pleased with everything he'd heard and seen, he said. "Well now son! That was worth the stopover, didn't you think?"

"Aye." I introduced my dad to Dennis, and they shook hands warmly. Then turning back to me:

"Are you ready for a spot of lunch yet, Winter?"

"Dennis was about to introduce me to young Jimmy, Dad."

"Young Jimmy?"

"Yes, Mr. Crowley," Dennis said. "And of course you're welcome to come along, too."

"Call me Colm. That's all right son. You go ahead, and do what you want to do. Do you remember that wee pub, across the way from where we left the car? I'll meet you there. That'll be all right then. You go ahead, and I'll see you after."

"You really should come with us, Mr – Colm," said Dennis, in his most winning manner. "You won't be sorry you did."

"That's all right, that's all right," said my dad, with perhaps just the ghost of a hint of exasperation. "You two boys go on. I'm tired from all the walking. Take your time. I'll see you in a while."

Dennis then led me across the main foyer, where as advertised there was a crowded gift-shop, and down a short corridor to a room marked, EMPLOYEES ONLY. "That's all right," said my guide. "The boss knows we sometimes bring tourists here, me and the other docents. In fact it's kind of encouraged, although there would be hell to pay if anything went wrong. Good for public relations though."

"Well," I said, by now thoroughly intrigued. "Lead on!"

Dennis unlocked the door – which was heavier than it looked – and let us into a room about the size and height of a squash-court, including a small observation gallery, where we'd come in, which was cordoned off from the rest of the room by a thick pane of Plexiglas. The space was spotless, painted white, cool from air conditioning, and through invisible speakers somewhere came the quiet strains of classical music – I recognized one of the charming duets sung between Princess Pamina and the bird-catcher, Papageno, in Mozart's Opera, *Die Zauberflöte* – floating in the artificially cooled breeze. On the other side of the Plexiglas an ancient man turned towards us, and tossed Dennis a friendly wave, raising two fingers, as though to say he would be with us in a couple of minutes. I approached the glass wall and stood before it, gawking in speechless wonder.

"Surely that isn't what I think it is," I finally managed to whisper.

"'tis!" Dennis snorted.

In the middle of the court, cradled in some sort of green velvet cushioning, and resting on an elegant wooden table, possibly of French design was a sphere of Clonmel crystal the size of a sizeable beach ball – the size of one of those old-school medicine balls – a yard in diameter if it was an inch, held stationary by four moulded white stops, so that on the off-chance an earthquake should come rumbling across Southern Ireland, the big ball wouldn't roll off the table, and get smashed to smithereens on the carpeted floor, though even so it looked precarious. I must say, it took a while for the reality of it to sink in. The sphere was truly enormous. It glittered under a series of futuristic-looking lights, its fine, rounded surface splitting the spectrum first here, then over there, a series of small rainbows dancing about as you moved your eyes, modified your point of view. Young Jimmy – dressed in saggy corduroys, a wrinkled shirt he swam in, rolled up to his scrawny elbows, with a white, full-body apron tied around his wattled neck, and large pockets bulging with tools – leaned over the big ball with some sort of delicate, whirring implement, either etching or buffing away. It was only then I realized young Jimmy, with a loupe, or jeweller's eyepiece, screwed into his face, was slowly but surely cutting a map of south-east Asian into a region of the sphere. It wasn't a beach ball, or an old-school medicine ball. It was a globe of the world.

"How thick is the crystal?" I asked Dennis, who'd stepped up beside me.

"Pretty thick."

"It would need to be, just to bear up under its own weight," I whistled. "It must be worth a fortune."

"It's priceless, man," Dennis said. "It's the only one of its kind."

"What of the cost of the crystal to blow it?"

"That I don't know," Dennis laughed. "It gives me a headache, just thinking about it. But the raw crystal aside, the value of Clonmel crystal lies in the perfection of shape, the elegance of design, many different things. Young Jimmy blew this one personally, after he retired twenty years ago. Countless attempts it took, I'm told, and a lot of help to get it to his liking. The Clonmel top brass were starting to think the entire enterprise impossible. But young Jimmy proved them wrong."

"What if the table broke?"

"It's stronger than it looks, and the engineers have it well reinforced from the underside."

"Still –"

"We keep a close eye out on the table, and everything else that goes on in there, although no one's allowed in but Jimmy and a few of the higher-ups. The unspoken worry is that one of these days, Jimmy will have himself a stroke, and collapse, bringing the entire works down with him. But he's careful and very fit for a man his age. He's been cutting that globe for nigh on two decades now, as a post-retirement project, only three or four hours a day, and not every day. It gives him something to do, since cutting and blowing crystal is the only training he's ever had. He began at the factory at sixteen – more than seventy years ago – and attained master status at both the blowing and the cutting. He was legendary during his time, and now is reputed to be the most skilled craftsman Clonmel ever employed. Oh, there's a lot of pride in that globe. Jimmy's little way of saying thank you, I suppose."

I laughed.

"Thank you to a company that had the use of his mastery for fifty years, the gift of a priceless, one-of-a-kind object, built over an additional twenty years, while living on retirement wages."

"Ah! The working class hero, is it?" Dennis smiled and winked. "Young Jimmy knew what he was letting himself in for."

"If young Jimmy is ninety years old," I asked. "How old is old Jimmy?"

"Well now, old Jimmy died sure, Winter. God bless and keep his soul. He passed away a year or two ago."

"Peacefully, it's to be hoped," said I.

"Boating accident."

Young Jimmy never did come out of his magician's lair, to say hello – either he'd become so absorbed in his work he'd forgotten we were there, or I'd misinterpreted his hand signal. Either way, I was disappointed not to have a word with him, but shook hands with Dennis, after we'd left the squash-court, and returned to the gift shop, thanking him for his trouble, bidding him wish young Jimmy all the best on my behalf.

"Will do, Winter," Dennis laughed cheerfully, with a wave, as I departed. "Winter – a funny nickname. Winter Crowley, the working class hero, off and running to see who else is in the way of needing a quick rescue!"

After the bright sunshine of the brief walk from the factory gates to my Aunt Esther's car, then across the busy little road, the interior of the pub seemed not only unusually smoky and smelly, but unusually dark. I found my old man at a table beside a pillar, cradling what was left of his pint, and looking vexed. For a lunchtime the place was crowded, mostly, I assumed, with tourists, and when the waiter came I ordered a coffee and asked to see a menu. I told my father about young Jimmy and the priceless crystal globe he'd been cutting, lo these many years.

"Then your friend was right," my father sighed, while our waiter dropped my coffee off, and put a fresh pint on the table, as well as a couple of menus. "It would have been worth my while to join you. I'd heard stories about that globe. I guess I'd assumed it had been long finished by now, and put on display somewhere."

"Maybe we could go back, and Dennis could give you a look-see for yourself."

"It's no matter, son. You saw it, and that's all that counts. Look, are you all right, Winston?"

"All right?"

Just then, as my eyes adjusted to the gloom, I caught sight of a girl sitting at a table with two of her friends. They were dressed in what appeared to be nurses' uniforms, washing down their lunches with Cokes in a particularly busy corner of the pub, awash also in golden light, but this girl would have stood out even in a crowd twice as large. She had the longest, most lovely wavy hair – scarlet-red and strewn with highlights from the candles – of any woman I'd ever seen. A real Irish rose, as my grandfather might have said. She exuded sensuality from every pore as she sat there, chatting and laughing with the other girls, and I found myself thinking of Cassandra, whose voluptuous nature had so smitten the god Apollo that he'd given her the powers of divination, only after having been rebuffed to have cursed the gift by ensuring that none of Cassandra's visions of the future would be believed.

"What do you mean, am I all right?"

"That boy, Dennis," my dad said, frowning. "He was a homosexual."

That thought, I admit, had crossed my mind too, but unlike my father's, having crossed, it had exited as quickly as it had entered. What did I care if Dennis was a homosexual or not? I'd encountered a few homosexuals at the tender age of (almost) twenty, and they'd always seemed harmless enough. Besides, there'd been no signs of flirtatiousness from him, and even as I'd thought the thought I'd considered it unworthy and irrelevant.

"Well, what of that, even if it's true?" I suggested, sipping my coffee. "It's a harmless thing."

"Is it?"

I laughed, all the while watching my Cassandra out of the corner of my eye.

"Some would say it is not," my dad continued. "Some would call it a sin. And a vice."

Oh dear, thought I. Here we go. I wrestled with my emotions for a moment, then simply shook them off. "I know that's true, dad," I replied lightly, attempting to keep the conversation from taking a turn into a brick wall. "But the condition of homosexuality isn't contagious – and as you know as well as anyone, homosexuality isn't one of my problems."

At the tender age of (almost) twenty, I'd had a few run-ins with pretty girls, several of which my dad was painfully aware of, not least a Jewish beauty by the name of Ariella Kaplan (whom I've written about at length in the story *Entangled*) who, even as my father and I were sitting there, was awaiting my imminent return to her loving arms, back in Canada. "Come on now, dad," I said, as cheerfully as I could muster. "We're having a great time, and now I feel a row coming on. Let's not bother with it, shall we? I'm perfectly all right, none the worse for my encounter with Dennis, and enjoying the company of a father who's trying very hard to be a loving man, and a protective father. I appreciate the effort. So let's have our lunch in peace, then push on. I'd still be interested in hearing more about the Poor Clares, even though we're a week or two outside Galway just yet."

So the conversation returned to more neutral territory, and I decided to order a beer, after all. After the waiter had brought it, and disappeared, I noticed that the red-headed woman in the nurse's outfit had caught me ogling her, and had half-turned around in her chair, to bequeath upon me with her painted-red lips the most voluptuously inviting smile she could conjure, her green eyes sparkling in the candle-light, her breasts now well turned my way, as on display, one of which she slowly grazed with the back of her wrist, as though to draw my attention to it, and I found myself envying Cassandra her God-given ability to divine the future, even as I sat there wondering if my father wasn't a little insane.

VII

By the tenth of June – which was to say my twentieth birthday – we had long ceased sailing due south, and now had made the great turn in a south-westerly direction, around the southernmost extreme of the island where we would continue to follow the coastal route as it zigzagged around multiple estuaries, inlets, loughs, bays, harbours and even the odd fjord or two, adding considerably to our travel time, but not begrudged for all that, starting in the counties of Wexford and Waterford, then finally reaching county Cork, at the western extreme of which we would turn back north – and homewards – at county Kerry. In the meanwhile, we would pass through the towns of Dungarvan, Ardmore, Youghal, and a dozen smaller villages in between, finally arriving at the great city of Cork itself, and from there northwards at Bantry Bay. As I said, we weren't out to set any land-speed records, and we enjoyed the voyage thoroughly, though I perhaps a little more trepidatiously, in light of this recent homosexuality business. My old man was making a valiant effort – this much I could plainly see – and how was I not to love him the more for all he was doing? As we'd travelled south, the temperature had begun to increase imperceptibly, until now on average it was a good three to five degrees warmer than it had been back in Ulster, the sunsets went on for hours, and often I was taken aback to come upon the odd sign of near-tropical conditions – dazzling strands of white, sandy beach that might have been lifted whole from Fiji, or the Australian coastline, so eye-smarting in the sun you had to look away, peppered by little clusters of coconut groves and other fronded plants.

"Happy birthday, son."

"Thanks, dad."

"Twenty years old! Imagine that! That's a great age to be! What was it I would have been doing, now, at that age?"

Tarring and feathering faggots? Was the uncharitable thought which flitted across my mind.

"Just starting into work on my Chartered Accountancy accreditation, I imagine. That was a long haul. Playing tennis with me mates, and rowing on the river Lagan–"

"You played tennis when you were a young man?"

"Sure, didn't you know that, Winter?"

My father still seemed not quite to get the picture – I knew almost nothing about him at all. These little dribs and drabs of autobiography he let slip, from time to time, were as a great deluge when compared to the arid Sahara of non-disclosure that had always passed as his default position. We hadn't started directly across the coastal route I've just described, but instead had taken a short detour north, up into county Kilkenny, where the old man had taken a notion he wanted to visit, on account of some family connection or other. That was fine by me – everywhere we went the scenery was equally breathtaking, and in three weeks' time, whether we stopped to visit Kilkenny or not, I would be on that big bird again, and flying back to Canada. Not that I was so very eager to leave, but homesickness had begun to niggle at my extremities, like a sort of emotional frostbite, and I missed the rest of my family, my friends, especially Ariella Kaplan, she of the bewitching Old Testament eyes and the charming Roman nose, who had for the last year or so suffered me to fondle, kiss and otherwise play with her breasts, dry-hump her on the couch, with many even more satisfactory offerings beckoning from just over the horizon.

So up we drove to Kilkenny, stopping en route for a bite where we met a cluster of young electrical engineers – God knows why they were there – who got into a friendly debate with my father regarding, of all the unlikely subjects, a recent national election held in Germany, though with names like O'Malley, Sinclair and Boyle, what their interest could be in the goings-on of the Germans remains a mystery, never to be explained. My father on the other hand was just such a mystery, partially revealed; as little as I knew about the particulars of his biography, I knew he harboured an inordinate fondness for all things Teutonic, his love of Beethoven and the writings of Immanuel Kant being only, I suspected, the tip of the iceberg. Over the years he'd flattered himself he had mastered conversational German (he hadn't) and spoke of travelling in that distant land, once he'd retired, chatting with the *Herren* and *Fraulein* at length, in their native tongue, clambering through the Bavarian foothills like a mountain goat or a von Trapp, in lederhosen and feathered cap, drinking steins of good, hearty *Muenchen* lager. Indeed, so keen was my father on the Great Alpine Way, that in my very young years – knowing he had not served in World War II, but not knowing why – I had contrived an idle fantasy in which my father was, in actual fact, a German spy operating covertly out of Belfast, the better to keep the *Luftwaffe* and indeed even *der Fuehrer* himself – that hot-tempered rascal who had already served time and would again, once the German people had come to their senses – apprised of the goings-on at Harland and Wolff, Belfast's fabled ship-yards, where (at least according to my fertile, melodramatic imagination) the Fatherland's worst enemies were even now putting the finishing touches on a warship of such dreadful proportions, it had *Reichsmarschall* Hermann Goering himself pissing in his drawers at the *Plenarbereich Reichstagsgebaude* in Berlin, for fear of its evil potential. It was said to be the size of a small city, this nautical wonder of the world, armed to the teeth with a bristling array of torpedoes, turret guns, depth-charges, cannons and a system of laser-guided nuclear-tipped intercontinental missiles, which were feared would one day soon, upon completion of the mighty vessel, end the war and bring the Third Reich to its knees. That in my imagination my father more closely resembled Boris Badenov of *Rocky and Bullwinkle* fame, than anything remotely passing for a German spy, didn't stop me, every chance I got, from crouching over my schoolboy desk in my parent's house, and committing his derring-do adventures to paper (complete with illustrations) with a series of pencils and notebooks I'd filched from Holbrook Public School. By the time I gave up on the project the manuscript was eighty pages long.

"Do you see that great pile of stones over yonder, Winter, in the field beyond the stone fence?"

"Aye."

"That's Kilkenny Castle. Or everything that's left of it, at least."

"Huh," I said. "I thought most of these medieval castles were built closer to the coast, to defend against invasions from the sea."

My father nodded his head in sage agreement. "Aye," he said. "Many of them were. A great many of them were. But sure old Cromwell and his boys didn't confine themselves to causing vexation only by the sea. They had vitriol enough to spare for land-locked places, like Kilkenny, as well, which on top of everything else is also a great tourist attraction, for all its ancient religious architecture. St. Canice's Cathedral and roundhouse is around these parts, somewhere, as are Rothe House, Shee Alms House, Black Abby and St. Mary's cathedral. In ruins now, most of them, but still worth the look."

"You think the Crowleys might have lived in these parts, once upon a time?"

"No, but the Landrys did, for certain, and up until not that long ago. Nathan and Pete Landry started a sort of cooperative here, at the turn of the century – the turn of the 20th century that is, of course – which did well and helped the local economy considerably. A lot of this was on Nathan's initiative, but between the two of them those boy-ohs even founded a fish farm, for the raising of trout and whatnot, to replenish the waters, and nursed it along until by the time the Great War finally broke out, the cooperative and the fishery were employing something like a hundred of the locals, which was a blessing at the time."

"Huh," I said again, for want of anything more intelligent to say, and lit a cigarette.

"But sadly, with the coming of war things quickly turned sour, Pete being all for supporting the British effort, and Nathan firmly against. So when Pete's son – I can't rightly recall his actual name, so I'll call him young Pete – when young Pete went off, and got himself blown to bits almost immediately, at the Somme, at seventeen years old, there was much recrimination and blame and I-told-you-sos, so much so that the whole bloomin' family was near to shook asunder. Things went from bad to worse, with the *coup de gras* coming in the form of the simultaneous disappearance of Nathan's son, only seventeen as well, whose name I also can't remember, so I'll call him young Nathan. Young Nathan disappeared under highly mysterious circumstances, and so quickly after young Pete's death, in the war, that their elder counterparts took to suspecting some kind of foul play – even if divinely ordained – which did little to assuage the bad blood that was building up between the two factions of the family. Of course the greater likelihood is that young Nathan just got stinking drunk one night – the Landrys were the great ones for heavy drinking, God help them – and walked off a pier, or else fell face-first into a bog. It wouldn't have been the first time. But no. I guess that explanation was too obvious for Nathan and Pete Landry, and even the local townspeople who worked for them at the cooperative, and the fish farm, began talking blatherskite about the Little People having come down one night, for to be carrying young Nathan off to his heavenly reward."

"The Little People!" I laughed. "The leprechauns?"

"Sure, don't be talking nonsense, Winter," my father scolded me sternly. "Everyone knows the leprechauns is just a fable. No, the real fear was that the wee space aliens had come down from the sky, and instead of their usual dirty business of mutilating the cattle, or filling the fields with their crop circles, had this time around come for young Nathan, for to be carrying him away for scientific experimentation, to Alpha Centauri, or what."

"Oh, come on!"

"Say what you will, son. But in certain pockets of Ireland, even to this very day, there are folk who believe in the existence of the wee space aliens, orbiting away up there in their rockets, which goes a long way towards explaining certain known earthly experiences, as well as the mysterious lights that sometimes show up in the night sky. I myself remember one evening, while I was walking up Orby Road – this in the days when I was courting your mother – I thought I saw a great light in the sky, a bright, shining orb, and by gum it made me jump! When I turned my head, it flitted away, faster than any earthly object could ever hope to travel, and no matter how I tried I couldn't keep it in me line of vision, so fast did it streak, east to west, or up and down, defying the laws of physics, and I don't mind telling you, son, it was passing strange to behold, this interstellar celestial phenomenon. That is, until I realized it was just a wee droplet of water – probably a raindrop – that had adhered to the lens of me glasses, and had been caught in the lamplight as I passed under. But even so –"

We spent the evening of my twentieth birthday booked into a very posh little hotel by the sea in Dungarvan. Normally, we contented ourselves with bed and breakfasts – themselves not establishments to be disparaged – but for whatever reason my father had decided on the Celtic Seabreeze Hotel, a stone's throw from the crashing waves of the Atlantic, and after we'd settled in my father insisted on taking me out to a nearby pub of his acquaintance, for to be having a celebration of the sacred event of my birth. Needless to say, the place was hopping – as any Irish pub is wont to be, day or night – with a Gaelic quartet done up identically in Aran sweaters, and tweed caps, singing the traditional songs of their fathers, both in English and Irish, and we had a beer and chatted about the wee space aliens, then we had another beer and waxed elegant about the likely true fate of young Nathan Landry, then yet another, and by now others of the pub's patrons had joined in the conversation, wanting to know what an American boy was doing, so far from home, so we bought a round and toasted my dearly beloved home, the United States of America, land of the free and home of the what-not, and then with the ground beneath me starting to wobble a little, I told my dad I was going to step out for a moment, to catch a breath of fresh air.

"Right, son," laughed my father, who was having a hell of a good time. "And when you come back, we'll telephone your mother. I promised her we would."

I checked my watched. A few minutes before nine. Just four o'clock local time. "Good," I said, then tottered through the crowd, and out the door.

The air was sweet and refreshing, and I breathed in large lungfuls of it, while I stumbled down to the crashing water. I loved the ocean, and always had. I loved its sounds, its smells, and being in its proximity was ever a source of great comfort, though what I needed comforting from at this particular moment I didn't know. Probably nothing. Still I needed comforting as a child needs comforting, in the reassuring arms of a loving mother, and here was our great mother, our great sweet mother as Joyce had called her, and so I went to her and stood admiring her, admiring also the enormous full moon that floated maybe thirty degrees above the horizon, sinking fast, painting an arrow of golden light onto the waves that pointed directly at me. Had my father made up this story of the wee space aliens, as a way of atoning for the prior business with Dennis, and the homosexuality, as a way of saying that he was just a man after all, a man with a sense of humour, who wasn't all thundering criticisms and harsh judgements? That, even though it was late in the day, it wasn't too late to learn how to enjoy each other's company, and maybe even like each other a little?

When I got back to the pub, my father explained that in order to make our long distance call, we'd have to say goodnight and return to the hotel, which we did, and we were both much heartened to discover the hotel itself didn't only have a wee pub of its own – although for guests only – but that their pub didn't have to abide by the rule of last call, and could stay open until the final guest had to be dragged out by his feet, back to his room, swimming in vomit. Like the hotel itself, this wee pub was a very posh wee pub, and when we inquired about a telephone, for to be making an important intercontinental call, the barman – this centuries before the use of wireless technology – brought a telephone over to our table, which my father, fishing a paper with a long list of digits from his wallet, now used to dial back home. He spoke with my mother for a minute or two, attempting to sound more sober than he was, and then handed the telephone to me.

"Winston?"

"Mom!"

"Happy birthday, son! I miss you!"

"I miss you too!"

"I love you!"

"I love you too, Mom!"

Things went on in that lively vein for a moment or two longer, and then my mother changed the subject, from our mutual adoration, to my father.

"Is everything all right with him, son?"

"All right? What do you mean? Everything's fine. We're having a great time, a grand time!"

"OK. Good," said my mother, from far away. "It's only that – well – he has a lot of high hopes for this trip, Winter. Perhaps unrealistically so. And you know – well – you can be a little short tempered sometimes."

"Me?" I laughed. "*I* can be short tempered?"

VIII

You might think from what I've said that as a teenager I was some sort of freakish music prodigy – an idiot-savant without precedent – if not in the playing of an instrument then in the appreciating of a performance, who listened only to the great works of the classical and baroque masters, but that wouldn't be true. My interest in the music of the Ancient Academy had undoubtedly been inspired from an early age by my father, but as with so much else (including the acquisition of conversational German, which I'd learned in order to complete my honours degree) as I grew older, bolder and more self-confident, I quickly outstripped my dad's musical interests, and indeed the interests of almost everyone else I knew or had ever heard about, and thus – with no threshold of effort-to-congratulations to hold me at bay – I was soon impressing the hell out of the adults with my knowledge in many an arcane field of endeavour, from serious music and literature to Captain Marvel and Batman comic books, higher algebra to the most lurid 70s porn movies, from remedial chess to advanced shoplifting, basketball and gymnastics. God knows what else. During my university days I was as close to entirely self-taught as you could get – and starting to do a lot of writing for the school newspaper – while still managing to make the Dean's honours list. I paid just enough attention to the required reading to collect my silly wagon-load of 'A's' and devoted the rest of my time – every other waking hour of the day – to whatever aspect of this mad, complex world happened to capture my attention at the moment, from cosmology to Gregorian chants. I listened to popular music too though, I admit. and even found some of it interesting. I especially admired this relatively new frontier called 'progressive-rock,' of which I approved for its complexity, its ambitiousness, and its nuttiness in general. But for all progressive rock's bold strokes and variation, when compared to the bone-chilling ice-blue flame of American jazz, or the great towering inferno the classical (and baroque) composers were able to ignite, so-called popular music seemed a tepid affair, a sickly-sweet concoction whipped-up by children for the edification of the disenfranchised.

But now, as the midnight hour approached of the first day of my twentieth year, I was to be accosted by a music such as I had never heard before. By ten-thirty or eleven that night, I think it would be safe to say my father and I were officially three sheets to the wind, stinking drunk even while standing on solid ground, in the posh wee pub at the Celtic Seabreeze Hotel, and in the process of disentangling ourselves from the knot of fellow patrons with whom we'd been blathering away for the better part of two hours, my dad to stagger off to his wee bed, and I – still wide-awake and feeling restless – to skip out for a long and (hopefully) sleep-inducing walk down by the waterline.

"Are you sure that's a good idea, son?"

"Sure," said I. "Why not?"

"Well – the hour's late, you're blind drunk, and this town is full of scallywags."

I laughed.

"The walk will sober me up, and I'll deal with the scallywags as they come."

"Don't be too long, Winter," said my father. "Seriously. This can be a rough little town."

I scooped up my Bushmills and ice, and headed for the large ornate doors that led out onto the hotel's gardened property. "That'll be all right, sure," I said, giving my dad a waggish wink. "That'll be all right."

The moon, by this late hour was, if not quite completely down, only a shadow of its former glory, although the night was clear and by the starlight and the street lamps there was enough illumination to see by, even down by the water, so I toddled along, sipping my whisky (with which I'd been forewarned I mustn't leave the hotel property) musing over this bizarre observation my mother had made on the telephone. Of course I'd said nothing of it to my dad – and if she'd said anything to him, after the Presbyterian manner, he wasn't letting on. I would have been glad to let it go as a not atypical example of maternal over-protectiveness, but I couldn't, you see, so there I was fuming over her remark, and listing in my head all the many reasons why she was wrong, wrong, wrong. In ten minutes, well below the hotel by then, I came across a large, flat rock, pocked with small pools of icy sea water, in which marine anemones wriggled about, where I placed my glass, then stripped down to my boxers, muttering and snorting all the while, at the unjustness of her accusation, and plunged into the lazy swells of the ocean, the better to converse with myself on the subject.

If either of us could be said to be short-tempered – and in my drunken magnanimity I wasn't conceding either of us were – surely it was my father, not me. His hard line on homosexuality was just for starters. The man was crazy with the potency of his temper, the potential foulness of his moods. At his worse he was a red Indian on the warpath, a loose cannon, an inside job gone dreadfully wrong, an airship up in flames, and that ship had sailed, the pot boiled over, the Alaska baked, the *coup de grace*. By the time I'd done with him, swimming alone down the dark coastline (I was also an excellent swimmer) I'd made my father out in my mind to be a menace to society, but was I any better? A multitude of small grievances and social sins started popping off in my head, like flashbulbs, not least the short shrift I'd given the barman at the Empire on University Avenue, with his remark about the carved lion's head not doing anything. And that wee firework display had cost me a fiver! Ooch, but you're both just a couple of short-tempered dunderheads, scallywags! You no better than he, not a speck of difference: cutting, belligerent and foul of mood. So I told myself, but convincing me was the harder matter, as I was no man's fool, not even my own. Who had I learned to be that way from, how to behave like that, hmmm? That was the real topic of debate. Who of us was the father, and who the son, after all? Any egg, when put under pressure, will eventually crack (I pointed out to myself, quite sensibly, while cutting through the ocean like a sea-otter) so what hope for the egg that someone drops a bloody pterodactyl on? Excuses, my better half – that traitorous swine – rebutted. Fancy footwork, nothing more. Evasions. Self-serving jibber-jabber. You're too old, at twenty, Winston, even if only barely twenty – and too damn good! – to be placing the blame for your orneriness at the feet of your poor oul' dad. That wouldn't do, not at all at all.

Just then I heard something which, in the darkness, sounded big and formidable whooshing by me in the water, and in its wake a shifting wave of sea-pressure that could only have signalled the close passing of a man-eating shark, or worse, which inspired me even though, swimming blind, I'd drifted a considerable distance from the shore, to exit those dark waters with an alacrity that would have made an Olympic athlete proud. I split the waves like a torpedo fired from that juggernaut out of my childhood stories, and turned around, with a weak laugh, once on shore – perhaps three nanoseconds later – to find everything just as serene and welcoming as it had always been. Cursing and laughing, I retrieved my clothes, finished off my drink (and threw the empty whisky glass into the water) then climbed back up onto Dungarvan's deserted main street, where a distant booming immediately caught my attention. It was music, I surmised. Very harsh, raucous music – young people's music – the sort of music guaranteed to bring out the jungle beast in every prim-and-proper country lass in the town. So naturally I had no choice but to track down the location of its source.

It was coming from the end of a narrow, dark alley, down a short flight of steep concrete steps, and within a door propped open by a cinder-block around which a small cluster of local boys were laughing, smoking and drinking their pints. I immediately switched over to Irish mode – by this late date my accent was so well-rehearsed, even the great Henry Higgins, or my mother, would have failed to divine the ruse – and down the steps I skipped, lighting a cigarette.

"Five quid cover, mate," one of these lads said, with an apologetic smile. I was about to protest, I'd planned only to stay for a single beer, but thought better of it. I knew a few starving artists back home, so I handed over the cash.

Another of this small group asked, "You been swimming, man?"

"A dip of just a moment's duration."

The little group looked around at each other incredulously.

"Well, it's your funeral, mate. There's barracuda in them waters at this time of year, and at night – when the sea calms down – they like to come out to play. One o' them cheeky wee buggers could have your nut-sack off before you said Jiminy Cricket."

Made fierce with strong drink, I laughed and said, "I heard something out there, sure enough. I thought maybe a shark. I got out right quick."

"You're not from around these parts, are you?"

"Up Dublin way."

"Huh," said my young inquisitor, scratching his scruffy chin. "A long way from home, then. There's no sharks here, man. The Gulf Stream comes in here – it fetches in flotsam and jetsam from all over the fookin' globe. Me da once found a crate of oranges, floated in all the way from fookin' Australia! But it warms the water too. Sharks don't like that. Barracuda, on the other hand–"

"What's the band?" I asked, having heard enough about the fookin' nut-sack-snatching barracuda.

"The Swankers," another boy answered. "From London, on tour. They're fookin' great!"

The other boys all nodded in enthusiastic agreement. I excused myself from their company, and made my way inside.

A death-trap, pure and simple, was my immediate first impression. A disaster waiting to happen. Three hundred boys and girls filled a space that would have been full at half that number, lit by a great multitude of candles, all the kids drinking beer and smoking up to five cigarettes each. In the corners, I could see some kids huddled around, furtively smoking pot – the room's low ceilings, and cedar-brick walls hung droopily with some sort of ghastly purple and grey bunting. The whole place was dry and fire-resistant as a bale of hay in August. Some of the kids were seated at tables, but a lot of them were milling about, or dancing with considerable animation, their arms and lit cigarettes flailing thither and yon in a frenzied abandon, in time with the great thundering noise that rolled down off the stage. All this hideous bunting, I supposed, was to give what was obviously just a large basement cellar a more cosmopolitan air, like the clubs the sophisticated Dublin boys and girls frequented further north, but it didn't appear to have glommed on anyone that the slightest spark would light the place up like a fookin' Viking funeral pyre, and in fact they were all just the walking dead – the walking, drinking, laughing, flirting, dancing, smoking deceased, waiting for the Grim Reaper to grow tired of their capriciousness, and throw the switch.

"Something from the bar, man?" a young waiter with a cigarette drooping from his kisser asked me, as I stood there, scanning the room. "You been in the water?"

"A pint of Harp for me."

"Ta! Back in a jiff!"

In the far, far reaches of the gloom I could barely make out a red sign, saying EMERGENCY EXIT ONLY, but if the emergency exit possessed anything near like the grandeur of the entrance, well, then these kids were just begging for an early death. Clearly, it was insanity to stay, yet I was loath to go – the whole damn spectacle was too anarchic and suicidal to turn my back on – so I came to an uneasy truce with my will for self-preservation, by deciding to linger close by the door I'd come in through, though even that seemed a mad risk. In the event of a panic, both exits would be so clogged with struggling bodies, I'd have been as safe out in the middle of the bloody dance-floor, with all the rest. Could it be these children had such little regard for their mortal hides? The majority of them were dressed in a fashion that was new to me – jeans and white tee shirts – but with great rips and holes gouged into them, as on purpose, and makeshift lettering on the shirts. PUNK RULES! FUCK THE QUEEN! ANARCHY IN THE UK! Their hair was spiked with gel, and quite a few of them had dyed it some outlandish colour. Large clothes-pins – 'nappy-pins' my mother would have called them – were jabbed through their clothing here and there, and more than one of them affected a pin or two in lieu of a nose- or ear-ring. Here were my father's wee space aliens, come to life, and come to call. *Hellooo* little space aliens! At a nearby table, I saw a bosomy teenager wearing a promotional Pink Floyd concert tee shirt, except below where it said Pink Floyd she had added in lipstick SUCKS! Just then the barman came back with my beer, and I paid him.

"How often does this go on?" I asked, or rather shouted at him over the din.

"Four nights a week, Wednesday to Saturday," he shouted back. "It's not often, but, that we get a band in here this fookin' fantastic!"

Then he was gone, disappeared back into the mass of writhing bodies, and I remembered one of the boys at the entrance had said the band was over from London, on tour, which I supposed gave reason enough for the anti-British sloganeering. Still, FUCK THE QUEEN? Way down here in Dungarvan? I took a large mouthful of beer and, still standing, with the exit ever in the corner of my eye, drank in the spectacle – a *dance macabre* or a recreation of something out of Edgar Allen Poe – in speechless wonder. Of course, I had no way of knowing

The Swankers, in only a few short months, would replace their current lead singer with Johnny Rotten, and change their name to The Sex Pistols, or at least they were destined to do so if any of them survived this starry night. But how much anarchy were they spreading right now in this nascent form? Enough to kill three hundred cheerful, willing children, in a gloomy basement in a little town in Southern Ireland? That, I thought, was a boat-load of fookin' anarchy! I checked my watch. It was only a few minutes before midnight. If I were destined to die in this place, at least it probably wouldn't be on my birthday.

Over the course of our westward travels, along the southern coast of Ireland, we had slowed down the pace considerably, my father and I, and now as often as not spent three or four hours in a place, instead of the normal one or two – saving the two days we'd spent in Dublin – when we would stop only for a bite to eat and a quick look-see. There was something in those southern climes that made us feel more generous with our time, I suppose. I had duly noted the difference in the pace of things, say, between Belfast – where everyone was fleet-of-foot, their eyes glued firmly to their watches – and Dublin – where things moved along smartly enough, but where a good time with your fellow man seemed the higher priority – to here, where hustle and bustle of any sort seemed as foreign as the great conflict – the Troubles – to the north. In a little village – I forget which one – we loitered so long a group of boys asked me if I wanted to join in their cricket match, but I didn't know the game and declined. Another time we found a bed and breakfast early, and spent a glorious five hours lolling around on a strand so bright it hurt your eyes, my father deeply immersed in my copy of *A History of Irish Poetry* at a picnic table, beneath an enormous tree, and me revisiting Dante's gleeful portrait of Heaven and Hell, spread out on a towel between two dunes, though after every canto or two I put the book aside and ran down to the sea for a wee splasheen in the waves, ever refreshing myself (though on the lookout for barracuda) before returning to the Maestro's vengeful passion play of the ways of God and men. Over a picnic lunch I asked my dad what more he could tell me about our relations, the Landrys and the Crowleys.

"Ach, sure by now you must be exhausted from hearing all that clap-trap," he laughed. "This is *our* time now, Winter," he added, stretching in his chair and turning his face up toward the sun. "Savour it!" he said. "Savour each blessed moment of it, son, for life is short and death lasts a good long while."

"Aye."

In yet another of these anonymous little towns, we came across an ancient church – though still very much a going concern, with a small cemetery which seemed to have more than its fair share of men killed in the war – World War Two – so we stopped a while there too, reading the names and the dates.

"James O'Hara," I read from one of the tombstones. "Born June 10th 1917 – my birthday! And died August 14th 1940." I looked up at my dad, woefully, shaking my head in wonder. "Dead at twenty-three years, two months old," I said. "A casualty of war."

"And not even his war."

"Aye."

We stood there for a while, contemplating a small scattering of bees busying themselves amongst the flowers, and then I said to my father, "But as a Belfast man, it would have been yours. Why didn't you go and fight during the war?"

"Och well," my dad replied, after what seemed like a long time. "As you know, Winter, my brother – your uncle Conrad – and I didn't participate. The Crowleys hadn't been in the north so long that we felt any compelling moral duty to put our lives on the line for it. We considered ourselves pacifists."

"Pacifists?"

"Aye. son. Or I suppose, to frame the matter in a more strictly accurate way, we considered ourselves Christians – good Christian men, both strong and true – and this coming war, being as it was between ourselves and other good Christian men, seemed a great sin against God. Of course this was during the time when war had yet to be declared. But everyone could see it coming. And many were the men of Northern Ireland, and even the south, who couldn't wait for the day. But my brother and I – and a great many of our friends – thought otherwise. As I said, we saw it through Christian eyes, as a sin, as a blemish on the face of two fine nations."

"You didn't see the Germans as a scourge? Not even after the Great War?"

"Och – now the Great War was a slightly different story. A different kettle of fish. There were enough causes and explanations to the Great War, to give a man the epilepsy, just trying to list them all. First, the Germans was allied with the Prussians, and then the Austro-Hungarians, against the English and the French. Then the Russians wanted in on the fun too. Next thing you know, the English and French are all for tearing each other to shreds – so that was business as usual – looking for support from the Ottoman Empire! The Italians was universally despised, and he is my friend who is the enemy of my enemy. Even the bloody Poles and Africans and Japanese wanted in on the action. The Greeks! No, no! The Great War was very much a different kettle of fish. In many ways, I would say the Germans were duped into that terrible war. But from a more God's-eye-view still, it would be accurate to say they was all simply confused into it. By a single gunshot. The whole bloody lot of them."

"Any regrets about it?"

"That I bowed out of the war?" my father laughed. "Don't be daft!"

"Still, as an Ulsterman – even newly arrived – it couldn't have been an easy decision to make."

"It wasn't. We paid a price for that decision – the lot of us. Conrad took quite the hazing on account of his views, and he wouldn't have been old enough to participate for years yet! I remember having to knock a few of the bigger lads' teeth out, on his account – this was at Methody – for to keep him from getting beat to a pulp for refusing to say he'd serve. There was one teacher in particular – a Mr. Wilde – Wilde by name and wild by nature we used to say of him – though certainly not to his face. That fellah would cane a boy for the crookedness of his smile. He was our Maths instructor."

"What branch?"

"Say again, son," my dad, who had been lost in thought, asked me.

"What branch of mathematics?"

"I don't remember, Winter. I was never the mathematical genius you turned out to be. Anyway, old Mr. Wilde had a face like a wrung-out sponge, and a disposition to match, and he took it into his head that if any boy under his command didn't show a sufficient patriotism, or love of country, then by God he was all for beating it into him. He had the lot of us black and blue, so he did, did Mr. Wilde. No relation to Oscar, at least to my knowledge. We weren't Irishmen, we were British!

Whether we liked it or not. And for anyone begging to differ, there was always the flat of his hand to answer to."

"But why didn't you report him?"

"To who, son?"

"To the Principal! To the authorities! To your parents!"

"Ach, Winter," said my father. "You're dreaming in Technicolor, man."

IX

As we came around into east county Cork, the first thing my dad wanted to do was detour north, up to the province of Munster, to visit one of Ireland's oldest and least-endangered so-called 'Gaeltacht' regions – the barony of Muskerry West – one of many small pockets of the country where Irish was still used in the majority, or a large fraction of it – an active concern although as a spoken language it had been on the wane for some time – and where the public signage was in Gaelic. "It's there we'll see the true old Ireland, son, and get to hear a language as pleasing to the ear as any contrived by men, while it's still around to be listened to."

"There are baronies in southern Ireland?"

"Still. Twenty-four of them, in county Cork alone. They date back as early as the sixth century, and were a convenient way of further sub-dividing the counties, for the meting out of the justice, and the tax collecting. The baronies were created after the Norman invasion of Ireland, though they haven't been used for administrative purposes since nearly the turn of the 20th Century. Even so, they make up an important part of the Gaeltacht, and take a great pride in preserving the old ways."

So up we drove, to the province of Munster, to the Barony of Muskerry West, in the heart of Ireland's

Gaeltacht – where I fervently prayed there might still be a few people who spoke English, as neither my father nor I had a word of Irish between us. We stopped for petrol at a garage, where we couldn't read the signs, and the young woman who came out to do the honours at the pumps got a kick out of my dad's sputtering attempts to *sprechen* the lingo, as did I. She told him, in a much friendlier manner than I'd been told the same, under similar circumstances, while driving through Quebec, that it was all right, she spoke English too, as did almost everybody under a thousand years old, and we needn't put ourselves out to accommodate the local culture. For this we thanked her, although I could see she was touched by my father's efforts to do just that.

"Where are yeas from?"

"Belfast," my father replied.

"Ah – a long way from home. You too?"

I nodded yes, then added, to account for my accent, "But raised in Canada."

"Canada!" She said something in Irish that sounded like a mouthful of songbirds chirping. "I have a cousin who moved to Canada with her husband." She told us the cousin's name, but I'm not even going to try to reproduce it phonetically. It was a long name, full of glottal stops, sibilant 'Ks' and coughing, though quite lyrical, in its way. "You don't know her, do you?"

"What part of Canada did she move to?" I asked.

"Is Canada divided into parts? Ooch, how stupid you must think me, of course it is! I couldn't say what part of Canada they moved to. Near no sea nor ocean, is all I know."

I smiled up at her. "Then likely not."

Back on the road, I noticed the country had flattened out a little from the usual rolling hills and dales, and besides the ubiquitous sheep, the fenced-in rocky fields also harboured small herds of cows, even horses. While in transit we saw a handsome young boy and a pretty girl, both on horseback, the boy chasing the girl towards a dell, or maybe a berm, their destination in all likelihood a covert bower for the making of wee Irish babies. Out of the blue my father said:

"So, it's off to university with you, in the fall! That'll be a grand experience for you. I know it was for me. Have you decided on a major?"

It felt odd speaking of such things with my dad.

"I don't have to declare one until my second year."

"Even so – mathematics, will it be?"

"In some form or other."

"You'll make a fine maths teacher."

"Like Mr. Wilde?" I asked him, as a cod, and he laughed.

"Who knows, maybe even better! You'll do well son, whatever your chosen field. This I know. I–"

I could feel him suppressing the urge to add more – no doubt remembering how poorly his flattering remarks had gone over the first time. "Aye, you'll do well. Though I must confess, I'd always harboured the fond hope you might find a calling in the Presbytery."

"The Presbytery!" Now it was my turn to suppress a laugh. It was no secret I actively disliked organized religion, which had been a thorn in my father's side for a long time indeed, as Sunday after Sunday he'd been forced to coldly order me out of the house, into the family sedan, for my weekly dousing in piety, whether I liked it or not, in the fond hope that some of it would stick. I think my father assumed my resistance was anchored in resentment at the loss of an hour's childhood pleasure, but it was more than that. Even from an early age, I'd sensed something essentially flawed, something fundamentally incorrect, about organized religion, which when I exited the church at the end of the service left me feeling dirty and hypocritical for the rest of the day. Of course my father's default position was that as a mere child, an urchin without an ounce of common sense, I knew nothing and required strict adult instruction, especially in matters which pertained to the salvation of my immortal soul. But he was wrong. As he had been in so many ways.

"Of course, maths is a fine profession too."

"Physics."

"Physics?"

"That's what I'm really interested in. I can earn my PhD in eight years – nine, tops. It's a strange world we live in, dad. Full of wondrous things. I'd like to get to the bottom of what makes it tick."

"And I certainly don't blame you for wanting to try, son. But sure the church is as good or better an avenue, to reach that goal, as the one you're proposing."

Had nothing of my essential nature been absorbed by this man, even after twenty years? I smiled, and answered, diplomatically, I hoped, "Well, on that we might not be entirely in agreement."

"Oh? In what ways do we differ?"

Back to the science! thought I. Or else this pony was going to canter right off the fookin' cliff. "Physics deals exclusively with the actual, physical world – not the moral or spiritual realms you speak of, though they're important too. And it's mind-boggling in its complexity, its strangeness. How, for example, can the universe be both infinite and limited at the same time? At first glance the two seem profoundly mutually exclusive. But science tells us to think of the universe as an enormous sphere, a ball, except in ten dimensions or more, and we as ants crawling along its surface. The ants could spend their whole lives crawling around and around on that ball, and would never see its beginning or end. To the ants the world appears an infinite place, but we can stand back and easily see its limits are well-defined. It's impossible to imagine what a ten dimensional ball would look like – no more so can the ants imagine the sphere – so we have difficulty with the concept on our scale. But the problem is one of perception, nothing more. That's what makes physics so appealing. You don't need to rely on the evidence of your senses. They're limited. The equations are not, and they don't lie."

"Well," my father answered, a little more coldly than strictly required. "In the eyes of God, your wee rubber ball is but a party balloon, for the amusement of children. Take care for the idols you worship, Winston. There's greater things at stake than the fate of ants."

That evening we stopped for dinner at a pub that seemed a bit rougher than the sparkling, bullet-riddled chrome-and-oak palaces you found in Belfast, or even the spun-sugar soufflés whipped up by the Dubliners, for their evening's entertainments. By then we were out of Munster again, out of the Gaeltacht, pressing down on the City of Cork itself, which, while no less urban than any other large Irish city, seemed to exude a sort of rural twang, a rough-honed pioneer primitiveness that was as fascinating to observe as the Belfast billionaires in their expensive cars, or the thoughtful Dubliners in their turtleneck sweaters and tweed sports jackets. As always, they were a jolly, welcoming lot in this pub, but they had dirt beneath their fingernails from tending the land, and a few of them were in desperate need of a shave. We willingly joined in their banter, and answered all their questions – me still in Canadian mode, in deference to my father, though I soon regretted it. It was a jolly good time, but as with so much else about these more urban southerners, their sense of humour seemed rougher-honed when compared to the average, so when they decided to play a wee cod on the Canadian boy I decided to play along, my father following my lead, just to see where they thought it would get them.

"This is not well known in the north," one of them said. "But it was right here in Cork-town that St. Patrick began his mission in Ireland." My father and I cut each other a glance, both of us knowing full well that St. Patrick had begun his mission in Ireland in the north, and in fact had been buried in Downpatrick cemetery, not a stone's throw from Belfast. "It was here that the Great Saint began the purging, for to be driving out all the turtles from Ireland."

"Turtles!" I laughed. "I thought St. Patrick was famed for driving the snakes from Ireland."

"Ooch, but that's just a legend. Sure Ireland is a closed – a closed – what is it again, Garvin?"

"A closed ecosphere?" Garvin suggested.

"A closed ecosphere. There are not, and never was, any snakes in Ireland, any more than there was ever kangaroos. But turtles? That's a different story. Why, time was Ireland was crawling with the little buggers, crawling! Some years you were waddling knee deep through 'em, while they clogged up the fields and pastures, threatening to turn the livestock into stripped-down skeletons. A curse, I tells yeas, and ever bolder in their ways with the passing of each season. There are reports in the county records of innocent Irish women and children being awakened, in the dawn, to the sensation of wee turtles nibbling at their fingers and toes, or attempting to climb up on the tables, for to be inspecting the fookin' pantry. And every year the situation just kept getting worse, until even the cows in the barns and the pigs in their sties were bloody terrified to go outside. The cow's milk production tapered off, and the consensus was that the ham and bacon those years was of a decidedly inferior quality."

"Jeepers," I whistled. "That must have been terrible hard on the locals."

"It was."

"What year would this have been around, now?

"Oh! Ah – sometime in the twelfth century, I think, if memory serves me still. Or earlier, maybe."

Another cut glance between the northerners. Or earlier, definitely! These boy-oh's were having trouble even keeping their cod straight, let alone their faces. "So anyways," the chieftain of the Codders continued, from beyond the pale. "The great St. Patrick hears all about it, from Spain, or Africa, or wherever he happened to be serving the Church at the time, and over he comes straight away, to see what's what. And within a year's time there wasn't a single turtle to be seen in all the land, from Bantry Bay to the Belfast harbour. Clean as a whistle, from stem to stern."

"But," says my father. "But what did St. Patrick do with all the wee turtles?"

"Drove 'em into the sea!"

"But," says I, "aren't turtles amphibious? That is to say," I added, in case they were unfamiliar with the term, "don't they live both on land and water? What was to stop the wee turtles from splashing out to sea, having a nice swim around for a bit, while they waited for St.

Patrick to calm down, then climbing right back up on dry land to be continuing their cheeky ways? No, what St. Patrick would have needed was a big pit, a thousand tons of something flammable, like peat, and a torch. I wonder, is there such a pit anywhere in the vicinity? It might be worthwhile to check the parish deed."

Stumped silence for a moment, then, "Sharks!" one of the others erupted, banging his fist on the table.

"Aye, sharks. The sharks got the turtles, before they had time to climb back up on dry land."

"But," I laughed. "Everyone knows the Gulf Stream comes into these waters, and makes them too warm for sharks. Barracuda maybe, but–"

"Barracuda, aye."

"Aye."

"Aye."

"Aye, it was the barracuda, right enough." So we all agreed it must surely have been the barracuda, and to celebrate we bought another round, but by then the wind had gone out of their sails, these boys, and they were much dispirited to have been out-codded by a smartass Canadian and his da, their feelings hurt you could tell, one or two of them, for which I was truly sorry as the Irish take great pride in their wit and their story-telling abilities.

Cork.

"Welcome to the rebel city, son." I remembered Cork vaguely from a childhood visit, and was surprised to find it much more cosmopolitan than I remembered. The streets were very wide, a leftover from bygone days when horse-drawn vehicles required a large turning radius, but paved, whereas I had a memory of cobblestones and gravel. A lot can change in ten years of course, but one thing hadn't changed. Cork was still the

pharmaceutical capital of Ireland (though not nearly the powerhouse it would become once Pfizer had developed Viagra there) and a general air of large-business prosperity was nicely balanced against the smaller family shops that littered Patrick street, Cork's main drag. It was not lost upon me that Cork was also the stated destination of Becky McNamara, who had said she had family there, and no sooner were we within the city limits than I went on high alert, on the look-out for the short-bobbed blonde hair, or the swaying ass I had admired so long when she had ventured down off the Martello Tower at Sandymount, in Dublin.

"Listen to the accents, son," my dad suggested. "They're different from any other Irish accent you'll hear. That's the Hibernian influence. They don't call Cork the rebel city for nothing. Many an Irishman considers Cork the true capital of Ireland, due to the role Cork played as the centre for the anti-unionist forces during the civil war, as well as its support for the Yorkist cause during the War of the Roses. As Irish a city as you'll find, with a culture rich and deep, and many fine examples of ancient architecture too. The Red Abbey. St. Mary's Cathedral. St. Fin Barre's Cathedral."

Why won't you come to me, woman of my dreams? Warrior priestess, damsel in distress? Why hold back now, so coyly, you with the fruit-bearing banded arms, you with the sun-bronzed skin, the true, original Cassandra of my longings and imagination? While my father blathered on, I scanned the crowded streets, and indeed there were one or two shops with the name McNamara in the window, above the signage. Of course McNamara was a common name in the south, but even so it was a promising sign. So why won't you come to me, angel from the realm of things unseen, woman of my dreams, my soul's desire?

"Cork is home to the Everyman Palace Theatre, and the Granary theatre both – both venerable institutions – and a lovely great Opera House. There's an Academy of Music here."

"I heard Rory Gallagher was from around these parts," I added. "Him and his bandmates, Taste."

"Should I know those names?"

"No," I laughed. "No, I guess you shouldn't. Look dad, it's a bit early yet for lunch. Let's poke around for a while first."

"Agreed," my father said. "Together, or should we split up?"

"Oh, let's split up," I suggested. "I want to have a look down Patrick street, and you–" I almost said he'd be wanting to find a pub. "You'll be wanting to explore the architecture."

"Back at the car in an hour?"

"An hour." And off he went.

The first business I came to with the name McNamara attached to it had never heard of a Rebecca, though they pointed out McNamara's Upholstery and Leather, much further down the way on Patrick street, where an unrelated McNamara clan was said to have been fabricating saddles and refurbishing furniture for nigh-on sixty years. I thanked the old man behind the cash register and stepped back into the sunshine. It was eleven in the morning, yet the streets were bustling with children. Then I remembered it was probably summer holiday here, and the kids set loose from school to help in the shops or the farms. I remembered meeting an acquaintance of my father's back in Canada, a teacher at the University of Toronto working on his doctoral in education, who told me of a cutting-edge school – a really radical experiment – recently opened in County Armagh, where forays were being conducted into the integration of Catholic and Protestant students into one program. An integrated school. It was quite a radical idea, in Irish pedagogical circles. I smiled to myself in the coolish sunshine, and watched the children chasing each other about, clumps of old men in dark clothing talking earnestly to each other, gesturing with their pipes for emphasis, young men gallantly strolling to the right with their young ladies, so to protect them from splashing water from passing motorists, though the streets were dry today, and shop-owners in long aprons, their sleeves rolled up to their elbows, sweeping the sidewalks in front of their businesses with straw brooms. A milk-truck tinkled up the street, stopping here and there at private homes to drop off two fresh quarts in glass bottles, and pick up the empties in return. They still did that down here. Somewhere in the distance was the smell of freshly baked soda farls, and I thought, this Cork of 1975 could be the Dublin of 1904 – the Dublin of *Ulysses* – it had been trapped in a time-warp and nothing ever aged. And would you take that trade-off, Winston, I asked myself? Would you content yourself to live here, amongst these good people, in exchange for eternal youth? I laughed, because of course I knew the answer was no.

Expensive, tailor-made suits from Seville Row were a common sight up in Belfast, but here it was all morning suits, tweeds with open collars, even the odd straw boater, and I thought Stephen Dedalus would have been perfectly contented here, trapped in a time-warp, thinking his esoteric thoughts and writing his books with only a letter of the alphabet as a title. *Did you read his C? Oh yes, but his W was wonderful!* I laughed, and pushed on to the upholsterers and saddle makers, McNamara, where I learned that Becky was indeed one of theirs, a cousin recently returned to the fold from Australia on account – at first – of her mother's grave illness, but now on account of her mother's recent passing, and I was shocked and saddened to hear of this, for certain, especially in light of all the dirty thoughts I'd been harbouring since that fateful encounter in Dublin. Now here Becky was, a motherless daughter, and all I could think about were her breasts! I asked the young man behind the counter if Becky's current whereabouts were known, and he replied by asking me who wants to know? I told him I was an acquaintance, that I had met her on her first arrival up in Dublin, and that I was very sorry indeed to hear this tragic news, wishing to express my condolences. He asked me how it came about a Dublin boy was down in Cork, and I told him I was from the north. So I was originally from Belfast then, he next asked, with an unseemly suspiciousness. I admitted I was.

"Dunno where Becky might be right now," he said. "And I dunno as I'd tell yeas if I did, mate."

I smiled and nodded. I understood, I said. That would be all right. I thanked him for his time, and once more offered my sincerest condolences to the family for their recent loss.

"Thanks," he replied, softening towards me a little. "I appreciate that."

Come lunch it was the ubiquitous pub once again, and I wondered once more if you could cross Cork without passing one, any more easily than you could cross Dublin, Belfast or all of bloody Ireland for that matter. The likelihood seemed remote. Some days it seemed the consumption of beer and whiskey was the prime moving force behind the whole economy, and never mind the pharmaceuticals or the ship-building. I still had no intention of sharing any new intelligence regarding Rebecca McNamara with my dad. I don't know why.

"There was a falling out, was there?" I asked him instead, over my stew.

"A falling out! Between who, son?"

"The Crowleys and the Landrys. There must have been. Why else would the Crowleys suddenly decide to pull up stakes, change their religion, and move north?" And why else, I though, would my father not wish to shake the hand of William Landry, back up the road? Though of that I said nothing.

"There was no falling out, Winter," my father told me. "There's never been a falling out in this family. Blood is thicker than water, sure, so rest your mind easy on that account. No, it wasn't that simple. You're asking me about things that happened well before I was born, son, my only source being either kin who didn't much want to talk about it, or kin I never met. Yet there are some things that can be deduced from what little I do know." He looked around, as though to be certain we weren't being overheard. "There would have been no need for a family altercation, to give rise to the Crowleys' decision to move to the north. We were Protestants, living in a Catholic Republic, and relatively well off, compared to some businessmen and land-owners, educated people. There was always the possibility that we might have been Loyalists too, a suspicion not entirely unjustified in certain quarters. I'm not going to sit here and tell you that the Landrys and Crowleys were persecuted, on account of their religious beliefs, son. It was nothing as ugly as that, and besides, religious persecution seems to be confined to the north, for the most part, especially in these troublesome times.

But there were suspicions and resentments to be contended with, which no doubt served to draw the Landrys and Crowleys even closer together, who weren't so much one big happy family as a loose coalition of cousins, in-laws, business partners and the like. Even so, what they had in common helped keep them stuck together, the enemy of my enemy being my friend, as it were, and even though they had their differences, say over the matter of the British – as seen in the example of the death of young Pete Landry, but pre-dating the Great War by half-a-yard or more – it was nothing to be shaking them asunder. They were made of sterner stuff back then, maybe, good Christian men, strong and true, plus maybe there were just too many strong connections, both financial and connections of the heart."

"So what, the Crowleys got tired of even a subtle persecution, on account of wealth and status, and fled north, while the Landrys – good Christians strong and true – stuck it out down in the Republic?"

"They were both factions made up of the same stern stock, Winter, and don't forget it! But you're looking for simple answers where there aren't any. For one thing, the Landrys' money was more firmly anchored to the ground, in the form of real estate and other investments in the land. Whereas the Crowleys were more town folk, with multiple businesses and interests that could be more easily liquefied. Not that the Crowleys loved the land any less than the Landrys. They were all of them fierce patriots in their different ways. But the Crowleys only ever owned the one piece of land – the farm down at Carnalynch. Just the one, but it was a big one! You remember it, surely. You've been there several times. By tradition, the farm was passed down to the oldest Crowley son, so by rights it should have fallen to me and of course, eventually to you, but I deferred it over to a cousin, who was eager to farm it. I was in Canada by then, and in mid-career, with no desire to move back to Carnalynch. And by now I'm guessing the same could be said for you, in spades."

I laughed.

"But it was important to me that the land be kept within the family, so I handed the deed over to Willy Crowley, a cousin once removed I guess, in your case. And everything's been running smoothly down there – or up there now – ever since. Do you remember that farm, Winter?"

"Aye."

Did I ever! The last time I'd seen it I would have been ten or twelve, when it was still presided over by a pair of ancient sisters, Daisy and Lily Crowley, doddering, ancient, blind as bats, crippled with the arthritis and one of them with a goitre, but no less indomitable for all all that; every morning, feeding the chickens and collecting the eggs, tending to the goats and sheep, even a pig or two, for the slaughtering of which they brought in a local handyman with an axe. The floors of the old farmhouse were raw, poured cement – nothing more – with throw-rugs laid down on top, and the only source of heat or for cooking, summer or winter, was a cast-iron, wood-burning stove, dating back to the early days of Queen Victoria, although the sisters kept an ancient, Coleman-like gas burner in the drawing room, which they could light for the boiling of water for tea.

"We should stop in there, before our trip is done."

"I'm glad to hear you suggest it, son. Though I confess it was already on my agenda."

In light of all the terrible things that were about to happen, we never did get to make that side-trip to the old farm at Carnalynch, which is a pity for it harboured some fond memories for me, especially of the old sisters, who were very good to me: and also I think harboured my first inkling that there was such a thing as the past, even a distant past, which I was connected to in ways I didn't understand, by chains of a tensile strength my own feeble strength would never be able to break. After lunch we were back on the streets of Cork again, together this time, though I would have preferred to be alone, meandering from historical site to geological wonder, and it was all very interesting but I wasn't likely to lose sight of the fact that Rebecca McNamara was somewhere on those same streets, except there were so many I despaired a chance encounter. Even so I kept my eyes open for a girl with short blonde hair and tear-stained eyes, with an Australian accent and an orange in her pocket, flown in fresh from Oz, mate.

We ended the day the way we always seemed to – in a pub. We drank our fill and chatted with the locals, as pleasant a way as any to get to know such distant people, far removed from life as I knew it, and listened to what they had to say about this wicked world with all its delightful surprises, its fearsome turns-of-events. Come eight o'clock dad asked me, should we just push on for Bantry now – which wasn't far – or wait until morning, so as to make the great turn and start up the western coast? I surprised him by saying I wanted to stay a while longer in Cork, yet, as even though it counted little in the annals of our family's history, and had no literary significance for me, I still found a wondrous place, somehow, and wanted to take some additional time to look around. My dad was puzzled but willingly agreed. We had two weeks to spare, more, and every mile we travelled, once we turned northwards at Bantry Bay, was a mile closer we'd be to Belfast, to Canada, instead of further away.

X

The next morning I was up very early indeed – the break of dawn – and it did me good to know the roosters could still be heard here and there in the far distance, announcing the beginning of a brand new day. I slipped out quietly and walked the streets, having left a note for my father, and was soon lost in thought until I came upon an old beggar woman, sitting cross-legged on the sidewalk like a witch on a toadstool, shivering a little in the early morning light. I had almost no silver in my pockets, so I pulled a quid from my wallet, and handed it to her.

"God bless you, sir!" she cried. "God bless and keep you!"

"'Tis nothing," I laughed. "Nothing at all."

"Is it the north yer down from?"

That surprised me. Henry Higgins, move over, you've met your match! This old woman might have been dressed in rags, but there was nothing shabby in the keenness of her ear.

"Belfast."

"Well," says she. "God bless you anyway"

I laughed. "Just a trifle," I said, "for the feedin' of the birds."

She caught my allusion immediately.

"Tuppence a bag, is it? I know that play! You have a generous heart, and a princely soul, sir."

I laughed. "There are some who might disagree, mother," I told her. "How old are you, if I may ask?"

"Seventy-eight, or seventy-nine," she said. "Depending who you ask."

"And are you a Cork-woman all your life?"

"Born and bred."

"Then maybe you can answer me something that's been on my mind." I was thinking of the little church, with its cemetery full of dead soldiers, soldiers who died in a war that wasn't even their war, and something my father had said about southern Irish being eager to fight. During the Second World War, do you remember, was there a lot of excitement for it? In Cork? Were the young men eager to join and go fight the Germans?"

"That's a funny question, from one as young as yourself!" she said, gathering up her features as in deep concentration. "But in all seriousness, no, not really. Of course everyone knew the war was coming on, and that it was fixing to be a big one. But sure, there was no love lost for the English down in these parts – in fact the English was the more immediate peccadillo. So in answer to your odd question, I would have to say no. No one was eager to go fightin' any Germans."

"And what of things in the north? Now, I mean. Are the good citizens of Cork paying heed to the Troubles?"

The old woman looked up with saucer-eyes, cast a glance up the street, then smiled thinly and shook her head as in wonder. "I'll advise you," she told me, "to have a care who you're asking questions like *that* question, in these parts, young sir. You're likely as not to ask the wrong person, and get your block knocked off."

"You're joking, right?"

"Either that," the old woman said, "or a bullet to the knee."

After parting ways I continued my solitary wandering, with no goal in mind except to see the town and hope for a miracle. As the morning wore on the streets got busier, and I began wondering how it could be that, on a week-day, there should be so many able-bodied young men out and about, evidently without a care in the world. It reminded me – as did so many things – of *Ulysses*, where aside from Bloom (who's in advertising) and Stephen (a part-time teacher) almost no-one is seen to be gainfully employed, even though there are hundreds of characters. Maybe I was right, I told myself, when I surmised it was the consumption of beer that kept the economy afloat. I passed a schoolyard where a group of kids were kicking around a ball – one of them lofted it in my direction, which I was obliged to step off the kerb to field. A horn blared, and as the car passed the driver called angrily, "Mind where you're walking, man, or you'll get yourself flattened!"

I had breakfast in a tearoom down a long side-street full of gaily-coloured shops, their windows festooned with flowers, and a butcher's shop where a line of small pig carcasses had been strung up by their hind legs, from the ceiling, also on display in the windows. The Irish bacon was especially good, and I lingered over my pot of tea, eavesdropping on a group of well-dressed men embroiled in an animated discussion of things financial, hedge funding I think. Pork belly futures. But my thoughts were never far from Becky McNamara. Even if you were to catch a glimpse of her, what could you possibly say? Remember me, the idiot from the Martello tower? I heard your mum croaked? Very sorry, very sorry. It all seemed so trite and calculated. So second rate. How could she mistake my intentions for anything else but sexual? She might even think I had contrived to be down here, in Cork, for that purpose, though I'd known nothing of her circumstances at the time. Then I remembered I'd told her about the trip with my old man, and Cork was a reasonable distance for us to have travelled by now, although we were only still here for my personal, nefarious reasons. Oh give it up, man! I ordered myself. In three weeks' time you'll be back in Canada, and she'll be a million miles away. Life will go on, as usual, and no-one the worse for wear. I tottered on, up and down the streets aimlessly, getting lost a time or two, needing directions back to Patrick Street, until come lunch I made my way back to the same pub my dad and I had eaten dinner at the night before. I hadn't suggested we meet there in my note, but the place was close to our hotel, and the likelihood of finding him there seemed good. But my father wasn't there. Instead, Becky McNamara was there, sitting at the bar drinking a beer, in jeans, a woollen beige cardigan, and an eggshell blue tee shirt She faced towards the bar, chatting with the barman, but even so I could tell it was her by her hair and her ample hips. I suppressed a sudden urge to just turn on my heel and skedaddle, approaching the bar instead.

"Well," I said, my voice wobbling with nervousness. "It is indeed a very small world!"

She wheeled on her stool and smiled, brow arched. "So it *is* you!" she cried, quite pleased, though I could see her eyes were red from recent crying, the muscles around her mouth tight from tension. "Kevin called last night and told me an Irish boy from the north had been around asking for me. I don't know why I thought it might be you. He said the boy was Irish. Then he said the boy was on a trip with his dad, and the coincidence seemed too great. But why," she added, "would Kevin think you were Irish?"

I switched on the Irish accent. "There seems to be some confusion, as to exactly where I'm from."

Becky giggled.

"Why the deception?"

"It saves me from having to answer the same questions, over and over again."

"Clever. A man of mystery. I must say you have the brogue down tight. You could pass for a local. I could never manage that."

"It's an art," I said, with a smile, in my own natural voice. "Look, Becky – Kevin told me about your mother."

She dropped her head for a moment, then shook her emotions off, and looked back up with a mischievous smile. "Why were you looking for me?"

I felt my cheeks reddening. I ordered a beer.

"It's complicated."

"Is it?"

"Well," I laughed. "Maybe complicated's not the right word." My beer arrived and I took an enormous mouthful.

"What's complicated about it?" she asked me. "I was looking for you, after all."

"You were?"

"Well," she laughed. "For whoever the mystery man was, who had come calling the day before, though I was hoping it was you. This pub is popular with tourists, and there's a hotel not far that's popular with travellers. Like you, Winston. Winter. I've been thinking about you for quite a while. .Winter Crowley. You made me laugh at

Sandymount, and I was a girl in need of a laugh." She snickered a little, then added, "Plus there was all that Joyce."

"Aye. The Joyce."

We drank beer after beer at the bar of that pub, the barman diplomatically retreating from earshot, and my father kindly obliging me by not showing up. We told each other about our lives. Her mother and father had moved to Australia not long after her father graduated from medical school, he to run a medical clinic two days a week, and she to help, the remainder of their week devoted to out-patient work among the Aboriginals, towards which end he had the use of a Piper Cub – both he and his wife, and now Becky too, were licensed pilots – and flew hundreds of miles each day into the Outback, to tend to the sick and distressed, though if any case were urgent – and in that wild country there were always a few – the Piper could be sent with an assistant to bring emergencies in. Becky loved growing up in Oz, where she had learned to swim, to shoot, to fly, and eventually even how to kiss boys, though the town they lived in was small and the pickings few and far between. Her mother – who was an accredited nurse – on the other hand disliked the place, and with homesickness gnawing at her heart the marriage and the fresh start in a wild and mysterious land were soon over, the mother returning to Ireland, the father remaining and remarrying, and Becky and her brother flown back and forth for agreed-upon occasions. Her life situation so mirrored my own – the divorce aside, which had been acrimonious – I remarked on it, and Becky smiled and lowered her head, put her hand on my wrist – on my watch – which gladdened my heart. I could see she didn't want to dwell on recent events, so I avoided them, choosing instead to lift her spirits by making her laugh, the clueless dunderhead from Canada who didn't properly know which side of the pond he owed his allegiance to. She was easy to amuse, this pretty Australian girl, and I went well out of my way to make her smile, to cheer her up but also because she had a lovely smile, and she laughed frequently, and she rested her hand on my knee, and then her forehead on my shoulder, which gladdened me even more. Then at about the fourth beer, she squeezed my knee, as though calling for silence, lowered her head, and in a low voice said, "Winston. Winter –"

"Call me Winter."

"I'm going to ask you something, Winter, and I want you to consider it carefully."

"OK."

"I want you to take me back to my place, and make love to me."

"Ah."

She looked up at me with a wane smile. "Does that surprise you, that a girl would just come out and ask a boy that?"

"Well –"

She laughed.

"You're so sweet! But you mustn't feel pressured, if there's a girl back home – or a boy?"

"There isn't," I said, a bald-faced lie.

"Are you shocked?"

"A little," I said. "But I'll get over it."

"I don't want you to do it, if afterwards you're going to hate me for tempting you into betraying a loved one back home."

"There's no-one, Becky."

"OK, good," she said. "These past few days have been hell. Just *hell!*" She looked up at me most grievously, but then smiled. "And as a result, you see sitting before you a fine example of a girl in need of a right, proper *fucking!*"

I laughed, but in wonder, in wonder. "Do all the wee Australian girls," I asked her, "talk that way, out in the spinifex, amongst the yellow tailed rock wallabies?"

"Yes," Becky laughed. "Yes, we do. You're sure you're OK with this, Winter?"

"Yes."

"And you won't be angry, or hate me afterwards?"

"I won't."

"Well, all right then," Becky said, hopping down off the stool. "What are we waiting for?"

She reached into her pants pocket for money, but I beat her to it, and paid our tab. Then, hand in hand, we walked out into the sunshine on Patrick street, giddy and smiling and a little tipsy. We walked east for a block, me commenting on the various shops, making her giggle, and then she dropped my hand and took my arm, pressing up against me, slowly moving a breast back and forth against my arm until I could feel the nipple, which was distracting in the extreme, but in a good way. Fifteen minutes later, we'd reached a row of single-story bungalows, of a kind I'd seen before – quaint but hardly of historical interest – with nondescript front entrances but broadening out into spacious back yards, the Irish being great ones for the gardening. We turned into one, and Becky told me it belonged to her cousin, and her cousin's husband, who were at work and not expected home too much before seven. Why she wasn't living at her own, family home seemed puzzling, except to say the family house was out in the country somewhere, and this one conveniently located in the heart of Cork, a stone's throw from everything. Hospitals, and funeral parlours, for example, I thought grimly.

Becky let us in, and we were met in the parlour hall by a small black cat – more like a kitten really – which purred and looked up at us quizzically. Becky chucked it beneath the chin and scratched its head, called it Corduroy. Then she took me by the hand and led me into a bedroom, closing the door behind us before turning to face me, to kiss me. That went on and on, that kiss, but soon enough we had each other down on her bed, where I peeled away her clothing in layers, like teasing the petals from a daisy-wheel, kissing her lips and ears and throat and breasts, and on and on, until finally she took my head in her hands and raised it up. "Not fair," she whispered. "You still have all your clothes on."

I soon rectified that, and then we made love, took a rest, then made love again. And that was how things went. Between our love-making Becky lay recumbent and gasping, radiant with sweat in the afternoon light, and we returned to talking about our lives, our hopes and dreams, while Corduroy scratched softly on the other side of the door, mewing. Then the sight of her would get to me again – those breasts, her belly, her bewitching eyes – and we were making love again, and that was how the afternoon passed. Becky was a few years my senior – not many – and knew some things I had only the most rudimentary knowledge of, specifically fellatio, which she performed with a grace of motion and an abandon I could only marvel at, performing as though in willing submission to an enormous, primordial command echoing within, both eager and wanton. Not that the act itself seemed so hard to master, if you were so inclined, and neither was I such a connoisseur that I could have told the difference. Even as she worked me over, I found myself thinking, this is a girl who has just lost her mother, a girl deeply immersed in the throes of grief! And what we were doing was despicable. Then, just as quickly, my better angels piped up, reminding me that we were here at Becky's own suggestion, that I had not uttered the command, and in fact I was playing the role of the good Samaritan and should be commended for the nobleness of my deeds, the goodness of my princely heart.

"Hmmm." Becky sighed, looking up at me. "Is there anything I'm not doing, that you'd like me to do, Winter?"

"Ahh."

"Would you like me to make you come in my mouth? Oh yeah," she added softly, with a mischievous smile, kissing my belly. "I'm going to make you come buckets! When you're ready, this time just let it go, just let it go. I want you to, Winter!" she whispered. "I want to give you so – much – *pleasure*."

Yes. That's the ticket, I told myself. Think of yourself as the good fookin' Samaritan! Yes—think of Gandhi! Think of Mother Theresa! Think of anything else, but not of this lovely Australian girl, hovering over you and moaning, who just asked you to pick up your legs a little to give her more wiggle-room. Yes I said Yes I will *Yes!* Think of *Gandhi!* Mother fookin' *Theresa!* Think of all the hundreds and thousands and millions of the –

XI

A cold-front rolled over the western seaboard of Ireland that evening, turning the ocean to glass while freezing the breaking waves in mid-curl. Snow was in the general forecast, and when it finally came it drifted down with a powdery, luminescent consistency that glittered in the moonlight and limned the hills and valleys in white silhouette. Caught unawares, leprechauns from Killarney to Galway Bay retreated by the thousands, to the comfort of their covens, scratching their wee heads and cursing, while cows lowed and sheep baaed in mass confusion. In pocked rocks all along the coast, sea anemones by the quadrillions froze solid, consequently perishing, and out on the Giant's Causeway old Finn McCool had taken to slaughtering sheep for their hides, to supplement his winter cloak. No one had ever seen the likes of it before. It was an unheard-of climatological wonder, especially for that time of year. Even the sharks found the water too damn cold, and walruses took to scraping icicles from their coats with their tusks, like barnacles, honking angrily in protest. The injustice of it! The wee space aliens fled back to Alpha Centauri, sputtering in their heathen brogue, and the crystal globe at Clonmel flash-froze and exploded into a million shards. The rainbows tumbled from the sky.

I arrived back at our hotel a little before eight, only to find a note from my father telling me to meet him at the same pub we'd been at the day before – the pub where I'd happened upon Becky McNamara that very afternoon. I was getting to know that wee pub too well. I checked my watch and grimaced. The old man would be angry, and rightly so, I thought. I'd been unaccounted for since the first light of day, and the message I'd left had been sufficiently vague as to not include a probable time of return. This business of short absences was not unheard-of on this trip, but the unspoken proviso had always been that we would meet for lunch. Now the sun had been set for an hour – or more accurately was an hour into the arduous process of setting – and here was I, with little to offer by way of explanation for my disappearance except the truth, and that was out of the question.

The pub had begun to gear up for the evening's entertainment. Small clusters of men clumped and gathered here and there, beers at their elbows, smoking their pipes, and on the stage a band of young people – brothers and sisters I'd wager – were setting up their equipment. This was a common thing in Ireland, where children were immersed in music by their families almost from the moment they were born, schooled in the playing of multiple instruments at nightly family gatherings, from penny-whistles to hurdy-gurdies, the nightly sessions a mainstay in what made many a family tick: then, when reaching a certain age, breaking away to form their own bands, some of which did spectacularly well. Tommy Makim and the Clancy Brothers had started out that way. So had Enya. The Corrs. It was the natural progression in a country bursting with music.

"Have a seat, son," my father said, clearly vexed. "Are you hungry?"

I was, but lied about it. A waitress came and I ordered a beer. My dad already had a full pint before him, as well as the remains of his supper, which the waitress took away.

"So..." he began.

"So what?"

"So what do you think, man!" my father snapped, in no mood for games. "You've been gone all day! I was worried! When you didn't show up at lunch-time, I got more worried still."

"Look dad, I wasn't 'gone' anywhere. I was doing just what my note said. You saw the note, right?"

"Of course I saw the note."

"I was poking around the shops and walking the streets. I met some people."

"You met some people."

"That's right."

"You spoke with some people."

"At great length."

My father sighed and rubbed his eyes under his glasses. He radiated exasperation. At a table not far from us a group of young men appeared to be engaged in a clandestine conversation. The band was tuning up on the stage. The prettiest of the sisters turned out to be their drummer. My beer arrived and I took a mouthful.

"You've been drinking a lot on this trip."

That irritated me. Of the two of us my old man was the heavier drinker by far – starting in at lunch which I almost never did – and ever on the lookout for a pub to drop in and see. I told him as much now, and his mood darkened further still.

"How much have you had to drink today?"

"Not much," I said, feeling defensive. Something more than my disappearance appeared to be afoot. "Just this. And a pint or two earlier."

"A pint or two earlier." This habit he had, when vexed, of repeating what I'd said was getting on my nerves. "Is that all?"

"What difference does it make?"

"The barman said a Canadian boy got here around noon, and nigh-on drank the afternoon away. Don't look. He's gone now. Shift-change," he added bitterly, as though this too was my doing.

"What else did he say?"

"Are you denying he was talking about you?"

"No," I said. "What else did he say?"

"That you were with a girl – a local girl – and that the two of you were getting mighty sweet on each other, and mighty drunk."

My heart was suddenly in my throat, though I couldn't say why. A boy meets a girl in a pub. What could be more natural? It's not like I robbed the bloody till at gun-point. Yet I knew there were multiple issues surrounding this scenario, that my father would have disapproved of. First and foremost the sanctity of the sexual act, as an adjunct to the sacrament of holy matrimony. My father had not been reticent over the years in demonstrating how doggedly he held to the strict law of the scriptures. Still, I held out hope that it wouldn't come to that.

"He said you left together, hand in hand, around three-thirty," my father looked down at his watch. "And it's near eight thirty now."

"Now look here!" I began, in a burst of petulant anger, but got no further.

"Her name?"

"What?"

"What was this girl's name, her name, man! You got a name out of her, surely!"

I could feel my molars grinding, and made a conscious effort to calm myself. The group of shady-looking gentlemen had disbursed, and the band were having a pint at the far end of the bar. The drummer caught my eye across the room and gave me a wink.

"Becky," I said, through clenched teeth. "McNamara."

"Becky McNamara." My father nodded grimly, as though I'd confirmed his worst fear. "Some local girl you met at the bar. A Cork girl."

This was not going well, but I found I didn't care anymore.

"I didn't meet her here, I met her in Dublin."

"In Dublin!"

"At the Martello tower," I said. "The Joyce museum at Sandymount."

"You met her in Dublin?"

"Yes."

"At the Joyce museum."

"That's right."

"And said not a word about it."

"What was there to say? A chance encounter, an hour long. I lit a cigarette for her. She gave me an orange."

"An orange."

"That's right."

"You met a Cork girl in Dublin."

"Stop calling her a Cork girl! You make it sound like a crime!"

"Settle down, man. You'll be making a scene."

"You're the one making a scene. I met a girl in a pub I'd previously met in Dublin. A strange coincidence. Hail fellow, well met. We had a few beers. What of that?"

"So now it's a few beers."

"How many have *you* had today?"

"Settle down. I was worried for you, that's all."

"Look, dad," I said, struggling not to let exasperation and anger get the better of me. "I fell off your radar for a few hours, and for that I apologise. It wasn't my intention. But I'm a grown man now, able to take care of himself. What more would you have me say?"

"A grown man." The condescending way he said that made my blood boil. "Did you have sex with this girl? Are you *that* grown now? Should I be worried about that too?"

"That's none of your business."

"So you did. We'll need to make an appointment at the general in the morning."

"What are you suggesting?"

"Did you use protection?"

"Are you saying the bloody Cork girls are all addled with the pox?"

"Settle down, man!"

"No, I don't think I will," I hissed angrily. "Look, this conversation can serve no further purpose. I'm going back to the hotel."

"Stay and finish your beer."

"I don't want to finish my fucking beer."

That took him down a notch. "Well," he said, finally, "I guess that makes you feel like quite the grown-up, using language like that to your own father."

"I'm going," I said. "We can talk about all this, if we must, in the morning. Don't knock on my door at the hotel. I'll be asleep."

"Stay," he said again, more insistently. "There are some things about your wee friend, Becky McNamara, that you ought to know."

"Oh, go to hell!" I said, then left the pub.

I started down the road, grinding my teeth, nearly in tears. I was so angry with my father I could have killed him. If I'd had a knife, I would have stabbed him. If a gun? A bullet in the eye. But more than my father, I was angry at myself, because I knew this mess was my fault, and could have been predicted down to the smallest detail, had I but been aware of the portents and signs. Instead, I'd chosen to allow my judgement to be clouded by a pretty girl, and now it was all this. Yet how much leeway did I have – any more than my dad – to do anything other than exactly what I'd done? I was twenty, and brimming with hormones. I was flesh and blood. And my heart had gone out to this girl. This pox-addled abomination from Cork. My father needed me to be a child, just as surely as I needed to be a man. All either of us were doing – all we had ever done – was play out a destiny that had been carved in stone. How right I'd been to have misgivings about this trip! Its folly was carved into that same stone, plain to any with eyes to see. And where was I now? In the company of a crazy fool, in a city as far from home as I had ever been. But there were other cities farther away still. The thought occurred to me I could go back to that bungalow, knock on the door, kick Corduroy to one side, and ask Becky if I might not be allowed to come with her in the morning, flying out to London to rejoin her brother, and from there to Australia, to live out my own madman's fantasy of a life amongst the feral wallabies and vampire bats. Where there were cities so removed from my father and my kin that you could find none further, and must start getting closer if you insisted on looking.

I stopped beneath the lamplight to calm myself, and took a look around. The streets of Cork were far from deserted – many people seemed out for no better reason than to admire the sunset, which was certainly worthy of their admiration. The clouds hung balloon-like far above, enormous, self-contained abstract sculptures, painted in varying shades of gold, crimson and grey, foreshortened all the way to the far horizon, the stars between them beginning to twinkle in the darkening sky. It was a breath-taking spectacle, this nightly occurrence, and the people of Cork were far from taking it for granted. These good people of the rebel city – who would as soon knee-cap me if I asked the wrong man the wrong question – had seen enough of the perils of life to appreciate its beauty too, and that thought made me inexpressibly sad. I was a stranger in a strange land. More. A dangerous land. A Canadian surrounded by Irishmen. An Ulsterman from Belfast surrounded by unionist Catholics, probably even a few radical unionist Catholics, as willing as not at the slightest provocation to knock my block off. My father had called Becky 'a Cork girl,' but you didn't need to be a linguist to divine that 'Cork' was a euphemism for Catholic. Not only had I disgraced myself by my conduct with some syphilitic tart from Cork, I'd disgraced myself by my conduct with a Catholic! Even a Jew had drawn less ire from my father – he had tolerated Ariella Kaplan's special place in my life for years, without a word against her – but a Catholic? That was a thousand times worse. Bad enough the Jews denied Christ's divine nature, his sacred purpose in their lives, but the Catholics, who should have known better, had taken that purpose and distorted it into something grandiose, vulgar, even monstrous. That's what Becky represented to my father, a desecration of the sacred heart of Jesus and a corrupter of his son's immortal soul.

Further down the way I saw a small cluster of nuns, and I wondered what the odds were of them being Poor Clares. For a moment I was tempted to approach and ask, then thought better of it. I'd already asked one too many strangers a potentially inflammatory question, here in the rebel city. What if I asked, and for reasons unknown they took offence, flocking around me like a murder of crows, punching and flailing away madly while cursing the blasphemy of my presumption? I laughed weakly at myself, and shook my head. You're a head-case, son, a rare half-wit and always were. A proper scallywag, no error. There was a cheerfully-lit pub across the way, and I both did and didn't feel like popping in for a quick drink. I also both did and did not want to linger a while longer, admiring the sunset, as I did and didn't want to return to the hotel. I had no clue what I wanted to do, so I just stood there doing nothing, listening to distant voices, the muffled music. For an uncanny moment I had a sensation like the passage of time were brushing up against me, her bridal-train carried in the clenched fists of Death's Dark Lord, then there was that dreadful sadness, once more, never so far removed after all. What was to become of us all, of my family, my brother and sister and mother and father and I, in time? Well, in a hundred years we'd all be dead, so that was good. I laughed. In the meanwhile, you have a doctoral degree to earn, and a universe to figure out. All those invisible dimensions weren't going to unfurl themselves.

I was soon back at the hotel, and when I opened my door, I found my father in my room, smoking a cigarette and reading my copy of Dante. I resisted the urge to snatch it from his hands. Instead, I just sighed. He was looking from where he sat in his chair as woeful as any man I'd ever seen. "This is hopeless, Dad," I told him. Bitterly I added, "A fool's errand."

"You don't mean that."

"It's not your fault," I said, sitting down on the bed and clasping my hands between my knees. "It's not even my fault, though more mine than yours. We're just too different. On every level. Beliefs. Morals. What it means to be a man. What it means to be good. Even our taste in music. We're sitting here in the same room, but we're a thousand miles apart."

"There's much we have in common, too."

"Not so very much," I said. "Not enough. Whoever first suggested there's such a thing in this world as free will, should be horsewhipped, then locked away in a lunatic asylum."

"I'm still your father, and you my son," my father said. "We have that."

"That's no great thing."

"There's never been a falling out in this family, son. And as for free will, why, we all have free will. It's a divine gift from God. The right to choose. And the responsibility to become better people."

I laughed, but woefully, woefully, and with my face buried in my hands I shook my head no. I had nothing more to add to that. My father tried again, "Look, son," he began, but I cut him off.

"I'm leaving in the morning," I said.

"What do you mean?"

"Back to Belfast," I said. "Back to Canada."

"How on earth do you propose to do that?"

I looked up at him for signs of condescension – there were none. But I reacted as though there had been. "What do you mean, how do I propose it? Do you think me a helpless infant? We're in Cork! There are express buses from here to anywhere in Ireland. If I left now, I could probably be in Belfast by first light. I know where the damn airport is, man. I'm not a fool, and I have my own resources."

"That money was intended for your university!"

"Alas for me."

"You're not serious!"

I laughed.

"This is not in keeping with our agreement," my father said.

"Well, somehow or other our agreement got broken," I said. "As if by divine fiat from God."

"Winston, I didn't stop in here to argue with you. If you're hell-bent to go in the morning, then go. I don't want you to go, but I won't try and stop you. As you said, you're a grown man now. I'll even give you the money for your passage, and, when you get back to Belfast, and if you still want to, I'll pay for the early flight. But I need for you to listen to me now, son."

"I don't need your money."

"I know. I know that, Winston. But just listen."

I lit a cigarette then crossed over to open a window. The sun was nearly down, and the clouds dispersing; rain felt not far away.

"The barman told me much more than I've let on. He told me the girl was in from Australia, that her mother had died. That her brother was in London, and her father back in Australia, but there's more."

"You knew that all along, but never let on?"

"As did you," my father said.

"It was my business to know. And yours, I suppose, to snoop around in."

I picked up the copy of Dante, and checked to see what my father had been reading from it – the *Inferno*. Of course. That was the part everyone read.

"I'm reluctant to tell you what else he told me," my father said, "for fear you'll question my reasons for doing so."

I laughed.

"You might have done well to question them yourself," I said. "Before telling me that."

"The girl's father, James McNamara, is a doctor. A medical doctor, recently graduated, when he emigrated."

"What of it?"

"He was also provisional IRA, Winter. The whole family is. Brothers, cousins, the lot. The father got mixed up in the assassination of two British soldiers – two officers – up in Phoenix Park, in Dublin. A cold-blooded execution, son. This would have been back around nineteen sixty-two, or three. The papers didn't say the father pulled the trigger, but he was involved. He was scheduled to be indicted on charges of first-degree murder, two counts. He didn't emigrate to Australia, to start a bloody medical clinic. He was a refugee from the law."

I let that sink in a good long while, wishing I had a drink.

"You're lying."

"I'm not."

"If it's true, what of it? He was a soldier, engaged in active combat. The British were the enemy. It was war. If those men got shot they probably had it coming."

My father considered these words of mine a long time too.

"That's hard of you, Winter," he finally said. "Very cold-blooded."

"You want me to think the world a horrible place, which I know nothing about. So little that I'm still in need of a father's protection from it."

"No." My father ran his fingers through his greying hair. "What I've told you is the truth."

"This barman of yours, he's quite the tout." 'Tout' was Irish slang for informant. "A veritable fountain of forbidden information."

"He only confirmed what I'd already known, Winter. And even then not directly. When he mentioned to me that this girl's father's name was James McNamara, and that he was a medical doctor long since relocated to Australia, it rang a bell. The coincidence was too great. The executions up in Phoenix Park had caused such a sensation, it was even reported in Canada. And the father's name stuck too – James. It stuck in my mind, after reading the accounts in the papers. Our own family is full of Jameses, sure. James McNamara, fled to Australia, a refugee from the law. It stuck in my mind."

That last part was all too true. Both of my grandfathers were named James. I had an uncle James. My own, full name was Winston James Colm Crowley.

"I mentioned this to yer man at the bar, and that shut him up right quick. The look in his eye was confirmation enough. But by this late date, it was all water under the bridge. Events of a decade past. So the barman was no tout. Only a little indiscreet with his facial expressions, you could say. Also, I think he was angry."

"Oh?" I said. "At who?"

"At you," my father said. "And at the girl. I think he was sweet on the girl. Then in walks you, and snatches her away, lock, stock and barrel. Just like that."

"You think he might have lied to you, to make trouble between Becky and me?"

"Son," my father sighed, shaking his head no. "I read about it in the papers! All those years ago. The man's a bloody terrorist."

XII

By ten-thirty the next morning we'd made the great turn at Bantry Bay, and had started north, my aunt Esther's car still humming along like a finely-tuned sewing machine, but with barely a civil word expressed within its confines. The morning was overcast, gloomy, and threatened rain with each breath, though nothing came of it. The temperature had dropped as well, so we were obliged to unpack a couple of heavy sweaters from the boot of the car. The wind had resumed. While travelling westward, the wind had tapered away, until I'd nearly forgotten the continuous thrashing it had given us coming down the coast. Now here it was again, except it was a confused wind, uncertain which direction it wanted to blow. That didn't deter the Atlantic from kicking up its former fuss, though, and the further north we travelled the more boisterous the waves seemed to get. The west coast of Ireland is a wild place, resembling the profile of an old woman, caught in a car crash; longer than the east coast, full of twists and turns, into harbours, the mouths of rivers, most notably the Shannon; bay inlets, estuaries and all the rest. We stopped to admire very little of it. What I was even doing in the car would have been hard to explain. Certainly I wasn't there for the pleasure of my father's company, and his running commentary on the history and geography all around us had fallen off to near nothing, neither of us certain how to reclaim the ground we had lost, nor even certain, at least in my case, if the ground was worth reclaiming.

As Cork fell away behind us, I could only hope my reluctant decision to continue the trip with my father wasn't yet another colossal blunder. From Cork, a direct bus link to Belfast was a simple matter, but almost everywhere else there would be side-stops, layovers, even transfers to other means of transportation. I was not so familiar with the terrain of southern Ireland that I didn't fear a postponed decision to abort could result in anything but headaches. Still, this was my father, his misery plain to read on his face, in his demeanour. I could be civilized if he could be. We would limp home quickly as we could, preferably with no more drama. Over the course of the next four days, we passed though Killarney, Tralee, Listowel – departing the coastline briefly to say how d'ya do to Newcastle West – Kilrust, Kilkee and Ennistymon, tiny coastal towns and villages with not much to distinguish them from each other. If it's possible to become acclimatised to charm and extreme beauty through overexposure to it, then Ireland's the place to do it. And compounding the awkward situation with my old man was a growing homesickness, the yearning for family and friends, for sure, but also just for the sound of a Canadian accent, the extreme weather, the flat terrain, the reasonable winds, the television, the taste of Canadian cigarettes and beer, a juicy Canadian cheeseburger, the familiarity of the old haunts or the feel of a Canadian tit beneath my hand. I wouldn't have thought, at just twenty, I'd have accumulated enough memories to miss so much in their absence, but I had. Mostly though, I missed Becky. The image of her, stretched out in the golden glow of her robust, youthful animal-health – recumbent on her bed, or diligently attending to the aforementioned buckets she'd committed to filling, glistening with post-coital satisfaction – none of it was likely to fade from my imagination any time soon, and I found myself whiling away the hours in close contemplation of the many, various parts of a beautiful woman's body, contemplating also the great mystery of how they all conspired to stitch together into this one, perfect thing. Then I had a weird revelation, an epiphany Joyce might have called it, both transcendental yet compellingly real. A revelation that I was thinking about these ethereal matters all wrong. Becky wasn't beautiful because her whole was greater than the sum of its parts: the whole was absolute and irreducible! I had, indeed, I thought, been looking at her – at everything – through the wrong end of an electron microscope. The wholeness of all things, this thing we think of as transcendent beauty, was not built from the ground up, but was preceded via a transcendent iteration. For a boy predisposed to think scientifically, with an intuitive understanding of higher algebra, this was odd territory indeed, for within it was contained the implication that Plato was right, that everything was spirit, that we lived as within a cave, observing but the shadows of things unseen. That we were radiant beings, irreducible and whole, everything else a delusion, and if we were, so then too was everything else. Even the universe itself.

I won't get all Oral Roberts on you, and suggest that, at that moment, I 'found God,' because what I had found instead was the quantum possibility that an even more fundamental reality existed, upon which rested a construct of 'God' that could both exist and not exist at the same time, whose parameters might not be beyond human calculation. A god, like the ten-dimensional sphere, both infinite yet well-defined. It was all just a matter of perception. There was little comfort to be had from such an unconventional insight, and I doubted its veracity, but I wasn't in the business of seeking comfort from the spiritual realms. That was my father's area of expertise. The mathematics of it would require ten years, minimum; a decade of blood, sweat and tears to straighten out. I barely had an inkling where to begin, but would arrive somewhere near it just in time for it to stand in as my thesis in theoretical physics. If my insight were correct, it should turn a few fookin' heads in mathematical circles, if not theological ones. Thus we passed through the counties of Limerick and Clare, my brain dancing with numbers, struggling to make theoretical infinities cancel each other out, arriving at Galway, where, as I suspected, my dad wanted to stop and make inquiries regarding the Poor Clare nuns. My old man and his nuns! Very deferentially, he asked me if that would be all right, and of course I said it would. We'd been driving a long time now, and a stretch was very much in order.

"Will you come with, son?" my father hopefully asked. "And have a look around?"

"No. I'll just wait over there, in the park."

"I can't say how long–"

"That'll be all right. Take your time, have a good look-see."

"If you get hungry –"

"I can look after my own lunch."

We parted company then, and the first thing I did was find a shop that sold cigarettes. Then I strolled across the wide street and into the park – some sort of municipally sanctioned botanical garden, I would wager – with great, softly rolling hills of brightest green, punctuated by enormous trees, and further ornamented with long rows of flower-beds, flowers of every variety and colour. The air was fragrant with them. It was a work-day, yet the park was quite busy – tourists mostly I supposed – and I was gratified to see a sign on the lawn saying *Keep Off The Grass* being cheerfully ignored by numerous clusters of gleeful, small children. I walked around for a good long while, smoking and admiring the gardens, which were quite elaborate, thinking of Becky, and the dual nature of a god who could both exist and not exist at the same time. It was the first sunny morning in a few days, and everything looked fresh and new. Eventually I found a bench in the shadow of a tree, and took a load off. A few minutes later a fat, ancient priest waddled over and joined me. "Good morning, lad!" he said, with grand jocularity.

Lad?

"Good morning, Father."

"Lovely day!"

"Aye, Father."

He stretched himself out, arms along the back of the bench, and sighed a sigh of deepest satisfaction.

"You've not been up to anything, have you laddie?" he asked me roguishly, with a smile. "Not up to any mischief, this fine day?"

I smiled. Was this old fool blind? Yes, judging from how he squinted through his spectacles. Or partially so. Blind in one eye and stupid in the other. Either he was codding me, or he'd mistaken me for someone much younger. The latter, I decided.

"Oh, no, Father!" I declared. "I would never!"

"Good! There's a good boy, now. A lovely day indeed. Full of God's good sunshine, and dew. Your face is not familiar to me boy. Are you not from around these parts?"

"From Killarney, Father."

"A fine town. A fine town. Are yeas up here with yer ma?"

"Alone, sir," I said, starting to enjoy this little game. The priest was ancient, weathered as an old boot, a large, ornate gold cross dangled on his vest. Except for the collar he was dressed formally, in black. He smelled a little waxy, as from candles. His teeth were not great, and he emanated a vague air of precarious health in general. His fingers were bejewelled with many rings, that glittered in the shadows of the tree. "Up to sit with a sick relative, sir."

"Ah," he said, as though that explained something. "You're a thoughtful boy. A good boy. Have you been to confession yet today?"

"I have not, Father."

"And is there anything troubling your mind?"

"There isn't, Father."

"A virtuous boy!" the old bastard chuckled. "I guess there's a first time for everything."

"Yes, Father. May I ask you something, Father?"

"Of course, my boy, of course!"

"Are there Poor Clares, here in Galway?"

"Poor Clares! Why now, aren't you the odd duck, asking after Poor Clares."

"It's for me sister, Father," I said. "She's after thinking about joining the order."

"And so she should! Aye, there are Poor Clares here, boy. They're one of ours."

"On Nun's Island, is it?"

"There and other places besides, aye."

"That's a place I'd love to see, Father."

"Nun's Island, is it?" He looked around a little cagily. There was no one else in the immediate vicinity "Sure, I could take you there to see it! It's not far, boy. We wouldn't be gone but an hour at most."

"You wanna take your fookin' hand off me leg, mister?"

The priest had laid his hand on my thigh, where it had started sliding up, in the general direction of my Unit, Monty Python.

"Why – I – I –"

I hopped to my feet, and turned to face him.

"Go on," I growled. "Get out of me sight, you old pervert, before I stove yer fookin' brains in!"

The priest sputtered and shook and rattled about, then tottered off, grumbling to himself. I lit a cigarette and looked around, laughing. No one had witnessed the altercation. My hands were trembling a little. This park was full of children, and I was angry at the priest. A few minutes later, the old dodderer returned in the company of two uniformed officers, a man and a woman, though they couldn't have been too much older than I was.

"Here he is, officers!" the priest cried, extending an accusatory claw. "That's the young swine! He threatened me with bodily harm, so he did!"

"The priest is mistaken," I said, dropping the Irish accent. "I was merely defending myself from his unwanted sexual advances."

"You never said he was a tourist, Father," the male cop said, a little confused. The old priest spluttered some more.

"I'm not a tourist. I'm a journalist, on assignment from *Maclean's* magazine. Are you familiar with *Maclean's*, officer?" This question I directed towards the female officer, who looked damned sexy in that uniform. I pulled out a pen and a small notepad I'd purchased in Dublin, and opened the pad to the first clean page. "It's a weekly glossy. The largest circulation of any weekly news magazine in Canada."

"You didn't say anything about him being a *Canadian*, Father!"

"Perhaps I could get your names? Yours especially," I added, flashing daggers at the priest. "For inclusion in my story. If you give me a mailing address, I'll see to it the issue it's in gets to you, when it's published."

I told them *Maclean's* magazine had a circulation of twenty-five million registered subscribers, though of course I had no clue what the true number was. For all I knew it was in the billions. Five minutes later, the priest and the uniformed officers had dispersed, having decided the entire thing was just some silly mix up, and no hard feelings. They'd asked me my age, and I told them twenty-four. Young, but not young enough to be a temptation to a paedophile. Young-looking as well. I found myself wishing I'd beaten the hell out of that old bastard, consequences be damned. I walked to the closest pub, and ordered a pot of tea, and a bite to eat. I was a little shaken up, but it was all great fun. It wasn't quite noon yet, but the place was filled with cheerful men. My father was not among them.

Up and up and up, while the sun rolled across the sky, and the sea pounded the shore to a bloody pulp. My father flipped on the radio and, petulantly, I flipped it off again, then thought better of it and switched it back on. I found a station playing traditional Irish folk music, and lowered the volume. Better this than all the deafening silence, I calculated. I thought long and hard about what my father had told me, about James McNamara, and the provisional IRA. The fact that it involved an execution didn't faze me too much – not as much as my father had perhaps hoped it might. Those men were British soldiers. Officers. On Irish soil. If they'd been caught in Phoenix Park with their pants down, who was to blame? Piss on 'em – they were in the wrong place at the wrong time. Still, there was no denying that this land I loved so well had a long and violent history, as much or more so now than at any other time, and we were all bound up inextricably in it, one way or another. A land of poets and warriors, sometimes forced to be both. I suppose I though such things because we were on our way back to Belfast, where the streets were curtained off by barbed wire, and the wee military helicopters bobbed in the sky, keeping a close lookout. I knew that as a Protestant – and a Protestant with a Canadian accent at his service, to boot – I was safely cocooned in Belfast, where any harm that might befall me would need to be brought down by my own, foolish doing. It would be unwise of me, for example, to walk the war-torn streets of west Belfast, say the Falls Road, at midnight, shouting, "Fuck the Pope!" at the top of my lungs, but what was the likelihood of that? Unlike those officers, I knew better than to find myself in the wrong place, at the wrong time. Safely ensconced in east Belfast, with its Royal Gardens and Universities, cafés and art galleries, you could live as in any other of Europe's great cities, more or less. Yet it wasn't just the poor and ill-educated caught up in this drama. Men like James McNamara had gotten caught up too, men better educated than average by a wide margin. I think, as a boy, I harboured the quaint belief that war was the doing of savage people, of stupid people, but of course it is not. Sometimes the most savage among us are the brightest, and wisdom is no firewall against a bullet in the back of your brain. Indeed, maybe it requires wise men and women to see with clarity the brutality that needs to be carried out, if ever we are to render a more just world for the as yet unborn, who flutter on angels' wings in a realm where God can both exist and not exist at the same time.

One fine afternoon we arrived in county Sligo, and without a word about it, my father turned off the coastal road, and made his way to Drumcliff, and the church at Ben Bulben, where the mortal remains of William Butler Yeats are buried. My father hadn't needed to ask. He would have known I'd want to go there. The grave was a nondescript affair – nothing ostentatious – its headstone not even marble, but a local Irish stone of which Yeats had been fond. All was as had been decreed, in the poem, *Under Ben Bulben*. Even the birds in the trees seemed to sing the lovelier, in joyous tribute to this great man, lying there. Yeats as a writer held no great sway over me – he was the pale-faced settler to Joyce's red Indian on a rampage – yet his mastery of the verse form was hardly in contention. If he represented the Establishment, it was an establishment of his own devising. An ever-supportive enthusiast for the New Irish Theatre. A ground-breaking playwright in his own right. A politician of great wisdom and skill. Beloved by the people of Ireland, and indeed the people of the world. And, if that weren't enough, Stockholm even threw in a Nobel prize for good measure. I was so close to tears, I wanted to tear my eyes out, to stop them from flowing. What a baby I was being! This hard land might have created the provisional IRA, but it had created Yeats as well. And that was no mean feat.

"Are you all right, son?"

"Sure."

"Do you want to stay or go?"

"Stay a moment longer."

"That'll be all right."

I found a small, smooth pebble and in pen drew a rudimentary Celtic cross on it. This I placed on top of Yeats's headstone. We just stood there for a moment or two, my father and I, and listened to the birds.

"What's to become of all this, I wonder?"

"Well," my father replied. "All is not lost."

"Isn't it?"

"Where there's a will, there's a way."

"Huh," I said, smiling. "You're spouting poetry. Yeats would be pleased."

"God bless him," my father said, near tears himself. "And God bless us all."

"Aye."

Now that my ladder's gone
I must lie down where the ladders start
In the foul rag and bone shop of the heart.

By the time we reached Donegal – even more northward than Belfast, but still part of the Republic – we had only five more days before my flight, so my father and I became mindful of the time, and where we were. I know I haven't done the same justice to the west coast of Ireland as I'd done to the east, which is a pity for it's an unbridled territory, wild in the extreme, but without my dad's running commentary on everything we saw, there was that much less for me to report. Plus, our central concern no longer lay outside the car, if I may put it that way. Not that we stayed cold as ice the entire time: it seems to me now, as the days passed, we thawed out here and there, as humans will. The side trip to Sligo certainly hadn't hurt. I don't think it was my father I felt so much the desire to castigate – and perhaps forgive – as myself. For being human. I had been young and foolish and impetuous, and I had let things get out of hand. So I wasn't angry so much as mired in a great sense of hopelessness. To say 'things got out of hand,' is to suggest they were ever in hand, in the first place. And they never are. We are who we are, all of us, you who read these words no less than I – horse-whipped and off to the lunatic asylum, straight away – that was the much-deserved fate of the first man to have suggested the preposterous fig-leaf of Free Will. With the hopelessness came the sadness, and with the sadness the desire to get out! Get out! Get out! My father and I would never understand each other – it was a lost cause. A fool's errand. I remember one time, when I was only nine or ten, my dad took me down to the Irish Canadian Club of Hamilton, to watch a live taping of a television show that starred the Irish Rovers, and aired weekly on CHCH-TV. We sat with a group of his cronies, the men drank beer and praised the quality of the entertainment, all things Irish. After the first number, one of these men leaned over, and asked me what I'd thought of that, now, and the conversation around the table stopped, so everyone could hear what Colm Crowley's boy had made of the music. I liked it, I said, except the harpist – one of her strings was out of tune. That got a laugh. Listen to the wee Canadian boy, playing the part of the great know-it-all! Puttin' on the high hat! The bloody harp out of tune, says he! And him but a Mutt! Except, ten minutes later, the MC stepped forward, apologized, and explained that the first number would need to be re-taped, as the harpist was not happy with the tuning of her instrument. My father's wee klatch of Irishmen now looked at me like I'd just stepped off a spaceship. And you'd think that would have taught the old man to have a little faith in my judgement, but it never did. Not even a little. On the contrary. Of the lot of them, my father had laughed the hardest. I'd thought that unkind of him at the time.

XIII

We buried my father on February 13th 2005, on a bitterly cold morning out in a little town called Hope – thirty miles outside Hamilton. The cemetery was flat and featureless, and the wind swirled the powder-dry snow around the attendees in short gusts and bursts, not least around my mother, in a wheelchair with a bottle of oxygen in a pouch on the chair's padded rear. She was beautifully dressed, my mother, as always. Her hair carefully set, but the wind didn't care about that. So after the brief ceremony we persuaded her to retreat to the warmth of the car, for crying out loud, before she froze solid. Then I went in search of my uncle Albert's grave, and my uncle James's, who wasn't really my uncle – just a friend of the family – though I had a real uncle James too, alive and well in Ireland. A lot had changed since we'd buried Uncle Albert, thirty years earlier, though that had been a cold day too. It seemed we were forever burying our dead in the winter, right here in Hope, and to me, back then, it had seemed the cemetery had been better landscaped, and contained only a dozen graves. Now the trees and shrubbery were gone, to make room for more graves I supposed, and there were hundreds and hundreds of gravestones, big and small, ornate or simple. Uncle Albert's grave was especially modest, in keeping with his wishes, and someone – my aunt Kathleen most likely – had put out fresh flowers in defiance of the weather. A number of graves over I noticed a teddy bear half-buried in snow, at the gravestone of a little girl who had died of cancer at six. Somehow her photograph had been affixed to the stone, as though embossed on it. She looked to be a cheerful, pretty little thing. She deserved better than this.

Hope. Knocking snow from the little girl's toy, I found myself thinking of Pandora's box, which had contained all the evils of the world – Pandora, in keeping with the origins of her name, had been blessed many times over by all the gods, but this one gift had been the exception to the rule. When it was opened, and everything save one thing flown out, it started a chain-reaction that spread misery, grief and suffering throughout the world, and no matter how Pandora tried she could not get all that suffering back in the box. So the story goes, and it accounts for a good deal, it seems to me. The one thing remaining in the box, once it had been opened, was hope. So whatever else had been loosed on the world there was always hope. And Hope was where we buried my father, with all the rest of them. Likelihood is, that's where I'll be buried. A week earlier, on the Sunday, and after sixteen weeks in hospitals both here and in Ottawa – where she'd been airlifted to undergo a radical new surgical procedure – my mother was finally scheduled to be released and sent home. With only ten minutes remaining of his long and remarkable life, at their regular Macnab St. church service, my father had leaned over and asked my brother if they would be going downstairs, to have a coffee after the service. So he never saw it coming, and hope springs eternal, which is perhaps for the best. Sure, my brother said. Why not? An hour later, at St. Joseph's hospital, in spite of all the best efforts of so many people, not least the ambulance paramedics my brother had summoned immediately upon my father's collapse, the old man was pronounced dead. And it fell to the three of us – my sister, my brother, and myself – to take that long ride up to the fourth floor of St. Joseph's, on the elevator, to inform our happy wee ma that her husband of sixty years was now dead, and that the life they'd led on Hamilton's west mountain – the life she'd fully expected to resume the very next morning – was over forever.

And still hope springs eternal.

With less than five days to go my father and I swept up around the northern coast of Ireland, to Malin Head, geographically the furthest point north in all of Ireland, before uneventfully crossing the border from the Republic back into Ulster, the wee Protestant sheep and their Catholic counterparts taking no notice, having more important things on their minds. Then it was around to Ballycastle, and down the Antrim coast, a wild and precarious place in Ireland, reminiscent of the cliffs of Dover, where the narrow roads wound around sheer rocky drops of a hundred feet, down to the crashing Atlantic (my leg already getting sore from all the pumping on the imaginary brakes), the wind rushing up so fiercely, so unrelentingly that even the sheep – well used to the wildness of it all – tended to take shelter in the lee of ancient, broken stone fences. And that was how things went. Another day's travel, and we were back in Belfast, greeted not as foot-soldiers in the generational wars, come limping home to tend to our wounds, but as generals and conquering heroes returned with a great fanfare of feasting and celebration. Everyone wanted to hear all about it, in the smallest detail, leave nothing out, and it was now that my several small notepads full of facts and observations came in especially handy. At one great feast, at my uncle Conrad's house, I couldn't help but notice that not a single one of my many cousins bothered to show up, but I didn't resent them for that. They had their lives, and I had mine; if our situations had been reversed, I would no doubt have done the same. Decisions made many, many years ago had recast me in the role of the Spy Who Came in from the Cold, and as with every other aspect of my life, both past and future, there was nothing to be done about it. To my aunt Esther, for the use of her car I suppose, I gave my copy of *The Divine Comedy*, which she protested at first, but relented to receiving if I would inscribe it to her. I scribbled something sentimental in the fly-leaf which, when she read it, she thanked me for, gave me a hug, and kissed my cheek.

"We'll miss you, Winston! You should try and come over more often."

Strangely, when I dug out my expensive, imported copy of Neil Young's *Harvest*, bought so much earlier at The Queen's University, it had been cracked – sleeve and all – as though someone had broken it in anger over a knee, or had inadvertently sat on it. I never uncovered its ultimate fate, but threw it away, unremarked upon, and bought another later in Canada.

I gave my copy of *The History of Irish Poetry* to my dad. God knows I'd had enough Irish poetry for one fookin' lifetime – enough Irish poetry to last forever.

Two days before my scheduled flight – my father's wasn't due out for another week, something to do with vacation schedules – I had one last goodbye to say, and that was to an older childhood friend, the only friendship I'd kept of all the friends I'd made in Ireland in years gone by: a guy named Alfred Moore – Alfie to his mates – a freshly PhD'd mechanical engineer who worked for British Rail, Ulster division. Alfie was a fine example of what I'd mistakenly thought of as that rarest of breeds, a well-educated, middle-class Catholic living in Ulster, and quite content, thank you very much, with the status quo. I phoned him at work and we agreed to meet for lunch the next day, at the Europa, Belfast's poshest hotel, and over the years such a magnet for attacks by both bomb and bullet that getting in through the front doors was a little like a maximum-security jail-break, in reverse.

Having been frisked twice, once by British soldiers and a second time, more scrupulously, by the Europa's own private security people, then passed through a metal detector for good measure, I finally found myself (a little indignant but none the worse for wear) in the bar of the Europa. The security was so airtight, an ant couldn't have crawled into that bar, through a vent, without first undergoing a colonoscopy. I was early for our scheduled lunch, so I ordered a coffee, which the barman delivered to me at an ornate round table beside a grand piano. I scanned the Europa's patrons for celebrities, or undercover agents. I even fancied I'd located one or two, by the bulge riding on their hip, or a face that looked familiar from the telly. Then I saw someone at the bar whom I did know, for certain, and I felt myself clench up in disbelief. I smiled as cheerfully as I could manage, as though delighted by this unexpected surprise, then hopped up and approached him at the bar, all the while my mind racing to stay on top of every conceivable angle of this bizarre turn of events.

It was Becky's cousin, Kevin McNamara – at least I assumed that was his last name. We shook hands warily, and he looked me over, both amused to see me, yet tense. Stupidly, I reverted to Irish mode without thinking – that being the way I'd last addressed him – though I found myself wishing I hadn't.

"Kevin, isn't it?" He nodded coolly. "Your cousin told me your name. Did Becky get off all right, to Australia?"

"Aye," Kevin said. "You must be a bit surprised," he added, "to see me here?"

"Why?" I asked him, trying to sound as genuinely puzzled as I could.

"Being who I am," he smirked. "And where I'm from."

I laughed – playing the innocent naïf – and waved off the remark as absurd.

"No more so than you should have been surprised, to find me in county Cork, man, I would say. It's a free country, and a small island."

"Aye," Kevin said. "A free country."

My nonchalance seemed to be doing the trick, or so I hoped. Time for a change of subject. "She'll have been back a week and more by now," I opined, signalling the barman. "Becky, I mean. Lovely girl. Drink?"

"Guinness," said Kevin.

"Good," I said. "And just a half for me. I'm meeting an old friend for lunch in a few minutes. In fact we're meeting for a goodbye toast. I'm off to Canada for a while. Student visa."

Kevin seemed to take that in his stride, and I relaxed a little. Evidently Becky had told this cousin of hers very little about me, praise God. I'd regretted the Irish accent from the moment I'd opened my mouth, and had even considered recanting the entire ruse, and coming clean, but here was the thing. If what my father had said were correct, and Kevin, along with his family, were mixed up with the provisional IRA, 'brothers and cousins and all,' then he'd just been 'made' – identified by time and location – by me in Northern Ireland's leading terrorist attraction – the favourite stop-over for famous travellers from Sean Connery to Harold Wilson – and I didn't think I could afford to recast myself at this late date as a dissembler, let alone a bald-faced liar, no matter how innocent my motives. As a potential tout, I'd made myself a target simply be being in the wrong place at the wrong fookin' time. Perhaps I was being paranoid, but what other business could this provincial lug from Cork have in Belfast's flagship for international glamour? Having passed through the same security I had, I had no doubt Kevin was clean as a hound's tooth, and I in no immediate danger, unless the IRA were preparing a full-frontal attack on the building even as we stood there, drinking our beers, but that prospect seemed unlikely. Belfast was heavily militarized – indeed, it was a war zone – and the British wouldn't have allowed it, if for no other reason than to spare James Bond and the Prime Minister of England from being subjected to colonoscopies of their own, every time they visited Northern Ireland. Even so, I couldn't spend the rest of my life as a political refugee in the bloody Europa Hotel. Eventually I was going to have to hit the streets again, where touts were routinely kidnapped, driven across the border, and 'disappeared' in the nearest convenient bog. Hence the second little ruse. "At dawn's first light," I'd as much as announced to Kevin, "I'm leaving this place and flying a long, long distance away, to a land where no one gives a shit about the Europa, Belfast, or the Troubles. Least of all me."

We chatted and drank our drinks, Kevin all the while becoming less guarded and suspicious-looking, if indeed he ever had been, and I remember thinking that if there were Academy Awards given out for sheer moxie, then I was that year's winner, no error. Eventually I checked my watch, and with a great show of regret slapped

Kevin's back in my most comradely fashion, and told him I had to shove off. I wished him well in whatever his endeavours in the north might be, then exited the Europa's bar for her restaurant, half-expecting a bullet in the back at any moment. The last thing Kevin said to me seemed odd, though I thought nothing of it at the time.

"You have interesting qualities, man," he said. "Many interesting talents. Stop by and see us, if your ever down Cork way again."

"Will do."

"You've got sand, mate."

Then down the broad corridor, stage-right into the Europa's spacious, ultra-posh five-star restaurant, where my life took a turn from merely terrifying to downright bizarre, for there at the table was my old friend, Alfie Moore, in dress shirt and tie, with the sleeves rolled up, looking every bit the football player he'd been in school, and beside him, celebrity-casual in sneakers and white khakis, tieless but with his snappy L.L. Bean dress shirt also rolled up to the elbows, was the writer, actor and comedian Michael Palin, positively aglow with a recently-acquired tan. I smiled as Alfie hopped up from his chair, and extended a hand. As if my day hadn't been strange enough, it had now transmuted into a full-blown sketch from a fookin' Monty Python movie! The actor got up too, but politely hung back, awaiting the introductions.

"Great to see you, Winter! You smell like a bloody brewery, man, that's not like you. Can't wait to get on that big bird, and off back to Canada, I suppose."

"A half of Guinness," I croaked. "Drunk under extenuating circumstances."

"Winston Crowley, this is Michael Palin. Michael's over from London to perform tonight in a comedy festival. We've known each other maybe a couple of years now, isn't that about right, Michael? Michael's dead keen on British Rail, and we sit on a couple of committees together. Imagine my surprise finding him here!"

"No surprises, really," the actor said good-naturedly, shaking my hand. "Where else does anyone stay, when they're in Belfast?"

"You want another beer, Winter? Or shall I just ask for the menu?"

"Coffee," I said wearily. "And menus would be grand."

We sat down, and the Great Comedian furtively checked his watch.

"Of course, comedy festivals and choo-choo trains aren't the only things Michael's interested in."

I laughed as Palin dropped his sun-tanned noggin modestly, and smiled. Michael Palin's keen interest in British public transit had pre-dated his rise to fame and fortune at the BBC, anchored in his train-spotting days at Oxford. He'd leveraged his celebrity in support of this most egalitarian of public goods, and Alfie's own relationship with 'choo-choo trains' made them a good fit, as mates, though the actor was a few years older. I was warming to this guy. He seemed like a genuinely nice guy. Too bad for him, in a few hours' time, the nightly news would be reporting that one of the last people to see the mysteriously disappeared Canadian student alive had been Michael Palin, from Monty Python's Flying Circus, in the Europa Hotel.

"I'm guessing everybody knows that," I said, looking around. "You'll be happy to know, I named my Roger in honour of your crew."

Palin laughed. "Your Python, is it? I'll pass that on to the others, they'll be thrilled!"

The next day, after a final tearful round of goodbyes, my father drove me out to Aldergrove, and after parking the car I suggested we say our goodbyes here. "Sure, I'll come in and wait with you, son."

"No. There's no need. That'll be all right."

"You have a while still."

"I'll buy a book," I said. "Let's just say goodbye here. Look dad, you were right about a few things. When push comes to shove, you're still my father, and I'm your son. And proud to be so."

That shut the old man right up, and more importantly stopped him from making any further effort to open his door, and hop out with me. This was the IRA's last chance, by my reckoning, to take me out at gunpoint, before I boarded my flight and was forever after beyond their reach. A tout on the run. It was now or never, and I didn't want any collateral damage in the form of a wounded father, caught in the crossfire, in the wrong place at the wrong time. So we shook hands in the car, and I told him I'd see him on the other side, then I was out and walking, a little nervously I don't mind telling you, with my bag slung over my shoulder, in it the clothing I'd been wearing for the past five weeks, only slightly the worse for wear, awaiting the violent arrival of Death's Dark Lord, and, without incident, passed through the doors of Aldergrove Airport, where I checked in, bought a book – something fast-paced and absorbing by Robert Ludlum – and not long afterwards was boarding the plane that would fly me back to Canada. I never heard another word nor saw Kevin again, and now I have to ask myself if I was just being paranoid, though the danger seemed real enough at the time. Cocooned though I might have been, as a Protestant in east Belfast, the Troubles were very real in 1975 and as I say Kevin McNamara was as misfit to be in the Europa as a man could get. With his long, straggly hair and hard, flinty eyes – in direct contrast to his fine-boned features, and almost feminine beauty – he reminded me of no one so much as the rock star, Marc Bolan, though without a year or two of wealth and mass adulation to soften his harder lines – he could have played the part of the rebel foot-soldier well, though I suppose he could as easily also have been just a country bumpkin, there to see how the posh people lived. And if I were to learn that it had been Michael Palin who had disappeared, in a hail of gunfire that day, instead of myself, I would have been horrified, though not horrified enough to regret not reporting my suspicions to the British army. Touts were routinely executed in Northern Ireland, but even if they had not been, I was no snitch. I had my own, serious doubts about the wisdom of the British presence in Northern Ireland – as had my father – and for all its razzle-dazzle, if the Europa couldn't safeguard the mortal hide of one comedian – himself a bit of an anarchist – then who was I to interfere? Kevin was a Cork man through and through, and as anybody could tell you Cork was a fortress of anti-loyalist sentiment – the rebel city, beyond the Pale – the equivalent stopover, I would even say –- to Oliver Cromwell's Wexford. It wasn't my job to put the machinations of Mr. Harold Abracadabra Wilson's Great Britain in the right, or teach them how to do their fookin' jobs.

Of course I never saw nor heard anything more about Becky McNamara again either, though I imagine by now she's a happy old grandma, shooting kangaroos and skinning koalas deep in the Outback, teaching her granddaughters how to dress a broken arm and fly small aircraft. At least I hope so. As for my father, I couldn't say for certain whether those five weeks did any good, but they certainly did no harm, and it was left up to my mother's dire illness in the end to bring us closer together – the enemy of my enemy being my friend – an illness which seemed most certainly destined to kill her, but which killed my old man instead. So maybe God has a sense of humour, and wanted my father remembered, not as a good man or even a Christian man, both brave and true, not as an adventurer in wild places or an obedient son or even a thoughtful philosopher and historian. He wanted him remembered as a man of good intentions, whose wisest advice had been to savour life, for life is short and death very long. As for me, I didn't even want him remembered for that much. His fingerprints are all over my soul, etched in stone. I just want him remembered.

Sugar Mountain

If my alarmingly eventful childhood can be said to have had a high-point-- an apotheosis-- and if I were forced to point a finger at it, I would point to my family's 1962 crossing to Ireland aboard the Empress of England. The Empress was a palace of exotic wonders – a Toyland bristling with charming alcoves, quiet corners, elaborate entertainments, mysterious doors and secret passageways, set against a jaw-dropping ocean vista. For my seven-year-old self, well-used to austere living and a predictable life, it was a big revelation – that there was fun to be had in this world, if only you knew where to look for it. I know everything is exciting when your seven, and nothing life throws at you seems particularly extraordinary, since you're still working out what's ordinary. If you were to find the sun rising in the west one morning, well – what of that? You're just a kid. Not even a smart kid. Of course my mom, my sister and I were going to spend six days on this dazzling jewel, in the sea – it was all part of the natural order of things wasn't it? When you're small an abandoned barn can be delightful as Disneyland, and I put it to you that the Empress of England was a Disneyland writ large – in a word, kiddie paradise. To all you seven year olds out there reading this, I can't recommend it highly enough. What are you waiting for? Go!

During the first night on deck my sister, Shona, and I struck up a conversation with two young deck-hands who, for a lark, told us they were in a band called The Beatles. They were young Brits from northern England, and we, coming from Canada (and being children) had as yet not heard of Liverpool's best kept secret.

The Beatles?

This was still only 1962. We'd never even heard of Liverpool. The deck-hands – a couple of swabbos whose seafaring ways had probably begun humping crates in the dockyards of that fabled harbour town – were surprised the news had yet to cross the ocean, so caught up was Liverpool in the grip of a nascent Beatlemania, though it would soon enough. Tsunamis don't grow smaller, after all. But for all we knew, they were talking about Rimski-Korsakov.

Every hour a new adventure on the Empress sprang into being, bringing new opportunities for fun. It seemed there weren't enough hours in the day to contain them all, let alone assimilate them. Our tender little brains were zapped. There was the swimming pool, in the depths of the Empress, with tiled walls decorated in multiple aquatic themes; seahorses, cheerful bubbly starfish, bosomy mermaids and whatnot, but that was just the most superficial of its delights. The pool was a body of water on a ship floating across a much larger body of water, a ship which rolled, pitched and yawed even when sailing the calmest seas. When you paddled round and about in the pool, you could revel in the surreal optical illusion of floating in a stable environment, while everything around you sloshed thither and yon, rolling, pitching and yawing drunkenly to the rhythm of the invisible turbulence below. It was a strangely delightful deception, made the more so because, regardless what your eyes told you, you felt totally still – and for those prone to seasickness (i.e. my sister Shona) it was a blessing in disguise.

A steward in the ship's library, where I went to search out books (I know – I was bookish even then) taught me how to play chess. His patience was remarkable – it took about three thousand lessons before I stopped seeing the game as a confused jumble of individual moves, but a fluid progression of elegant combinations; a kind of mathematical ballet in ranks and files that ignited an enthusiasm that lasts in me to this day.

During the course of our adventures we met lots of other kids, including a little girl with the unlikely name of "Pippa," (there's a Middleton by that odd name, coincidentally, I know, but this wasn't her.) Pippa and I spent hours in each other's company, exhibiting a kind of proto-fascination with each other, akin to puppy love. We both loved table tennis and spent hours on the breezy foredeck of the Empress, batting a tiny plastic sphere between us, though sometimes batting them into the Atlantic as well, in hopes of clocking a mermaid.

Then there was the Atlantic herself. Our great sweet mother. Surrounded though I was by a thousand distractions of human contrivance – the pool, the library, the ping pong table – they couldn't hold a candle to the mesmerising, vast sweep of the gigantic waters through which our little boat bobbed like an ant traversing a meadow.

"It's so beautiful!" Pippa sighed.

"Beautiful."

"Have you ever kissed a girl?"

"Yes."

The ocean hypnotised me. It bedazzled me. Morning, noon and night, I would make my way to the guard-rail, to look out over that vast, complicated carpet of crashing, breaking glass, glittering in the sunshine, both ever-changing and constant in every direction to the distant horizon.

Pippa leaned in and kissed me.

"Well," she said. "Now you've been kissed by another one."

Of the prepubescent among us, it seems girls are more interested in the opposite sex than boys (though boys make up for lost time soon enough) and there were plenty of things on the Empress I was more interested in than kissing Pippa. There was the madwoman who ruled supreme over the games deck – a thousand-year-old crone as gnarly as a Joshua tree, who spent every waking moment cranking two-penny pieces into the one-armed bandits that became legal only after the Empress had passed into international waters. One time, watching her with my sister, the two of us hypnotised by her grim single-mindedness, my sister reached out and touched the handle of 'her' machine, and the old biddy went berserk, screaming as though we'd just strangled her canary. Something else that only became legal in the open sea was the formal gambling room, replete with roulette wheels, green velvet craps tables, dart boards, poker tables, baccarat tables, even an elaborate miniature motorized racetrack, including ceramic race-horses that moved along on metal rods. What is it about adults and gambling? And what is it about gambling adults that's so interesting to kids? Shona, Pippa and I, and a few other children we'd befriended, liked to play there before opening time, and one morning a slender young man dressed as though for a wedding confronted us and gave us a piece of his mind, for being where we had no business being. The most memorable thing about him was his painstakingly coiffed hair – the top of his head looking like a post-modern sculpture woven from fibre-optic cable. Later that night he was introduced to a full house, in that same room, as the Las Vegas crooner and dandy Wayne Newton. Wayne Newton and The Beatles. It was like we were on a Love Boat, but for headbangers! Of course I hadn't yet heard of Wayne Newton either.

For a few hours the Empress picked up an entourage of blue whales, too beautiful to be attacked even only with ping-pong balls, though that was my initial impulse. We outran them all too soon – either that or the whales got distracted by something else. Between the pool, the slot-machines, the library, the shuffle-boards and table-tennis tables, the candy machines and toy shops, the movie theatre and the little ceramic horsies, we weren't so easily bored.

And always – always – there was the Atlantic. Our mighty mother. *Fergus's brazen cars.*

One morning my sister and I were in an elaborate toy room we'd discovered, towards the bow of the ship, filled with plastic castles, jungle gyms, big stuffed teddy-bears and the like, when the constant humming all around us was complicated by another sound – distant, crumpling paper. Curious, we hoisted ourselves on some stacked toys, the better to see out a porthole, and before us there rolled an extraordinary spectacle. The sea had become caked with a jagged white frosting, and bobbing chunks of ice. The Empress had wandered into a small field of icebergs. Nothing dramatic enough to attract the attention of James Cameron, but there were clearly no limits to the surprises the ocean was capable of springing on us. The ice also meant we were getting closer to shallow water. Our little dream vacation was starting to drawing to a close.

Was it presumptuous of me to begin by calling my childhood 'eventful?' Probably everyone's childhood is eventful, just in different ways. And it's not as though, by comparison, my later years and adulthood were bereft of events. Just the opposite – a couple of times my life became so damn 'eventful' I was tempted to throw myself from a tall building. As though eventfulness were a tempestuous Niagara Falls, and I the poor sap bobbing in the barrel.

But now it seems I've made it safely ashore, and, with trepidation and wonder, I'm experiencing something I haven't experienced since that distant childhood – a carefree existence. What a pleasant surprise! It appears I survived the fray, braved life's mighty Niagara's, settled old scores and proved everything I had to prove, beginning with my first report card and ending with the decision to retire from teaching and concentrate on pure theoretical research. My academic career is over: I passed all the classes, got all the grades, landed the good jobs, impressed the right people, and, in general, fought the good fight. Against all odds I won. I had been wounded in battle here and there, but I soldiered on, and now, not unlike my seven –year-old self, I'm free to go where the wind blows me, pursuing the adventures of childhood, and reaping the rewards of a responsible life without a care in the world. How strange! How bizarre! When family and loved ones ask me what I'm doing, now that I'm retired, I answer, with more than a hint of breathless wonder:

"What am I doing? Why – nothing! Nothing at all! Nothing at all – *in abundance!*"

Oh to live on Sugar Mountain…

Of course Neil Young is right. He always is. The magic and glory of childhood is irretrievable – a Sugar Mountain-- and like sugar over time those innocent days melt into the sea and then are gone forever. That's what makes innocence heart-breaking, as we grow older, but it's also what makes adulthood triumphant, when we regress into the past. I spent a lifetime playing Hide and Seek with ghosts in God's quantum playground, and I'm pleased to report that adulthood doesn't replace the magic of childhood with the mundane. The mundane is magical too, just in a different way. Truth is, the whole damn thing is magical, from stem to stern. But the barkers and coloured balloons are of my own creation now... Like a child I've become impervious to the destructive forces of reality. Few people get the chance to rebuild their own Sugar Mountain. I'm a lucky guy in that regard. How could it ever have been otherwise?

Geppetto's Other Pinocchio

Here was my dad, a man of forty-one, visibly greying as he squatted on the toilet seat. And there stood I before him, with my pants around my ankles – my poor, battered eight-tear-old penis bobbing just inches from his nose. No incestuous paedophilic perversion, this – the year was nineteen sixty-three, and sexual perversion had yet to be invented. Then why was my old man fumbling around with my little guy, like he was trying to button a poorly tailored jacket?

In fact, why had he spent every evening of the past two weeks repeating the mysterious ceremony? Clearly, it had something to do with my last visit to our family doctor, a gruff, no-nonsense basketball of a man, who had shown the same interest in what, until recently, had lain innocuously enough behind the zipper of my trousers.

At eight years old, I think it's safe to say, I'd given no great thought to my 'private parts.' Freud notwithstanding, the thing was good for making pee-pee, and not much more. As the vent through which I routinely relieved the pressure on my bladder, it deserved hardly any notice at all – certainly not as much, say, as my nose, which I could pick; or my ass, through which I could fart. Now it was as though no other appendage was of more importance. The doctor examined my dick, then took my mother and father aside for a hushed conference. When they returned to the room where I crankily waited – the examination had left me tender and indignant – they had a stricken air about them, as though they had just been informed their middle child was about to expire. Then the new, evening routine. After dinner I would wash my hands, brush my teeth, and have my pecker pulled, poked and prodded at by my worried dad. *Why the sudden interest, hay?* Not that I asked. Even at the age of eight, it seems I knew better than to question the status quo. Whatever the problem was, I didn't *want* to know. But in just this undignified manner, I was formally introduced to my manhood, and of course we've been together ever since.

A month later, I was taken for a second visit to our doctor, and the next day my mother, bless her Presbyterian soul, told me that I didn't have to go to school that day. Instead, I followed her around the house, pretending to help her with her daily chores, until, after a lunch of tomato soup and pancakes (my favourite) she sat me down and contemplated me with her large, sorrowful eyes. We were going, she told me, downtown to see a movie, one she thought I might like. The movie was Disney's *Pinocchio*. My parents were not the movie-going sort, not even on weekends! What in God's name was going on here?

And was there a message for me, perhaps, in that choice of film? Disney's animation dazzled me at first, then slowly started to fill me with a horrified fascination. Particularly horrifying was the scene in which Pinocchio's bad-boy friends seduce the erstwhile puppet into joining them at the fantasy carnival, only to find themselves turned into donkeys. Who knows the difference, at eight years old, between whimsy and stone-cold truth? Was this really what happened to kids who were bad? Did Jesus Christ himself reach down from on high, and transform them into barnyard animals? That seemed at least as plausible as Santa Claus, maybe more. And, worse still, did that explain the doctor's visits? The nightly poking and prodding in the bathroom? My mother's stricken expression over her bowl of tomato soup?

Was I, penis first, being turned into a donkey? *Or worse?*

It didn't take much soul-searching to divine why I might deserve just such a punishment. I picked my nose. I farted, then giggled at the fart. Worse even than that, at cub camp the previous summer, I had made the acquaintance of that most pernicious of 'F' words, from a neighbourhood friend, and had learned also that it was a 'bad' word; a word, in fact, so bad my parents would have throttled me for using it, had they but been there to hear me utter it so casually – even for *thinking* it, had they but possessed the needed clairvoyance. The same friend attempted to enlighten me on what that word connoted, exactly, but I was nobody's fool – my credulity could be pushed only so far, and no further. He left me with a mental image of the way my dad might have lain a hot-dog in a freshly steamed bun, for dinner on a summer evening. I was too busy earning merit badges to further worry myself about that most elemental relationship between men and women. Yet maybe I'd learned enough, and as a result was now to be transformed, dick-first, into something which henceforth would need to be kept tethered to the support beam by the car-port, beneath my bedroom window.

When the movie was over my mother took me aside in the theatre, and told me the truth. I was to be admitted the next day to General Hospital, where I would undergo an operation. Hospitals I understood. They smelled bad and sick people went there to get well. Strangely, the idea of being operated on didn't faze me. It sounded like a bit of an adventure, and it would mean more time off school. No problem there. Of course after all these weeks of preoccupation with what lay between my legs, there was no need to clarify what was to be operated on, *why* might have been a more pertinent question. But that, being a question from the upper echelons of adulthood, didn't bother me much either. So long as I didn't have to return to my grade three program, clopping along on four hooves, and braying, let the operation commence!

The hospital was a dingy, impersonal place, yet I don't recall my spirits being dampened by its drab, institutional air. I had, after all, already missed some school, been treated to a movie, and much more seemed in the offing. My sister's nose had been put out of joint too, by all the attention lavished upon me, and really, what more could any younger brother desire?

There was a toy room where my sister and I played, while my mother and father signed my execution papers. They stayed with me until dinner, pale and teary-eyed both. I was more interested in the cowboy hat and 'authentic' six-shooter I'd discovered on a shelf, by a doll's house. I don't recall now whether I'd resigned myself to the inevitability of all that unknown territory, spread out before me, or whether I really was fearless enough to consider the entire thing an adventure, to be treated accordingly. Maybe I was just an unusually stupid kid. After all, this was a hospital, where sick people went to get well, and even back then I suspected that not all of them succeeded. Then there was what surely should have been at least a young child's understanding of *where* I was 'sick.' By rights, I should have taken a greater interest in the proceedings than I did, it seems to me now. I knew from taking baths with her that my sister didn't have a dick *at all!* If nothing else, this should have set off the warning bells. But strangely, I don't believe it did.

Physical pain, being supremely subjective, ultimately defies description. The closest we ever get to absolute honesty is when we say 'the pain was indescribable.' But somehow that doesn't do justice to what I woke up to, after the operation. It was as though I had stumbled in a wood somewhere, and accidentally set off a bear-trap with my penis. *Yah!* And then, having been dragged, let's say, to the nearest log cabin, getting the wound stoppered up with a 100 watt electric light bulb, which burned invisibly up through my intestinal cavity, and which was guaranteed to continue burning up there until I died.

Yah! Yahhhh!

I was astounded to discover it was still only the year nineteen sixty-three. In my agony I assumed many centuries must have passed. But it was indeed still the same day as the day I'd been prepped for surgery. Shivering, half naked on the slab, I had been instructed to start counting backwards from one hundred, after which the surgeon clamped a plastic mouthpiece over my face. That was ten o'clock in the morning, and it wasn't even lunch-time yet! All this searing, fiery damage to my mid-section, and it wasn't even noon!

Skip the pain. It's boring. Assume it continued throughout and, unendurable as it was, I endured it. Of more interest is the young nurse who now came to comfort me, as I lay groaning beneath the sheets in her section of the ward. Like the pain, I remember her well to this day. Perhaps it is the pain that forged that vivid recollection, acting on my consciousness as powerful chemicals are said to work on photographic plates. Her hair was straight and brown, glossy, and pulled severely back into a little bobbing pony-tail behind her nurse's cap. Her eyes were large and very lovely, very bright – regular klieg lamps – with an arresting tint to them, almost a lavender, though very pale. Conceivably, aside from my own mother's eyes, they were the kindest eyes I had ever encountered in my life. Deep wells of eyes, overflowing with compassion for my suffering. Her hand on my forehead was cool. For a moment, I thought we might both cry.

She was also pregnant, really far gone – she looked like she had a Zeppelin parked beneath her stiff, white uniform. Pregnancy I understood, more or less. After all, I had a much younger brother, I remembered my mother's pregnancy. But this little nurse was so big with child she might have climbed into the empty bed beside me, and delivered right then and there. Compounding my new-born respect for the frailties of the flesh, I devoutly hoped it wouldn't come to that. There was only so much agony the walls of a hospital could contain (so my eight-year-old brain reasoned) before the sheer force of all that contained suffering blew the windows out of their frames, and caused the entire structure to collapse into its foundation. My own suffering was plenty bad enough, thanks very much, without adding hers to the general malaise.

"You'll be fine soon, Winston, I promise," she whispered, smiling down sweetly at the pale, nauseated creature that trembled feverishly behind my eyes. I managed an inarticulate grunt. Fine? Soon? Hadn't I been fine before? Why were they torturing me, what had

I done to deserve this? There was an aspect of enlightenment here, a dawning awareness that all was not as I had assumed. Children indulge in 'magical thinking,' so the psychiatrists tell us: an unquestioned ego-maniacal super-belief that every aspect of creation is somehow geared and calibrated to their own, puny wills. Now, with a kind of negative rapture, I was discovering that the mute flesh has an agenda of its own. Undeniably it was a first step towards adulthood, the first great disillusionment. Here I was. I was here – and no matter how hard I tried, I couldn't wish it away.

In only a matter of hours I was strong enough to scrape myself up off the bed, and it was then that nurse Duncan and I engaged in what must surely have been the slowest footrace in Christendom – she waddling gracelessly with what looked like a sixty-pound medicine-ball in her belly, and me with a 100 watt light-bulb smouldering away where my wienie used to be. Oh, we tore up the corridors, we did, we two; we really cut a rug. You'd think I was pushing a Buick in front of me, instead of the intravenous stand I required to stay propped up vertically at all.

There were other children on the ward of course. My own living example aside, there was plenty of evidence that, when push comes to shove, body has it over mind hands down. One kid had a broken collar-bone, and his entire upper torso, including his right arm, were encased in a body cast. He groaned pitifully; the attendants had needed to strap him down to keep him from crashing his cast into the metal frame of the bed, in a fruitless effort to get at an itch. The ward in those pre-air conditioned days was roasting hot, and so there he lay, sweltering, twitching and pathetic, a monster from some Kafka nightmare. A monstrous insect.

In the early afternoon my parents came to see me, and, I'm ashamed to report, I was angry and disgusted at the very sight of them. This predicament I was in, you see, was their fault. I was of their flesh, and the flesh had rebelled. They moped about miserably, watching while nurse Duncan and I streaked neck and neck, down the corridor. At around two my own family doctor dropped by to see how I was doing. I blamed him too. What good was dutifully keeping those yearly appointments, if this was the result? Doctors and dentists represent a form of institutionalised worst-case scenario. Breaking even with them is the equivalent of a thundering victory, and bad news is the only realistic alternative.

Come four o'clock I was hungry, and had a craving for Cheerios, my favourite breakfast food. I had broken my fast, if the term applies here, on some form of foul, poisonous jelly – a regular modern-art masterpiece served up in a bowl that was cracked and faded. So I begged and cried for the Cheerios, until nurse Duncan relented. I wolfed them down, then almost immediately threw the tragic results right back up, all over her, for which let me take a moment to formally apologise to her now. Sorry, nurse Duncan, wherever you are. Less than thirty minutes later, however, with mounting horror, the realisation slowly began to grow in me that I needed – *to urinate!* That very soon now I was going to have to perform that *unimaginable act!* So it might be for the best if, on that sad note, I conclude my narration. The circumcision had been a resounding success, and the problems my freshly unsheathed manhood might get me into later in life were still a million light years away. But here was their beginning, and now we have arrived at the end of the beginning. *He knoweth the way that I take: when He hath tried me, I shall come forth as gold.* Thus spoke the prophet Job, but it was cold comfort to me, that cheerless summer afternoon so long ago, as my bladder slowly filled. The urination was fast upon me. I could not wish it away.

Welcome to the Motel Pandemonium

I did some ugly jobs putting myself through school – ghastly, quite. One summer I sprayed under-body paint on the assembly-line of an auto-plant. Have you ever read Dante? At the end of my shift, I would crawl from a sweaty pit, aching from stem to stern, while all around everyone laughed at the university kid who, splattered in goo, resembled the victim of a mining disaster. I shovelled soy beans one summer, in a dust-choked purgatory, and painted a live furnace so hot the paint combusted even as I rolled it on. I sold vacuum cleaners too; I even won a trophy for it – regional! My folks were so proud! I drained sludge – in the middle of the night, shivering and knee-deep in it– from beneath four enormous water-filtration tanks. (Ironically, a few years later, I wrote a series of videos extolling the virtues of industrial water-filtration systems.) None of these thankless tasks paid overly well, but each contributed to making me the cheerful anarchist you see before you now. *Thank you!*

Another such job, which I'll always fondly remember, was as handyman at the Motel California, south of Ancaster village. The motel itself was a classic rural stop-over, wrapped in white stucco and charmingly dilapidated, backed against a swamp towards the rear of an enormous, sloping property, framed by apple trees and tall pines, complete with gas pumps, a restaurant for truckers, and an ancient, concrete swimming pool with twelve inches of rancid water in the deep end, where the drain was rumoured to be. The place had been recently acquired by their ambitious son, but the true proprietors were Humphrey and Abigail Muntz, two of the loveliest people it's been my good fortune to have known; Humphrey, a tall, stooped Briton, originally from Blackpool, a veteran of Her Majesty's Royal British Air Force – he'd seen heavy action at Midway and witnessed from above the fire-bombing of Dresden – though currently he was a retired gentleman in baggy corduroy pants and cardigan, with an air of bemused old-world resignation. He bore a striking resemblance to the aged Bertrand Russell, without the pipe, but with a moustache even Einstein would have blushed to sport in public. His eyes were sunk in craters of wrinkles and folds, but sparkled with the lively natural curiosity of a child.

Abigail Muntz was Canadian – she'd met Humphrey in Newfoundland after the war. Back then she was a waitress who always had a snappy come-back for the handsome veterans' quips over rashers and toast. Now she was the diminutive, bespectacled, slender and pragmatic keeper of a stucco-encased pandemonium, with a golf-course to the south, and the village of Ancaster twenty minutes down the road. I had just turned nineteen and was starting to sock money away, to finance my first year at Brock University the following September.

"Winter! Quick! Tell me something about *Romeo and Juliet* I don't know!"

"Kissy!" I shouted back. "Like what!"

"I have a paper due next week, and I know you know this shit!"

Kissy McCaffery was a bright, peppy seventeen-year-old, getting a jump (God knows why) on her grade twelve year in high school – her real first name a mystery no less than how she divined I knew shit about Shakespeare. She worked part-time as a waitress at the Motel Pandemonium.

"Read the play."

"I've *read* the play! *Ooo!* Tell me something I don't know! I need an 'A' on this paper!"

"Why?"

"Just one teensy-weensy little-known fact, and I'll show you my breasts."

I laughed. At seventeen, Kissy was most certainly feeling her oats, and experimenting with being 'slutty' after the manner of high-school girls in bad buddy movies. Clearly, she wasn't too good at it yet.

"You should take her up on that," cackled Paula Motley, one of the restaurant's full-time waitresses, a single mom whose sense of humour was so marinated in lust, just thinking about it made the vapours bead up on my forehead, like I was sweating broom-sticks. *"I would!"*

"I don't molest younger women." Actually, Kissy was barely a year my junior.

"Oh all right. Juliet is a lesbian, and Romeo is a figment of her father's paranoid imagination."

"Really?"

Paula was ten years my senior, and had the slutty thing down pat; her sassy attitude towards life – enlivened by the superb figure she cut – kept her from harm's way when her dirty mind got the better of her.

"The only quality you need to look for in a man you're thinking of marrying," she once announced in the presence of a throng of paying customers, "is the size of the bulge in his *pants!*"

Kissy McCaffery, scandalized, managed to stammer:

"You mean – his wallet, right?"

I mowed the lawn and trimmed the hedges at the Motel California, lugged beer to the refrigerators and frozen vegetables to the basement. As time passed, my value to the franchise improved, however, and I was entrusted with more integral aspects of the business, like balancing the books and ordering inventory. But what I mostly did was work on the pool. That whole summer was a running battle with the pool. This dilapidated wreck had been installed around the time King James commissioned his Bible, and by now (like that book) it was beginning to show its age. The passing centuries had turned its concrete lining into a brittle, cracker-like substance, easily crumbled, and every time I thought – after long hours in the hot sun – the surface was sufficiently prepped to be rolled with a fresh coat of paint, the attempt would peel my hard work away like layers of an onion. It was a fool's errand – everyone knew it except the mild-mannered Humphrey Muntz, who, after each setback, would rub his chin, furrow his brow, and start dreaming up yet another solution. His fond desire to resurrect this artefact from an ancient civilization – and my fondness for him – only renewed my determination that somehow his wish would be fulfilled, though a good fire-bombing – like the one at Dresden – might have been a preferable use of my time.

"*C'mooon!*" Kissy whined, stamping a foot. "*Ooo!* Do me a solid!"

"A solid?"

"*Ooo!*"

"OK. *Romeo and Juliet* begins as a comedy."

"Winter!"

"It's true. An Elizabethan audience would have recognized the signs. It's like *The Birds* that way. That's probably where Hitchcock got the idea. First you have *Pillow Talk*, starring Rock Hudson and Doris Day, and the next thing you know everything's gone down the crapper, and there's a dead guy laying slumped in the broken crockery, with his eyeballs pecked out."

Kissy stamped her foot once again, then stormed off in exasperation to the kitchen.

"That was true, wasn't it?" Paula Motley asked me, while pouring coffee.

"Sure. *Romeo and Juliet's* a problem play, not a tragedy. But if Kissy put that in her essay, her teacher would flunk her for plagiarism, sure enough. A seventeen-year-old wouldn't know that."

"But an eighteen-year-old would?"

"I turned nineteen last month, Paula."

"I thought you were supposed to be some sort of math genius."

"Well shit, Paula", I laughed. "A guy can have a hobby, can't he?"

Time, as the poets and physicists tell us, passed; and with each passing day I became more hell-bent to find a way to realize this old soldier's dream of a pool of sparkling water glittering in his front yard, filled with laughing children and ringed with exhausted travellers, lounging in the sun. I would have moved heaven and earth for him, not just because of his service during the war, but because he exuded a kind of warm wisdom that, as a very young man, I found tremendously appealing, and feared was all too fleeting. So I chipped, swept, plastered and painted, but to no avail. I wrapped the pool's rusted-out filtration tanks in fibreglass, but they were beyond repair. Hour after hour I cursed and sweated in that pool, and every week or so Humphrey would optimistically order another truck-load of water, only to watch it leak away into the water table. Then he would rub his chin, furrow his brow, and invite me down to the restaurant for a beer, so we could problem-solve what we were going to try next.

"No beer for me." I said. "Your wife would kill me."

The summer was unusually hot that year, but between the Kissy and Paula show, the deliveries, the problem of the pool, and the coming and going of all manner of guests – from businessmen screwing their secretaries, to old married couples making their way south to the Canada/US border, to assuage their gambling obsession – uneventful moments were few and far between. By mid-summer, I was ensconced in the workings of the place, and an honorary member of the family. I was even entrusted on occasion with the baby-sitting of Their Majesties, Cleopatra and Alexander, two of the largest, ugliest dogs I hope never to lay eyes on again, outside a horror movie; two enormous sacks of cement that wobbled through the house thither and yon on spindly legs – identical bulldogs of Hindenburg-like proportions precariously balanced on pipe-cleaners. When I entered the house, these Frankenstein dogs invariably mistook me for someone who adored them, like their owners.

"Whoa – who's this?" I'd been in the office, reviewing requisition forms, while Cleopatra and Alexander slobbered on my ankles and staggered into the walls, when I glanced into the motel's register and noticed a familiar name.

"*Whoa, Nellie*! What's this?"

"What is it, Winston?" asked Abby, looking up from the linen she'd been folding.

"This guest – Al Purdy."

"He and his wife checked in this afternoon. They're down in the restaurant right now, having dinner. What about him?"

"There's a Canadian poet of that name."

"Oh?"

"Yes, a pretty big one." I picked up the phone and called down to the restaurant. "Paula, is Kissy still there?"

"She just finished her shift."

"Tell her to stick around for a minute, will you? Is she still taking that English course for school?"

"As far as I know. What's going on, Winter?"

"Well," I said, "unless I miss my guess, there's an A-plus essay to end *all* A-plus essays down there, just waiting to be written, eating his dinner."

Alfred Wellington Purdy was born in Wooler, Ontario, in December of 1918; he attended Albert College in Belleville and Trenton Collegiate, before dropping out of school at age seventeen. He served in the Royal Canadian Air Force during WWII and after that worked at all manner of thankless, ill-paying jobs until, during the sixties, he was able to establish himself as a poet, editor and writer. In a long, fruitful career he published thirty-nine books of poetry, a novel, and much else besides. He'd been awarded both the Order of Canada and the Order of Ontario, so yes, as Canadian literary figures go, he was a pretty big one. Even so, I was surprised I recognized his name, scribbled in the motel's register; it rang an ancient bell in the darkened corridors of my psyche, where high-school "Can-Lit" syllabuses lay stacked up, slowly rotting, along with the requisite anthologies that went with them. In high school I didn't much care for Canadian literature in general, let alone Canadian poetry, and my enthusiasm for Al Purdy's brand of it, let's say, burned less than incandescently in my fervent, adolescent breast. When I told Abby he was a big deal, that biographical crap-shoot was based on the fact that I recognized his name at all, and what I recognized it for had little to do with his writing. I vaguely recalled that Al Purdy (aside from a guy whose sentences didn't reach the edge of the page) was a hard drinking working-class bad-ass who tore up the sky during the war and knocked down trees after it, by punching them. That was my kind of Canadian poet. I wanted to meet him, so I could only hope this wasn't that *other* Al Purdy, regional rep for some dog-shit manufacturer from Wormhole, Ontario, here in Ancaster for a Jubilee.

"What's this all about, Winter?" Kissy demanded petulantly.

"There's someone here I think you should meet."

"Who?"

I told her the story, and Kissy turned about fifty shades of white, then headed for the restaurant's front door.

"Wait! Don't go!"

"Ooo! Do you have any idea who Al Purdy *is?"*

"Well, yah," I laughed. "Yes. I do."

Kissy stamped her foot crossly once more, then, without further ado, fled as in horror.

The restaurant was at half-capacity with the usual suspects – local teens washing down burgers with

Cokes; truckers drinking beers, exchanging horror stories from the road; anonymous travellers from the rural byways of Canada, some heading south towards the godless republic below, and still others fleeing it as one might flee a vengeful Godzilla, freshly resurrected from the ruins of a radioactive sea. But a poet? Nowhere I looked could I recognise the brow of a winner of the Order of Canada. Then, around the corner of the L-shaped room, there he was, Al Purdy, swigging Molson Light from the bottle (just like the truckers!) while the patrician woman who sat with him nibbled rabbit-like at a salad. Purdy looked older than I expected, which made sense since the last time I'd seen his photo would have been two or three years previously, in the pages of some old anthology or other. But it was him, sure enough. There was no mistaking the empyrean line of his profile, the Romanesque nose, the froth of swept-back, wavy hair, the high cheekbones that dropped dramatically into the haggard jowls and fearsome scowl of a street-brawler, with penetrating eyes keenly observing everything around him – including now myself – with the quiet reserve of a Plantagenet in exile. It was like looking at a combination Emperor/bowery boy, and it occurred to me that Norman Mailer projected that exact same image, and probably no less intentionally. He was dressed like a steelworker, just beginning his shift, and chomped down hard on the stub of a cigar.

"Hi – Mr. Purdy? Ahh–"

"How did you find me?"

"Find you?"

"How did you track me down?"

"Oh, I didn't track you down, sir. I work here. I recognised your name in the register, and just thought I'd come down and welcome you to the Motel

California. I'm not a stalker, or a fan, or anything like that, but I know who you are and I admire your accomplishment."

All this while, a condescending smile had begun to register on his companion's smug visage, and I felt my dander rising. The great poet, on the other hand, leaned in and squinted me up and down through his glasses, as though assessing a rival at the poker table.

"So you're not a fan?"

"Well – that's not exactly what I meant. I know who you are."

"You don't want my autograph?"

"No."

"Well, then, this is all just a big funny coincidence?"

"I think that's what I said. Look, Mr. Purdy–"

"Call me Al."

"Look, *Al,* I've said what I came to say!"

"Whoa!" he laughed. "Slow down. That's some temper you're sitting on there, son – you're no shrinking violet, I'll give you that. Sit down! Join us! Let me get you a beer!"

"You have a reading tonight, darling," his companion – I had to assume it was his wife – cooed, touching him delicately on his extended wrist. "You've had enough to drink for one day."

The cold disdain with which Purdy responded would have shattered a beer bottle at twenty paces.

"Why don't you go wait for me up in the room, *darling?"*

Ouch. Whoever she was, she'd been told, and rose stiffly – stiffened by mortification – and retreated while gathering her dignity back up, to staunch the sucking chest-wound from whence it had been blown-out at point-blank range.

Turning back to me, Purdy asked:

"You married, son?"

"No."

"I didn't think so. You don't seem like the type who has a lot of patience for the back-stabbing and ego-gratifying that goes into social intercourse."

Social intercourse? It occurred to me this guy was pretty goddamned tipsy, sure enough.

"You don't know me. You have no idea what 'type' I am."

He laughed.

"I wouldn't be so sure. You live long enough in the public eye, the public tongue starts whispering its little secrets in your ear, whether you want to hear them or not. Don't get the wrong impression. My wife's a wonderful woman. I don't know what I'd do without her. Normally, she doesn't come on these things with me. But after all these years, she still thinks she has to protect me from myself. So, are you really only here because you *work* here?"

I laughed.

"Mr. Purdy – Al – I assure you. I'm plenty impressed, believe me, but you're no Bob Dylan."

That got a chuckle out of the old coot.

"Or even Leonard Cohen, for that matter," he added.

"No. Not even Leonard Cohen."

"You like Leonard Cohen?"

"No."

Paula turned up just then to take our order, and Purdy asked for two whiskeys with beer chasers. Knowing I never drank at the motel, Paula cast an eye my way, looking for confirmation. I just shrugged. A moment later our refreshing beverages materialised before us.

"You talk about your public profile as though it were a burden that you resent. What's wrong with being a successful artist?"

Purdy drained his glass, then took a pull on his beer.

"Nothing usually. Better to be known than unknown. But it's a job, just like any other. What's your name, by the way?

I told him, but I don't recall him ever using it, and probably he forgot it five seconds later. Which is probably just as well.

"Most of the time we live out in B.C., or up at the house at Roblin, where mostly people just leave you alone, and you can think. Walk the trails. Enjoy the view. Chop wood. Then you come down here, and you're not yourself any more. You're this man everyone wants to meet. You're this man everyone wants to talk to! They ask you questions about your work. What was the inspiration for this, Mr. Purdy? What did you mean, when you wrote that? How the fuck should I know? They want to turn you inside-out, and then give you awards, and buy you dinner. They want your opinion on something they call *the current literary scene.* Whatever the hell that might be. They fawn and smile and drag you around, like a dog on a chain, and nothing you say can ever be too outrageous. They still insist on introducing you to their friends and colleagues, they want to interview you, to photograph you, to televise you, so they can write essays about you, to fulfil their *Can. Lit* options. Because God forbid everything shouldn't be complicated! So you have to oblige them, for a lot of reasons. You have to support your own work, first and foremost. Your publishers are relying on you to uphold the franchise. There isn't much money in what you do, so you do what you can to help out. And if that means drinking tea with arthritic old Chairs of literary Committees, day after day, year after year, then *that's* what you do! It's strange only at first; after a few years it becomes repulsive. There's more to it even than that – but that's where it all begins. Success isn't really the downside of being a writer. Success isn't the point. I could have been just as successful driving a truck, or slinging hash. But that's the name of the game, so I read my goddamn poetry, accept the accolades, smile at all the nice people who keep my books in print, and put up with all the bullshit. But that doesn't mean I have to like it. What did you say you name was again?"

"Mr Purdy, can I ask you a question?"

"Sure."

"Why are you telling me this? You're Al Purdy, and I'm just the shit-bird who mows the lawn."

Purdy laughed. "I guess I'm telling you this because you know who I am and aren't impressed by Al Purdy," he told me. "That's refreshing. Also, I'm drunk."

"I have to take a leak," I said. "And I should tell you, my ride will be here any moment."

"Invite her in!"

"It's my father."

On my way back from the john there sat Humphrey Muntz, at a table by himself, his head drooping, his hands shaking as they always did while he sipped his drink and stared off as into outer space, or maybe into the sun-capped clouds over war-torn Dresden, forty long years before, when boys were boys and men were men; or dreaming of how perfect everything would be when between us we finally got that damned pool up-and-running, the sun sparkling off the water while happy innocent people splash in the crystalline results of his beneficence.

"Winter! Join me! Have a drink!"

"Oh, hi, Mr. Muntz."

"Why so formal? Humphrey! I just ran into your dad, he went up to the motel to put your bike in the car. He'll be here in a minute. Why don't you invite him in for a drink?"

"Well – my mom will have dinner on the table by now. But come around the corner with me. There's someone I want you to meet."

"Oh?"

"His name's Al Purdy. He's a veteran. He was in the air-force too."

So Humphrey followed me on unsteady feet, and I made the introductions: two ancient airmen, nothing more; one British and the other Canadian, after which I bid my fond adieus, but before I could turn away Purdy looked me dead in the eye, and said:

"When you write about this, son, don't make me look like an asshole."

I laughed.

"I'll throw in a disclaimer."

I left then, leaving the famous Canadian Poet and the wizened owner of the Motel California to share their stories, and relive the golden years of their youth, while I exited the restaurant into the mild summer air to reapply myself to the task of inventing my own. The sun was setting with the moon not far behind it, so much so I wondered if a solar eclipse might not be coming soon. My dad was waiting in the car, idling in the parking lot, my ten-speed bungied into the partially-closed trunk.

"I had a word with yer man, just now," my father offered, not unkindly, as I got in.

"He told me."

"He was drunk."

"I know," I said. "I don't think I've ever seen him sober."

"Ach!" exclaimed my kind-hearted dad. "It's a pity!"

"Aye."

I'd seen one before, many, many years ago, in Nova Scotia – the very same total eclipse of the sun Carly Simon refers to in the song, *You're So Vain*. I saw that.

"Them two wee dogs would drive *any* man to strong drink!"

I laughed. We pulled out onto the highway, and then towards home. I dialled the volume of the radio higher. The CBC was playing Beethoven's *Eroica* – which movement I couldn't seem to put my finger on.

"You know, son. This job, are you certain it's for you? If you're worried about your education, you know your mother and I are always here for you. If you need financial help, like? Or just want to – you know."

"I know," I said, wiping the tears from my eyes. "And I appreciate it, dad. But don't worry about me. I don't mind the work. It's an interesting job – some days," I added with a laugh, "more than others."

The events and characters in this story – including characters based on people in the public domain – are entirely fictional, and any resemblance to real people is a contrivance of the author, or a coincidence. This is a work of fiction.

"Gerty"

The one good thing about commercial air travel is it gives you an excellent excuse to drink a lot. This flight was no exception. The trip to Ireland is usually six hours, but this one took seven, something to do with headwinds, or leprechauns sprinkling pixie-dust in the ailerons, some such thing. When we finally touched down in Aldergrove it was eight local time on a drizzly Irish morning, and I was in dire need of a bed. My folks met me and obliged me (they were thinking breakfast, my central nervous system was telling me otherwise) so we drove the forty minutes back to Dundrum, a fishing village-by-the-sea where they owned a caravan on a hill, and where they had been retreating every summer since my dad's retirement four years before.

"This is what you wear to travel, Winter?" my mom clucked, a little disdainfully.

I was wearing (OK, it was grubby) a white tee-shirt, jeans, and an admittedly pretty ratty denim jacket. Over my right shoulder I lugged a black gym-bag, loaded with socks, underwear, several 'good' shirts and pants, another dozen tee-shirts and two four-pound lead-lined batteries. Slung over the other was a Panasonic F250 three-CCD colour video camera – a hellishly expensive piece of technology (including tripod) which I'd rented in order to document the trip for cable TV. The camera was what the batteries were for. My mom's disdain for my dress didn't surprise me overly-much. She and dad dressed for travel the same way they dressed for everything, as though in preparation for a funeral, or a wedding.

I was asleep the instant my head hit the pillow, and awake just as abruptly three hours later, confused and groggy. Oh right – Ireland. The old sod. Scratching my butt, I looked around for my pants, which were neatly folded on a chair by the bed. I dressed and walked out into the dining room, to a disconcerting tableau. My mom looked up from the carrots and onions she was chopping in the kitchen, both defiant and guilty. Draped around the living-room, like so many articles of dainty unmentionables, were twenty fifty-dollar traveller's cheques slowly drying over the space-heaters. Behind my sleeping back my mom had collected up my travel-wear (probably with a clothes-peg on her nose) and ran it through a washing machine, without checking the pockets. Along with my disgraceful rags, she'd inadvertently washed a thousand dollars of my hard-earned dough.

I burst out laughing.

"Ma – you laundered my money? *Literally?* You realize that's just an expression, don't you?"

I inspected one of the cheques. Kudos to American Express. No harm done.

"That's *far too much money* to just be carrying in your pocket, Winston!" she scolded me crossly.

"You launder my money, and now you want to make it out that I'm to blame?" I laughed. "It's money! It goes in your pocket! Oh come here, I love you, you crazy ..."

I hugged her tight – she was beyond distraught.

"Sorry, Winter," she whispered.

"It's OK. The cheques were insured. Even if you'd ruined them, it wouldn't have mattered."

"Still ..."

I laughed.

"Thanks for washing my stuff."

My folks had been begging me for years to come back to the old sod – really, they'd been begging me all my life – to reaffirm my connection to the country of my birth, the country they still considered home, even though they'd raised three children in Canada. But there was more than that to my being here. I wanted to see the grave of William Butler Yeats again. I wanted to video myself visiting that sacred place. Anyone who can string three words together has at least a passing knowledge of the magnitude of Yeats's achievement. Poet and Nobel prize Laureate. Senator in the Irish government. Tireless advocate for Irish theatre. Champion of an upcoming crop of young Edwardian-Irish writers – Joyce, Singe, Sean O'Casey – destined to repay Yeats's advocacy with an outpouring of genius that would evolve not only Irish literature, but world literature in its entirety. Yeats died in 1935, in France, and was buried there at Roquebrune-Cap-Martin, but in accordance with his wishes he was exhumed a year later, in order to be laid to his final rest in Drumcliff, county Sligo, Ireland, where as commanded in the poem *Under ben Bulben* his tombstone had been carved with the words:

Cast a cold Eye

On Life, on Death,

Horseman pass by!

And then there was the Crowley connection. Oh yes. The Crowley connection.

Alistair Crowley (like Yeats) had interested me since I was a boy, and not just because we shared a last name. He'd been born into a wealthy Christian family, in Dublin, but quickly turned his back on his heritage and pursued all manner of strange, warlock-like peregrinations. He'd published the most lewd, graphic pornographic poetry, and smoked opium, drank absinthe and studied Satanism. He travelled the entire world, championing a truly nutty cult, the Hermetic Order of the Golden Dawn, which caught the attention of the ageing Nobel Laureate Yeats. In the Edwardian era Crowley – that other Crowley – was reviled as Satan himself, which Crowley regarded as high praise indeed, but there was something about him and his weird ideas that appealed to Yeats. Crowley participated (legend has it) in ceremonial orgies, and was rumoured to be involved in bisexual extravaganzas. Maybe that's what did it. Oh, and he was a mountain climber too, and not mountains in Ireland. Incredibly, Crowley wended his way 6000 meters up the frozen shelves and precipitous rock-faces of K-2, in the Karakoram range (from whence comes the K) between the borders of Pakistan and China – a mountain second in height only to Everest herself, which hitherto had not been climbed by man nor beast – but was forced back due to influenza, malaria and snow blindness. One can imagine Crowley gallivanting like a sexually aroused goat, up and down Lhotse, Annapurna IV, even Chomolungma, insolently renamed 'Mt. Everest' by the British, pursued by half-naked Jezebels while dancing through the Khumbu Icefall in the Himalayas, as though through the meadows of Elysium, in top-hat and sleeves, with an ancient book of Satanic spells in one hand, and a hash-pipe in the other.

The Crowley connection, oh yes, the Crowley connection.

After Sligo, my plan was to push on to Dublin, to research original documentation on Yeats's relationship to Crowley, and the Golden Dawn, at Trinity College, University College Dublin, and a Temple of the Golden Dawn which, amazingly, was still in existence. I'd done worse in the quest to satisfy my curiosity and pursue a story in this world. Word was that Crowley had humiliated Yeats repeatedly, to thwart his desire to join the Order. I won't go into detail but I suspected there was good cause for librarians, historians and hagiographers to protect Yeats's legacy from a chapter of his life story best left untold. The likelihood of discovering (or appropriating) something new was not good, but here I was, ready to give it a try.

Some of this I told my father that night, over beers in a pub down in the village, and some I didn't. Oh yes. I suspected he wouldn't approve, and anyway, it was none of his business.

The Crowley connection. Cast a cold eye, indeed!

I was in bed sleeping by nine that night, as dictated by my jet-lag, but awake fresh and ready to do some exploring by five the next morning. I dressed quietly, and walked down to the sea in the predawn starlight, breathing deeply of the briny air, a little amazed to find myself where I was. Ireland! The old sod! A parked car with two Irish kids in it, engaged in some unspeakable act in the back seat – as surprised to see me as I them. I walked west at the water-line beyond Dundrum harbour, admiring the enormity of the thunderheads building slowly in the east, the mountains of Mourne, painted purple, pink and orange by the peek-a-boo sun, which did indeed run down to the sea.

I struck out through a patch of long grass, to dip my foot in the crestless waves, and something truly Irish happened. I startled a nest of feral jack-rabbits, hundreds of them, and all in a blind panic they bolting like nuclear-powered pogo-sticks in every direction. Five seconds later (or less) I was a hundred feet up from the shoreline, in the shadow of Dundrum castle, laughing weakly while my heart raced like a sewing machine. Beside the ancient ruins of the castle was a paddock of broken stones, within which stood a lovely chestnut stallion, with a white patch on his breast and liquid golden eyes, watching me with considerable amusement.

"Geimhreadh Crowrentach."

"What?" I gasped, only now calming down from the manic bunny-attack.

"You're Geimhreadh Crowrentach. I know yer wee mammy and da. Lovely people! Lovely!"

"That's my name in Celtic," I laughed. Actually, 'Geimhreadh' was the Celtic word for 'Winter,' the season. This was one canny nag! "My friends and loved ones call me 'Winston.'"

"Irish."

"I beg your pardon?"

"Geimhreadh is your name in Irish. 'Celtic' is the Irish word for 'Irish.' Irish is the English word for 'Irish.' We're speakin' fookin' English, man! Ooch!"

I traversed the distance from the castle to the paddock, where I reached out to stroke this beautiful animal's muzzle. I tore a fistful of grass from between the paddock-stones, and held it out.

"Well," I said. "It appears I've travelled a long distance to cadge a language lesson from a horse. Thanks!"

"Ooch!"

"And your name is ...?"

"Gerty."

"All right then, Gerty. You've made my day. Thanks! Probably you've made this whole damned trip!"

"Bollix! It was me first owner what called me Gerty, a lassie's name! Twit! Twenty years before he sold me to this rummy Pom, then emigrated tae Australia, where 'e went on to become a world-renowned banana-bender, in the banana-groves of that distant land."

"Your former owner is now a famous banana-bender in Australia?"

"Aye – didn't I just say that? Do yeas not ha' bananas over there, in Canada?"

What made this horse think I was from Canada?

"Of course, but –"

"And do them wee Canadian bananas not come bent?"

"Well, naturally, but–"

"Ooch! There yeas ha' it, then!"

"And did this former owner of yours become a banana-bender before or after he torpedoed the Titanic, in the briny waters of Loch Ness?"

"Yeh regard yerself as a funny wee man, don't yeh Laddie? Did yeh kiss the Blarney Stone?"

"Many years ago. And you?"

"Ooch!" Gerty snorted, indignantly. "Sure yer worse than tha' wee felleh what wrote 'bout them Dingoes, or Day-glows or –"

"Wee felleh?" I laughed.

"Swift!"

"Yahoos," I said. "Which I guess makes you the last of the Houyhnhnms."

"Ooch! You come here from Canada?"

"Aye."

"Is it true what they say about Canadian lassies? That they have unusually large brrrreasts?"

I laughed.

"For a Houyhnhnm, you're quite a pig, Gerty."

"It's just me humble, rustic, unsophisticated way like – yeas want vulgarity? I'll show yeh vulgarity! Yeh see tha' wee mountain over there?" Gerty snorted in the direction of Slieve Donard, a large hill due-east of Dundrum harbour, overlooking Newcastle, part of the Mourne mountain foothills. "There's a coven o' leprechauns up yonder what brings new meanin' to the words sexual perversion! No lie! Never seen the like, in all me born puff!"

"Huh," I said, stroking Gerty's muscular neck absently. "That's interesting. Sexual perversion is one of the reasons I'm here too."

"Ooch! I know why yer here."

"Oh?"

"Yer here to tarnish the good name o' a great man, if yeh can! A poet o' timeless genius! An Irish nationalist! A champion of the Irish people! A saint! A visionary! A true son of Ireland!"

"I'm not here to tarnish anyone!" I protested, more heatedly than I'd intended. "I'm here for the truth!"

"Ooch! The truth – is that how yeh justify this vile thing yer here for tae undertake?'

"That's not fair!"

"Ooch! Yer here in the hopes of promotin' yerself, at the expense of a man who's shadow yer not worthy of *dyin' in*, let alone livin' in! And yeh call yerself an Irishman? Go home, wee Irishman! Go back to yer God-forsaken land, before yeh do somethin' yeh'll regret for the rest of yer life! *Ooch!*"

When I woke up the next morning, I found my father in the field beside the caravan, sipping a cup of tea and also drinking in the wondrous sea and sky, the Mournes, the architecture of the clouds, and all that lay beyond.

"I've changed my mind, I think," I told him. "About going to Dublin. There's plenty enough to record without going all the way down there."

My dad looked me over, long and hard. Eventually he smiled, as though in relief, and put a hand on my shoulder. Evidently he knew me better than I realized.

"Winston," he said. "You were always an ambitious, precocious boy. And it pleases me no end to see you've grown up to be a very wise man."

"Why, thanks dad!" I said, smiling but genuinely touched. "Now let's get ourselves down to Sligo, so I can dance a jig on this crazy Irishman's grave!"

Entangled

It was only when I got to third grade that I finally met the love of my life – the inglorious angel who (I suspect you're about to learn) would haunt my dreams and recollections like a radiant ghost from an ever-retreating, more distant past; a beacon, like a lone pulsar by the edge of the galaxy, transmitting its forlorn signal into the void, and awaiting the evolution of a technology which would allow even a single reception-point it could calibrate and recognise. Her name was Lucy Nelson, and there she was, newly materialized in Mrs. Pasternak's classroom when I returned, having been away 'sick' (i.e. recovering from my circumcision) only to find myself traumatised once again by Lucy's willowy loveliness, the demure tilt of her slender, alabaster neck, the sweeping black tumble of her hair, her sparkling eyes (shyly averted from the wounded warrior, only now rejoining his battalion after prolonged enemy resistance at the front) her modest wool-plaid skirt, concealing her athletic legs, her mohair cardigan (her arms forever a mystery) and black, patent-leather shoes. From top to bottom she was perfection. Better than perfection – she was the blueprint for a perfection yet to be arrived at – and I was thunderstruck. For all I knew the rest of that morning, Mrs. Pasternak could have been speaking Japanese, or Swahili, blathering merry mumbo-jumbo about long-division, or elephant husbandry, some such blatheration.

"Hi." It was Lucy, having come up tentatively behind me on the playground, at recess.

"Oh! Hi!"

"What did you do to your leg?"

"What do you mean?"

"You're limping."

"I was in the hospital. I had an operation."

"What sort of operation?"

"An operation on my leg." No medieval torture could have coaxed further explication across the battlement of my tongue. "I'm OK now."

"Ah. I'm glad."

It's lovely and sad, how the little tendrils – the microscopic relational threads – begin lengthening and tentatively reaching out from the darkness, to start the process of defining the world around us, and the person we become. We drop at birth like stones out of oblivion, into the arms of our mothers, self-defining and self-referential, and only as time passes do the tender strings begin groping blindly for other strings to entangle themselves with, until, with the passage of time, we ourselves become entangled with the starry landscape of the universe. A once-in-a-lifetime miracle repeated a billion times a second. Lucy and I were instantly transformed into a single unit, enveloped by an inexpressibly gossamer cloud, an ionized field of charged particles as impossible to separate, or contain, as the poles between two industrial magnets. Of course when you're eight years old your cohorts are likely to look askance at such transfigurations, with the jaundiced eye of the stupidly young. I don't know how that translated for Lucy, but in the world I inhabited girls were regarded as cootie-riddled aliens, comical witches just spooky enough to scare the bejeebers out of us, even as we laughed at their pointy black hats and the warty-carrots of their noses, concerning themselves with mysteries and subterfuges best left unexamined, except under the direst circumstances.

The year was 1964 and things were changing quickly. Not so long before, my mother had taken me aside one sunny morning and told me – in a state of obvious distress – that an important man (an Irishman!) whose name I didn't recognize had been shot in Dallas, Texas – why that mattered to the Crowley clan was a mystery to me – and in the past few weeks a unique phenomenon had begun rolling through our little neighbourhood, so portentous even an eight-year-old couldn't miss its rumbling progression. So feverish was the climate created by Beatlemania that even I – half-again too young to be a hippy, let alone an acolyte to the royal-sons of a nascent Hippy Nation – registered their incarnation as they dropped from the clouds to make a joyful noise amidst the wailing of the true believers. Overnight the airwaves were brimming with cheerful three-part complaints, from four working-class avatars, with funny accents, singing rapturously about holding hands, three-way adolescent melodramas, and dancing with that special someone, even while the Gemini astronauts sailed far overhead, making beeping noises right out of *My Favourite Martian,* and space-walking their way into history.

After school and dinner the kids in our neighbourhood would congregate in the street, or our backyards, to relive that week's episode of *Bonanza,* or *The Man from UNCLE*, chasing each other thither and yon through the Magnolia trees and strawberry bushes, playing war, hide-and-seek, Red-Rover, whatever prepubescent diversion drifted into our heads from the darkening sky. The Flintstones were a huge hit that year (bigger than the Beatles, as far as I was concerned) as were the Jetsons, *Gilligan's Island* and *Mutual of Omaha's Wild Kingdom*, while *The Mod Squad* and *Star Trek* yet awaited our whole-hearted endorsement a few years in the future. Girls were not banned from this twilight merriment – the more the merrier, after all – but Lucy's inalterable presence by my side became a source of some small teasing, endured with a giddy admixture of alarm and secret pleasure (it conferred a new-fangled social status on us, as yet undefined) and a jolly good time was had by all. We could be found in the shade of the big trees, at the foot of Holbrook school, analysing *The Lucy Show* (that *other* Lucy Show), *Z-Cars, Mr. Ed, My Three Sons* and *Petticoat Junction* with the same hermeneutical prescience an art appraiser might have brought to the Louvre, or strolling side-by-side through the leafy property of Chedoke hospital, out to the enormous neon cross (still lit in the evenings, in those days) to eat peanut butter sandwiches prepared for the occasion by my ever-thoughtful mom. That that hospital had housed so much suffering (and still did, to a degree) was lost on Lucy and me – it was our sanctuary, our Eden, and even a ten-month interruption while I was sent to Belfast for a (presumably) culturally invigorating dip in the chilly institutional waters of Orangefield public school (my dad thought the experience would be good for me) could not tamp out the glow of our ardour for each other's company.

Then one sad day – and didn't you see it coming? – the walls crashed down, and, like many an innocent Adam and Eve before, we were for evermore banished from the beautiful garden, not by a spiteful God, for partaking of the knowledge of good and evil, but by a restless father (Lucy's restless father) who had found better employment out on the west coast, and had arranged to transplant this most precious flower there forthwith. The night before she was scheduled to depart my life forever, we walked hand-in-hand down our sad, lonely street, under the lamplight and the pitiless scrutiny of the stars, two lost souls still united by a scant but fleeting handful of hours; she squeezed my hand, and, raven hair aglow in the lamplight, eyes brimming with tears, she turned to me and whispered, "You know, Winston, you can kiss me if you want." And I've been lingering over that kiss ever since.

The violent untangling of all those myriad tendrils – the carnage their sudden uprooting caused to my boyhood psyche – was as the collateral damage done by a mighty storm of Biblical proportion. God's own tempestuous wind rendered those billion fragile connections, leaving me torn and raw as a burn victim. The days passed, and stuff happened to fill those days, but it was all the same to me; Lucy's invisible smile was all I could see, the silky smoothness of her hair all I could feel, the sadness in her eyes after I had kissed her that night – my first kiss a kiss goodbye! – all I could remember. Mrs. Pasternak's class was now little more than a drudgery; weekly commitments – painting and music lessons, boy scout meetings – bleak chores to be endured. My sympathetic parents distracted me as best they could, and even my playmates backed off as in awed wonder and respect, for this new-found thing never encountered before – a boy's broken heart. Then, many months later, I divined a glimmer of light at the end of the tunnel – a whisper of hope in the form of our family dentist, an ancient Irishman with a rasp to his brogue that made Crocodile Dundee sound like Prince Charles, and who, elbow-deep in my mouth with many sharp implements and the whirring little drill that ground away at the cavity in my molar with frantic abandon, sweating and grunting over me in his tormentor's delight, planted a word in my ear that started my wounds to healing. "T'ink o' da Lord, Winston," Dr. Seamus O'Donnell grunted, bearing down on the drill. "T'ink o' da soofferin' o' da Lord, on da cross!"

And I began to feel better.

Breasts.

Need I say more? Does any other word better define what it means to be a boy, in his teenage years? To be a male of any age, really; big, perky titties, pretty little knockers – breasts with nipples like manhole-lids – the word alone enough to turn an otherwise level-headed adolescent into a drooling chimp, a muttering sociopath, a steaming tub brimming over with boiling hormones, just waiting for someone to take pity and pull the plug. God in his wisdom – 'da Lord' suffering on 'da cross' – did not put Anna Crowley's son on earth to write pornography (plug-pulling metaphors notwithstanding), but not drifting towards the graphically sexual to capture those engorged, sweaty years would be a coy exercise in futility at best, if not a downright betrayal of the truth. Ladies, do you have fond memories of that special dreamboat, with the wavy, auburn hair, the letter-jacket and the soul-melting smile, captain of the football team; the chiselled, steely-eyed athlete with the profile of a Navy seal and the disposition of a Hollywood movie-star, who transported you with seductive words, extolled your charms, brought you bouquets and chocolates in heart-shaped boxes, on Valentine's Day, ladling flatteries even while whisking you off on that transformational first date – perhaps a movie starring Robert Redford, or Richard Gere – treating you afterwards to bacon-and-tomato sandwiches washed down with Coke-floats? Remember the season-opening home-games, the high-school proms, the lover's leap under the harvest moons, where you cuddled in the backseat of his daddy's Chevy, while he crooned in your ear to a sound-track by Karen Carpenter, Ann Murray, and Olivia Newton-John on the radio? Remember all that? All that time, Prince Foxtrot Romeo over there was obsessing over your Winnebagos, girlfriends; fantasizing about them, itching to set them free, picturing in living Technicolor how they would look unadorned, how they would feel and smell and taste. Men are pigs, girls, and any man who tells you otherwise is a lying pig.

It was a warm summer in 1970 – I'd just turned fifteen – three-nickels-in and half-way to no-where – when I got up from the dinner table, tried to stretch out a phantom discomfort in my twilight zones (my belly was starting to feel like an industrial mixer in which cement was slowly drying into the rock of Gibraltar) and decided the best thing to do was go for a walk ("shower his brains" my adoring mother called it), as I had done many a night before. At fifteen, I was beginning to show creeping signs of being 'creative' in numerous, depressingly uncreative ways. I was a dedicated painter of forgettable landscapes, and well-rehearsed in the bare minimum of chords required to play ninety percent of all known popular songs, on the guitar. I read music well, consumed novels as though the last good one had already been written, had a pretty defensible tenor singing voice, and had begun to write – the only talent even remotely promising I could lay claim to.

I started north around seven that night down West 35th street, to the accompaniment of a soothing breeze which rustled the branches of the trees in our neighbour's yards, until I reached the mountain brow. To the west, a small woods, hidden within which was the top of the Chedoke senior ski-hill, a short but perilous killing-field of moguls that had nearly crippled me more than once, and to the east a winding path along the mountain which once upon a time represented the extreme outer-limit of my known universe. Within its cramped confines, I'd drunk a thousand Cokes, got fitted with the first of many pairs of glasses, played a thousand street-games with my friends (a coterie I'd assumed was immortal and unchanging, until one of them, Doug Maxwell, was reported dead of juvenile leukaemia at age twelve) attended parent/ teacher meetings, church functions and Boy Scout activities, including film-nights in the gymnasium of Chedoke school (where I first saw the Beatles' *Help!*, having attended with a cousin the premier of *A Hard Day's Night* in Ireland, a year or two earlier) and dances organized in the basement of the church across the street from the school. The geography of my childhood might have been limited, but the wealth of the experience it contained was enough to enrich the lives of a billion unborn souls. And if I live to be a hundred, I'll never capture the essentials of all its secret beauty.

When I reached the top of the Garth Street stairs, which wended down to the lower city – a destination already pretty far outside my fifteen-year-old definition of familiar territory – I made an unusual decision, and continued down the steps. For me that was a first, and the only explanation I can give is that the cement-mixer in my tummy was telling me the purpose of this outing had yet to be accomplished. Besides, it was a lovely night. The air was fragrant with the scent of wild flowers and ancient forests, wafting over the lip of the mountain-brow, no less comforting than the musty smell of our finished basement, or the pillow-cases on my bed. In short, I didn't feel like going home yet, and therefore pushed on.

At the bottom of the long stairway (and now I really *was* in alien territory), I came upon a small gathering of children – girls, I had deduced, on the strength of their muffled conversation – seated side by side on the curb of a sidewalk, smoking cigarettes, a habit I had yet to acquire. "Hay! You! Boy!" one of them called out from the darkness, to a jingling accompaniment of laughter. Oh damn – she was talking to me! Not only was I figuratively uncomfortable in the glare of this awkward social situation, there was something rumbling in my guts that was also making me literally uncomfortable too, so (like an imbecile) I decided to pretend I was deaf, and continued on my way.

"Hay! You there! Come over here for a minute, are you stupid?"

"No," I muttered under my breath, feeling my cheeks flush. "I'm not stupid."

"What's your name?"

"Winston."

"Wha'cha doing, Winston?"

"Out for a walk."

"You came down the stairs, or along the Chedoke trail?"

"Down the stairs."

"You OK?" my interlocutor further inquired. "You look like you just coughed up a hairball."

Giggles all around. As small klatches of high school girls go, this one had nothing much recommending it – four kids lined up in a row on the kerb, under the lamplight, smoking and whiling away a pleasant evening, dressed in cut-offs, tee-shirts and halter-tops (beneath which, not likely to go undetected by my observant adolescent eye, each possessed budding breasts of various size, desirability and perkiness) chit-chatting about school, boys, home-life, boys, last night's episode of *Charlie's Angels*, the newest top-forty hits on the radio, and of course more boys, boys, boys.

Introductions all around were called for, but of the four of them, each vying in her way for the attention of this welcome novelty in their midst, the girl whose attention I most wanted sat at the end of the row, almost invisibly, as though in deep reflection, her knees pulled up to her chin and cradled in her arms, partially obscured in the shadows, the least demonstrative of the four, and the next in line to lay waste to my idealized romantic fantasies – the fate of adolescent boys since time immemorial – for the next five years. Her name was Ariella Kaplan, and as in a revelation of Old Testament proportion she was the very embodiment of feminine allure and desirability; qualities that swirled around her as though she were glittering under a veiled shadow of seething, distant aloofness, coy yet erotically charged – both voluptuously beseeching after the manner of the concubine, Abishag the Shunammite, yet also demurely swaddled in an elemental, virginal uneasiness, like a fawn in the embrace of an unfamiliar primordial attraction. Her black hair, high cheekbones and smouldering almond eyes gave her a startling resemblance to a fully-formed Lucy Nelson, breasts and all (and what breasts!) as though reincarnated in a more perfect iteration from the distance past, not to be exaggerated but impossible to ignore.

Who is this that cometh out of the wilderness like pillars of smoke, perfumed with myrrh and frankincense? Tell me, O thou whom my soul loveth, where thou feedest, where thou makest thy flock to rest at noon; for why should I be as one turned aside by the flocks of thy companions? How beautiful are thy feet with shoes, O prince's daughter! The joints of thy thighs are like jewels, the work of the hands of a cunning workman. How fair and how pleasant art thou, O love, for delights; a garden enclosed is my sister, my spouse; a spring shut up, a fountain sealed. Thou art beautiful, O my love, as Tirzah, comely as Jerusalem, terrible as an army with banners! My beloved is unto me as a cluster of comphire in the vineyards of Engedi – go forth, O ye daughters of Zion, and behold King Solomon with the crown wherewith his mother crowned him in the days of his espousals, and in the days of the gladness of his heart.

We talked for an hour about small things – the tribulations of high-school, *Hogan's Heroes*, the recent near-catastrophic events of Apollo 13, on its way to the moon. When we parted company it was not before agreeing to meet again the next night, same time, same place. As I walked back up the Garth Street stairs that evening, under the starlight, it was as though uplifted by a choir of angels, singing Hosannas from above in 4/4 time, and I knew my life was complete.

Sometimes Fate plays the ace she deceitfully keeps up her sleeve, however, and in this case the diamond of expectation I'd been polishing in my mind began crumbling, and the heavenly host ceased singing their Hosannas. At the same hour the next night, instead of reuniting with the goddess of my dreams and her entourage, I was flat out on my back in St. Joseph's Hospital, and had been the entire day, resting comfortably in a semi-private room, beside myself with disbelief and regret. That morning, I had awakened in truly dire straits – running a fever and seeing quadruple – the cement-mixer in my bowels having not only completed its diabolical task, but for good measure turning radioactive, and so distressed were my parents when they realized how far gone I was (I think I was babbling incoherently from the *Song of Songs*) they carried me to the car and drove me directly to the hospital, where a young intern with hairy knuckles and a tattoo palpated my stomach, grunted disapprovingly (the skin concealing my kidneys as tight as a bongo-drum) and asked when I'd last had a bowel movement. In my delirium, I mumbled something about springs shut up, and fountains sealed.

"Yo, Winter!" the intern reiterated. "Pay attention! Your last bowel movement, dude – when was it?"

"My last – what?"

"A shit."

"Ahhh."

The only other time I'd found myself in a hospital was seven years earlier, when I'd undergone my circumcision – and that little caper made this seem like a waltz amongst the petunias. When I'd awakened after the dreaded surgery back then, it had been to the unspeakable realization that my innocent little pecker had been transformed into one of those cascading fireworks, that spit luminous globules of green and gold into the sky, where they burst in an awesome display of smouldering incandescence and mortal agony. By comparison, the appendectomy was nothing. Instead of an Armageddon between my legs, I had a urine-hued stain of anti-bacterial paint due-east from my belly-button, swabbed over a razor-thin scar made unseemly by a dozen gnarly, black stitches, the entire mess patched by a translucent oval of sterilized plastic – if there was any pain it was more like an itch than the eternal fires of damnation. My mom and dad were beside my sickbed when I opened my eyes from the procedure, and now they had a dilemma of their own. By an incredible stroke of bad timing (not the first that day), they were scheduled to fly out to Ireland in twenty-four hours, and my mother now wanted to cancel the whole shebang, even though it would cost the price of the tickets, and even though my sister (several years my senior) had already been entrusted in their brief absence with the New World interests of the corporation. Knowing full well I would be fine – and reassured by my sister, my aunt Kathleen, and my aunt Jo that all would be well in their absence – we were able to convince my anxious mom a costly last moment cancellation was extravagant and unnecessary – after all, I was fifteen! With maximum doubt (and my father's helpful prodding) we convinced her that throwing away an expensive, long-anticipated vacation was unnecessarily melodramatic, and here now a novel opportunity presented itself. My meddling sister Shona notwithstanding, I was free to experience a foray into independent living. Things were looking up.

Then, the next day, who should come shyly creeping into my hospital room, at the first permissible moment, but Ariella Kaplan herself, breasts and all, the perfect iteration of a previous incarnation, and the diamond I'd been polishing to dust in my imagination exploded in a multi-hued panorama of possibilities. Has youthful longing ever been so richly rewarded? Has bewilderment and loneliness ever been so lavishly dispelled? Has a hopeless adolescent fantasy ever been so miraculously fulfilled? It turned out, the explanation was less than miraculous – when I'd failed to show up the night before, as scheduled, Ariella's resourceful girlfriends pooled their detective-skills and looked up my family telephone number, and had been told (probably by my quick-witted sister, Shona) the cataclysmic news. And the rest was simple.

"Hi," Ariella said shyly, with a little wave, from the door. "Can I come in?"

"Ah."

"Are you OK? We missed you last night."

"I'm good. Fine. Never better."

Ariella giggled, and approached the bed.

The entanglements flourished and the little tendrils multiplied like a fast-growing garden vine, until the entire hospital felt as though bound and trussed in the heavy undergrowth of our love. The word 'love' doesn't really do justice to that magnificent outburst of growth. We bathed in each other's company for a blissful hour, and then I made a decision (one of many) that would get me in trouble with the grown-ups – hospital staff, my family (not yet my parents though – they were in Ireland) and even my family doctor. On a fearless impulse, I decided I was going home. I didn't sign myself out or tell a soul – I simply (and with great care) pulled on my clothing, and limped unnoticed out the door, into a blistering-hot summer afternoon, with Ariella by my side. We walked to the foot of the West 5th access, then hitch-hiked up to the corner of Garth street and Bendemere, from whence it was but a short walk to my home. Did my fresh wound and the merciless sun slow me down? I think not much. The power of love had rendered my infirmity and the scorching sunshine irrelevant.

That Ariella was Jewish and I was, well, not so much so, introduced a *caveat* into our bliss, in spite of the unstoppable attraction between us – certainly it was a source of concern to both our families, if less so to ourselves – from my unique viewpoint I'm happy to report the elder Kaplans and Crowleys approached this distressing development like two sides of a symmetrical figure. With maximum graciousness, and a minimum of obvious discomfort, I was as welcomed into Ariella's home as she was into mine, for which we were both grateful, if pleasantly surprised. Of course to me this small cultural misfire was as nothing – I was more an Irishman than a Christian, and my Canadianness (to say nothing of my horniness) trumped both hands down. Ariella's Jewishness pressed harder on her than on me. Through her family (even at such a tender age) she had been made aware of the history of her people; its centuries of forced isolation, suffering, and betrayal culminating in the rise of the Third Reich, and the unspeakable horrors of the holocaust. That Ariella had a tie to such misery only added depth to the mystery of her allure in my eyes – there was something wounded about this beautiful young daughter of Zion, with the almond eyes, the troubled smile and the firm, perky breasts, that I felt I'd been put here to comfort and assuage. She was my Abishag the Shunammite – my *cause celebre* – my New Jerusalem.

We made out. A lot. We explored each other's bodies, with trepidation at first, and then with mounting urgency, but the explorations never reached the finale – the glorious Ode to Joy – of their necessary biological inspiration. Like the intrepid souls aboard Apollo 13, I was destined never to touch down on that most yearned-after celestial bull's-eye – the whys and wherefores just as entangled as the infinitesimal strings that groped towards its achievement. I was forever held at bay from splitting the sacred goal-posts, crossing the radiant finish-line. We were still young of course – there were a few kids our age at our respective high-schools having sex, sure enough, but not by the bushel barrel-load, not by the thousands; lust was in the air (as it always is) but it was no Roman orgy – not in the locker-lined corridors of Sir Allen Macnab, and not the bathrooms or broom closets of Sherwood High. Then there was the little matter of our religious differences. Erotic and alluring as I may have found Ariella's 'otherness,' I suspected she was finding *my* otherness a source of confusion and distress. Both our families had raised us to be aware and observant of our respective religious contexts, and that my education in this regard had not taken as well as my elders might have liked, would be saying the least of it. When I was thirteen, I was required to attend Sunday morning lessons in Official Presbyterianism, in order to become a fully sworn-in member of the church. On the day of the ceremony, to complete my union with 'a sooferin' Lord' on the cross, Protestant-style, when asked the fateful question, I (and I alone of the dozen children standing before the alter) said thanks, but no thanks to the precious gift of divine mercy and life-everlasting. The collected congregation was scandalized, of course – not least my mom and dad – by my apostasy (to his credit our Minister was so impressed by my independence-of-mind he recalled the moment fondly each time our paths crossed, to his dying day) but I could be pushed only so far down the road towards the group-think and blind faith of a social institution that threatened to torture me for all eternity, if I didn't shut my big yap and behave.

So I had the suffering of the Lord, but Ariella had the suffering of the Israelites to contend with – a watermark that identified her as one with her history as nothing could identify me with my own. The incineration of six-million of Ariella's brethren in war-torn Europe, thirty-years previously, stood between her and the fulfilment of my longings, like the Keeper to the Gate of the Law in Kafka's celebrated little parable (another much put-upon Jew, though mercifully he didn't live to see his macabre fairy-tales made all too horribly real by the Nazis.) We found ourselves in a thorny, emotion-drenched predicament – with everywhere to go and everyone stopping us from going there. I mooned over her, I yearned, I lusted after her; her radiant visage provided the background to my everyday duties and distractions, and once or twice (after alcohol had entered the equation) I even made a bloody fool of myself on her behalf. We would break up for a week, a month, even a few months, only to be pulled back together, as though conjoined in a cat's cradle of rubber bands, the sweetness and delight of each reunion made all the more ephemeral because nothing had changed, and nothing possibly could.

After graduating from high school I had my choice of the three universities I'd applied to – McMaster, The University of Toronto and Brock. Toronto was an enormous metropolis – rapturously complex and potentially overwhelming – I had as yet to evolve an appetite for, and McMaster was my home school, the more reason (despite my family's perfectly sensible protestations) to give it a wide berth. Brock, chosen by default, was a small learning environment in a sassy little city named for a woman, and more-so than advanced algebra, or the plays of William Shakespeare, women were on the forefront of my pedagogical short-list of subjects to major in. So Brock it was, and on a chilly Sunday afternoon in 1975 I kissed my mom good-bye, shook my father's hand, and boarded a bus to freedom and independence, never to look back again. My life had undergone a sea-change, and I was in heaven; I'd been assigned to a double room I was resigned to sharing with an obnoxious Yankee from Kalamazoo, Michigan, with the square jaw and protruding forehead of Palaeolithic man, but even that wasn't enough to suppress my exaltation. Independence Day! University! University *life!* University *girls!* Let the Saints go marching in!

I don't want to suggest life in Brock's only student residence – necessarily co-ed – during the 70s was a Roman orgy, but it beggared the competition in the corridors, bathrooms and broom closets of Canadian high schools, from one end of this fair Commonwealth to the other. To keep things 'chaste' (I'm guessing) the boys' and girls' floors alternated, but there wasn't an armed guard in the stairwells, crying, "Halt! Who goes there!" and demanding the password, either. These were serious, intelligent young people after all, who devoted their days to attending lectures and seminars, writing papers and burning the midnight oil in Brock's undergraduate library: students of Economics, Business Administration, Philosophy, English Literature, Science, Dramatic Arts, Chemistry, Engineering, and every other avenue open to human endeavour for which there was a classroom – but they were horny (and good-looking) young primates as well. In their late teens and early twenties they were mature enough to know when to buckle down and put their noses to the grindstone, and sensible enough to know that when their hormones started bubbling, it was time to close the textbooks, crack open a bottle of wine, and commence fraternizing with the opposite sex. After only a few days the ubiquitous sound of protesting bedsprings, thumping headboards and the soft moaning of youthful voices, were competing with hockey games on television, or the latest record by Pink Floyd or Led Zeppelin, rattling the windows in their frames.

For my part, even now – pathetic though it sounds – I was entangled in that cat's cradle with my Abishag the

Shunammite. Come Friday afternoon I would catch the four-o'clock express back to Hamilton, from this wine-drinking, pot-smoking, high-brow Gomorrah, complete with rampant copulation, and return to the frail uncertainties of Ariella Kaplan and her doubts. My routine absences were enough to refresh things that might otherwise have gone bad, and the novel idea that I was a university boy (Ariella was a year younger, and hence still only a senior at Sherwood) made me desirable in a limited kind of way. As the academic year progressed, however, I found myself less inclined to go home on weekends, even inventing reasons not to. During the autumn months we played squash or basketball in the Phys Ed facilities, tossed a frisbee or football around in the quadrangle, or just sat around the common rooms, drinking beer and blathering about Nietzsche, Plato, Sir Isaac Newton, Schopenhauer or Bertrand Russell, like we knew what the hell we were talking about. That winter we were entertained by the sight of a dozen South African exchange students frolicking with open astonishment in this never-before-seen climatological wonder (snow), and after a particularly heavy snowfall, in the middle of a cold-snap bitter enough to chase the shadows back up the trees, the girls from the top floor of the student-residence – a notoriously bad-ass bunch – got half the population put on notice by organizing the erection of a penis in the quadrangle built from snow – a male sexual appendage (fully aroused) of such spectacular proportion and anatomical precision, down to the finest detail, that more than one of Brock's senior administrators, the ones comprised of straight-laced, pinched-faced, squinty-eyed grannies, arthritic as ancient apple trees, when they braved the cold to witness the desecration, keeled over in a dead faint among the drifts. It was excellent.

One night during that same cold snap I was out on the balcony of my room, overlooking the quad, drinking a beer and breathing in giant lung-loads of frozen, rejuvenating oxygen, when I noticed a girl I knew but slightly, opposite me on the balcony below. Her name was Alex Dreschel, and since the year's commencement she'd been the target of multiple amorous advances from every direction, rebuffing each in turn (she was in recovery, still, from a broken heart, acquired in her home-town of Barrie) and now here she stood beneath the starlight, staring forlornly off into space, lost in thought.

"Alex?"

"Oh! Hi!" she called up, laughing self-consciously, as though being startled were a *faux pas*. "I didn't see you up there. It's Winston, isn't it?"

"What are you doing?"

"Oh," she sighed sadly. "Not much."

"Well," now I was just making things up, "it's such a beautiful night, I was thinking of going for a walk. Do you want to come with?"

"Isn't it a little cold?"

I laughed.

We bundled up against the weather, and met downstairs at the front of the student residence, pushing off from there across the wind-blasted drifts towards the student parking lot, beyond which was a thin border of willows and elms, fringing a small man-made lake whose purpose and providence were a mystery to me, chatting about school-life and the people we'd met in the brief time we'd been here. Slowly, Alex seemed to cheer up, which was gratifying – I knew how it felt to nurture a broken heart, and anything I could do to lighten her mood I would do, so in the parking lot, as we approached the connecting road that led to the outer world, I threw out my arm, as in cautionate warning, and said, "Whoa-whoa-whoa – stop sign!"

Obediently we both stopped at the sign, with nary another soul to be seen for miles around, while Alex giggled and I turned clownishly, looking first up and then down the abandoned road, as though on the lookout for imminent danger. After a suitable time we proceeded across the road towards the lake.

"All clear."

"You're funny."

"Just erring on the side of caution, ma'am," I told her. "In these hazardous times we live in, you can never be too careful."

We scrambled through the snow and ice for a good sixty minutes, under the starlight, laughing and talking, until Alex told me she was getting a chill, and wanted to go back to her room for hot chocolate, or a glass of wine, perhaps. When we arrived back up on her floor, we began tugging and untangling ourselves from our heavy winter clothing, and when I was down to a woollen sweater and jeans, I told her I'd need to excuse myself and make use of the facilities. "Oh, but –"

"What?"

"The other girls on the floor."

Now it was Alex's turn to laugh.

"Winter, it's late. Go! Everyone else will either be out partying or asleep."

"All right, I'll only be a moment."

"Take your time."

I'd had several beers that evening, and after an hour performing my missionary work in the snow, the urination, partially impeded by numerous layers of tight-fitting clothing, seemed to trickle on forever. When I had myself safely tucked away and zipped back in, I returned to Alex's room – a large double, like my own, though her room-mate was nowhere to be seen – to find it awash in golden candle-light, and Alex herself, not content to stop at her thick, outer clothing, stripped naked and standing like an apparition with a glass of wine in each hand, in the flickering glow. Her head was tilted mischievously to one side, her long, thick hair cascading over a bare shoulder, and she boasted a sly, confident, irrepressible grin as she assessed my reaction, then started towards me, holding out a glass for me, and said:

"Are you going to live?"

"Ah –"

"Is it a girl?" she asked. "Back home?" That there might be such an eventuality didn't much faze her – after all, here stood she before me, naked and just bursting with animal sensuality, and home was far, far away.

"No," I managed to croak, nearly knocking a candle over with my erection, "there's no girl."

Alex laughed gaily, and pressed herself up against me.

"Then what are you waiting for?"

Here's something I've noticed over the years. There's a transformation that takes place in men and women from the 'before' to the 'after' of when that most intimate, momentous decision is mutually agreed upon. Before, men are the hunters and women their quarry – males the aggressor and females – knowing full well the value of their allure – left only with the decision to either stave off the attack, or acquiesce. But afterwards, the tables get turned. All of a sudden women reveal themselves to be just as aggressive and adventurous in the pursuit of their pleasures as men had been beforehand, maybe more, and now it's the men who resemble the wilting wallflowers, coy as virgins, baffled and baffling as *ingénues*. For the whole of that night Alex tossed me around in the candlelight like a rag doll, and when I thought I could take no more, she made it her business – with her hooded, almond eyes and her mischievous grin – to demonstrate how quickly and effortlessly that illusion of utter satiation could be turned aside, so the joyful adventure could go on and on – and on. There was a telephone call to be made, eventually, and when I finally made it several days later I was taken aback by how hard Ariella took the news, that whatever we had before was over, that I'd met someone in St. Catharine's, and that when I came back to Hamilton, she would not be hearing from me. Ariella wailed and carried on like I'd left her standing at the alter with infant in arms, but I was unmoved. Sometimes the disentanglement of loves little tendrils leaves you feeling like a burn victim, and sometimes they just wither and die. In any event, there's no end to the ways we complicate each other's (and our own) lives with them, no end to the entanglements, no satisfactory conclusion to their endless fascinations. Stop me from dreaming? Don't be absurd!

Orangefield

Children raised in bubbles might be forgiven for seeing the world through slightly distorted fields, and this must certainly be true in my case. Having been born in Ireland, but raised in Canada, by loving parents who never let go of their shared history – who made no effort, really, to embrace the New World or declare themselves born-again citizens of it – it seems in retrospect I never felt I had a firm footing on either side of the Atlantic. I grew up in a cultural no-man's land of mixed feelings and ambiguous loyalties, breathing the good clean Canadian air, admiring the fluffy Canadian clouds drifting overhead through an azure Canadian sky, attending Canadian schools, enjoying the tar-bubbling/brass-monkey polar extremes of the seasons, but never really feeling like I *was* a Canadian – and none the worse for the residual confusion. If you were to ask me outright my first instinct would be to say I'm Irish, even though (more or less) that flies in the face of my biography.

My parents emigrated to Canada in the winter of 1956. I was eighteen months old and my sister was five. Why they did so has long been a mystery left unexplained – young families mostly pull up stakes and relocate to foreign lands to improve their lot – better opportunities, more lucrative jobs – or even just to find employment of *any* kind. None of this was the explanation in my parents' case. My father had earned his Chartered Accountancy degree in Ireland, while a young man, and had landed secure, lucrative government employment thirty minutes down the road from Belfast, in a small town called Downpatrick (believed to be the final resting place of St. Patrick himself, patron Saint of Ireland, who is incorrectly credited with driving the snakes from Ireland centuries before.) There's an ancient church and cemetery in Downpatrick, with an enormous rock on its perimeter, on which the sacred name is cut in stone.

So what patron Saint drove the Crowleys from Ireland? Why the sudden departure from such an idyllic, comfortable circumstance? My mother had no interest in Canada – of relocating there or anywhere else – but she was a woman whose marriage (on her twenty-first birthday) had included a vow of obedience to her husband in the days when such vows were serious business. So now, in the winter of 1956, here she was – barely an adult herself – ploughing down Concession Street, pushing a perambulator through the slush and ice in which her first-born son lay drooling in contented indifference, swaddled against the weather, while her daughter, my sister Shona, rode behind on the axle-shield protecting the rear wheels, like the running-board of a Volkswagen Beetle, wrapped in her winter finery, my poor mother wondering all the while what unfair Celtic spirit had transported her from her comfortable, leafy bungalow in east Belfast, a short walk from the family home, the house she'd been born in, in 1931 , growing up a dark-haired, winsome lass in semi-rural Irish splendour, under the stern eye of her father (my grandfather James, a cabinet-maker who had worked on RMS Titanic while that vessel was under construction at the Belfast shipyards) and the Presbyterian church. Now she found herself knee-deep in a bitter Canadian winter, living in a walk-up, three-bedroom flat in Hamilton, Ontario, a light-year from everything she revered, adored and understood. What transgression had condemned her to this fate? What offence against the god of her ancestors had landed her in a country where the snow piled up chin-high in the streets, to the point where you had to crane your neck to watch for traffic, at risk of life and limb, her only relations her own mother's sister (my great-aunt Molly, and her husband, Bill), and a brother (my clever uncle Ken and his wife, far away in British Columbia, where he worked as a journalist, though soon would move to Toronto to become a High School English teacher.) In short, my homesick mom knew exactly no-one her own age, and her judgement on the Canadian weather was made the less charitable for loneliness. She suffered the disheartened vertigo of the culturally disenfranchised, yet she never complained – over the years her stoicism in the face of adversity would become the stuff of family legend, and it all started here, with the grim trudging of Hamilton's busy streets, up to her armpits in slush with her squabbling children in tow each time she needed a replenishment of Tetley tea, or a rasher for the next morning's breakfast.

The apartment itself, on the east mountain, was also a big downgrade from the stylish home she'd established for herself and her fledgling family back in the Old Country. Three flights up, if not quite squalid, it certainly wasn't what my mom had grown accustomed to; sweltering in summer and far from cosy in winter, the place had the anonymous air of an abode stamped from some everyday material, by a machine for the mass production of barely-adequate housing. The preparation of meals filled its every corner with an aroma that quickly turned unpleasant, and in the summer the corpses of bluebottles needed to be swept from the windowsills with dispiriting regularity, which (said windowsills all facing northward over the mountain-brow) compromised the grandeur of the shadowing sun, slowly sinking behind the city below. There were two ancient laundry machines rattling in the basement, but the clothes-lines were up on the roof, where my mom had to deal with her neighbours – if not vulgar in their Canadianness, more than a stone's throw from the refined daughters of Erin she was used to associating with (though not over wet laundry) and all as foreign as the Aboriginals of Papua, New Guinea, or the bunny-infested Australian outback. Eventually, she got a part-time job, not out of monetary need – my father's job was well-paying and rock solid – but the desire to meet other people her own age, and get out of the house. This in turn meant mastering the city's geography, as well as its public-transit system – my folks had just the one car, and my mother had never driven, not even in Ireland – which she stoically went ahead and mastered.

In the meanwhile, here was my father – a tax accountant for the Federal Government charged with the grave responsibility of keeping Ontario's largest industries – Stelco, Westinghouse and Otis elevator among the local examples – on the straight and narrow, tax-wise; a responsibility he approached with the gusto of a priest entrusted with the errant souls of a flock of unruly black sheep. When not thundering from his pulpit over the industrial heartland he could be found (too frequently for my mom's liking) in one of the pubs within walking distance of the old Federal building at Catharine and Main streets, in downtown Hamilton – assembled with the small coterie of fellow countrymen who might have shared his predilection for a cold draught of beer, and a little Old World companionship, after the long day's work was done. In this manner he met the five or six men who would become life-long friends, and with whom he established The Irish-

Canadian Club of Hamilton – an institution now venerable-seeming to me which honoured my dad a few years before his death with a plaque and a certificate recognizing him as one of the founding fathers of that little bit of the 'oul' sod,' which I remember so fondly, growing up, and to which he devoted so much of his energy and time, mostly filling the role of Chief Financial Officer. When not putting the fear of God into Ontario's more powerful CEOs, my father liked to chinwag over a pint with the lads – most not as well-educated as he, or so knowledgeable in the nuances of history, politics and classical music (fields of endeavour my father became more expert in with each fresh pint) – and who seem to have regarded him as an oracle, a fountain of wisdom. Well into my own adulthood, any time I ran across someone who found out I was Colm Crowley's son – and there were a lot of them! – I would be regaled with fond reminiscences extolling my dad's silver tongue, the unassailability of his logic in debate, regardless of the topic, and his maximum impressiveness in general – views I listened to with genial interest for the most part, until I couldn't help wondering just how legendary my father had become in the minds of these multitudes who praised his virtues over the years.

Could he really have been all that? This, after all, was the same man who too often left his wife to fend for herself (and his children) while he held forth on the blunders and misdemeanours of the western world, both Irish and Canadian, the British class system, the music of Ludwig von Beethoven; the man who would brook no argument or disagreement from any man or child – especially not his own children – and whose judgements on all matters tended to be harsh and final. I tread carefully here – the relationship of fathers to their sons has a long tradition, and my father is no longer here to refute my recollections, so what I say will necessarily reflect on us both, for good or ill – so let me hasten to add he was a good man too, a loving father, and something more – he possessed a restlessness of spirit that fed his curiosity about the world and somehow accounted for both his judgemental ways and his inexplicable decision to abandon the safe, comfortable world he knew so well, and at the age of thirty-three (my father was ten years older than my mother) struck out into the great unknown. He hadn't done so in search of a better version of himself, mind you – the bubble his children were growing up in was composed of his own irreducible self-confidence – but a newer version of society he could keep at arm's length, and like a mad Irish scientist study objectively from afar. In short, he was in search of a breath of fresh air, and of course he found that in Canada, in abundance.

Come the age of maybe two or three my own dim recollections of life in Canada – more specifically life on Concession Street – begin kicking in, if made misty by the novelty of existence (it was my first time here) galvanized with greater value for being first-hand. Unlike my elders, there was nothing 'foreign' about this country to me – I had nothing to feel homesick for, save non-existence, which I don't recall missing. Canada presented me with my first remembered experiences of life on earth, and with no point of comparison I was happy to find myself here, playing with my sister (my brother as yet not conceived) and the neighbourhood kids out by the wrought-iron railing that stood between us and the geometric vista of the Great City below. I vividly remember being impressed as hell by *The Wizard of Oz* when it debuted on network television – the Wicked Witch of the West so terrified me I'd literally flee the room each time she appeared – yet not impressed at all by the spell-binding view we had of Hamilton. Growing up I guess I assumed everyone had such views

– it was part of our common background, like the clouds and the noise of the traffic. We played hide-and-seek in the basement – or up on the roof – and while my sister attended kindergarten at Peace Memorial, I helped my mom with her daily chores: laundry, the shopping, the almost obsessive cleaning and tidying of her disappointing home-away-from-home; instinctively, I think I sensed there was something wistful and morose in my mother's youthful demeanour; I divined it in the way she cradled her cup of tea, gazing through the fly-speckled windows towards the lake; how defenceless and inward-dwelling she seemed when any song even remotely Irish came over the radio. Still, when the song was done, when the mood had passed, she would turn to me with a smile, and ask if I didn't want to come with her for a walk along the mountain brow, which of course, hand in hand with this pretty, forlorn brown-eyed girl, I always did.

My old man could at times be aloof and garrulous, but I never doubted his love for us all, even if poorly expressed – if he was gruff and judgemental it was part of his nature, but I never felt stupid or inadequate in his eyes. My shaky grades in the early years of my formal schooling disappointed him (those grades skyrocketed when my myopia was diagnosed, and I was fitted with glasses) but his judgemental disposition was always qualified (if never entirely suppressed) by his kindly nature. He was moved to tears one evening at parents' night for my scout-camp weekend when, during a talent contest, I delivered (solo and *a cappella*) a charming if quivery rendering of *Wild Mountain Thyme* ('Will ye Go, Lassie, Go') that pretty well brought the house down, and he remembered the experience fondly for decades. By the same token, when I came dead last – by half a lap! in a school-sponsored swim competition, he went to great pains to console me (needlessly; I'd agreed to participate only to fill out the team's roster, and that I'd lost so commandingly – comically, really – didn't bother me even slightly.) What my dad mostly did was worry about me. A lot. The business of the bad eyesight going unnoticed for so long seemed to heighten his concern; were my physical and intellectual milestones being met with alacrity? Was my evident indifference to organized religion endangering my immortal soul? Was my uncircumcised penis likely to cause me grief in the decades to come? Mostly however what my dad worried over was, for want of a better word – my *Irishness.*

This preoccupation with my 'Irishness' (and my sister's too, of course) became a source of considerable worry to both our parents, but to my father especially, which might seem incongruous considering the lengths he'd gone to drag us all (unwillingly in my mom's case) a quarter of the way around the world to get away from the place. Our roots in that distant, fabled land were something he was determined to nurture and strengthen in his children, at any cost. Not that I didn't remain plenty Irish unassisted, living as I did in a cultural bubble of indeterminate tensile strength, and from which I was reminded at every turn I was a stranger in a strange land, even into my late teens and beyond. I still recall the first time I'd heard the word 'gasoline' used to mean petrol, 'trunk' for boot, 'hood' for bonnet etc. etc. (in case you couldn't tell, my interests were turning towards cars and driving.) It was with considerable hilarity that my grade eight shop teacher, Mr. Benson, enlightened me that a heavy, metallic tool I knew perfectly well was a spanner, was in fact a 'monkey-wrench,' a sort of malapropism that conjured images of primates grunting gutturally over a rusted bolt, but that quirky revelation was as nothing compared to the mirth inspired by my sister – the superior philologist of the two of us – when she first told me the small, wheeled contraption our newly-born brother was being toured around in was not a perambulator but a 'baby carriage,' with all the royal associations thereof – four tiny horses bedecked in polished leather pulling a jewelled, golden vehicle fit for Cinderella, or Queen Elizabeth, or even (and who'd have credited it?) our chubby little newly-born brother, His Majesty the most Recently Arrived, Ben Crowley, giggling and squirming in all his princely-glory, even while his brother and sister rolled on the carpet, struggling for air from laughing so hard.

Yet somehow none of that was good enough. Our new house on the west mountain – a proper home by now on West 33rd street, though in no time we moved to an even more spacious house two blocks further west – had a television, but our father didn't approve of the programming we were beginning to absorb. In his judgement there was something vulgar (i.e. Canadian) about Bugs Bunny, Fred Flintstone, Marvin the Martian, Batman and Robin, Gilligan, the Skipper and the Professor too, and the rest of that motley crew – vulgar also after the manner of all things regarded as mere popular entertainment, and thus best avoided, Canadian or not. In good faith the old man couldn't very well forbid the watching of such trash, but he didn't like it and with his body language and frosty demeanour made his disapproval known, loud and clear. The same was even more true with regard to popular music, which my father despised with a virulent hatred. Again, he didn't ban us from listening to music – the Dave Clark Five, the Kinks, Eric Burden and War, the Who, the Stones, The Doors and by far the worse all – those kings of everything mindless, asinine and coarse in the world – the much-despised Beatles, clown princes of the frivolous masses everywhere. That almost none of these landmarks on the terrain of the Canadian culture – these unsightly blemishes on the innocence of his darling children's hearts and souls – were in fact Canadian (mostly they were British, as we were ourselves, technically, being from Northern Ireland) was beside the point. Vulgarity was vulgarity, and was to be kept outside the bubble as best one could. On the night the Beatles first played live in North America, on the Ed Sullivan show, our family was scheduled to attend an amateur play at our church – some sort of Pilgrim's Progress for tots – and bitterly resentful though I was, my older sister was inconsolable with anger and disbelief, even while our father shrugged off our childish protestations as nothing more than further proof evil was alive and well in this fallen world (in the form of a never-before-witnessed sociological phenomena rolling out right before our eyes all around the world and into the history books in real time) and shovelled us kicking and screaming into the family car, to watch a thoroughly forgettable and forgotten Passion Play, in three acts.

It was ever thus with my stern father – protector of the faith even though he had abandoned his post for a life of adventure in the frigid north. I recall one time when I'd come up to the family house, to drive him to McMaster Medical for a minor procedure he'd been cautioned not to drive to himself, Miles Davis's *Kind of Blue* was playing quietly through my car's CD player, and with a grunt my dad asked me what we were listening to. I turned up the player, told him what it was, and asked him what he made of it. 'Garbage,' he opined, flatly and with such finality I nearly burst out laughing. That my dad had no ear for anything so esoteric as jazz fusion and modal jazz – had I noticed the background whisper of Miles' most universally-loved opus, I would have turned it off as a courtesy to his rarefied sensibilities – was only the most obvious point, but what on earth did he think such a judgement was supposed to sound like to me, by then a grown man? If someone he knew – even someone he knew but didn't like! – had come up and asked his opinion of their family, would he have said, *"Your wife's ugly and your children are stupid."*? Some things you simply don't say, no matter whether you think they're true or not.

The task of maintaining and nurturing the Irishness of his children was not confined exclusively to minding what we watched on television, or listened to on the radio. My mother had taken part-time work not only to meet people her own age, but to have her own money put aside, so each year during the summer months (she detested the heat even more than the cold) she could book passage for herself and her children back home, to the world she had so reluctantly left behind in order to honour her duties of obedience to a restless, adventurous soul. I know for a fact I spent the majority of my childhood growing up in Canada, but so vividly do those regular, brief visitations – a mere month or two at each crossing – stand out in my mind (made the more memorable by their novelty and the sudden, dramatic contrast they provided to an otherwise typical Canadian boyhood) that in retrospect the two contrasting cultural reminiscences seem nicely balanced, evenly disbursed amidst the terrain of boyhood recollections, as though I had indeed grown up with one foot in either camp. I remember spending a dismal afternoon with my great-aunt Willa, on the busy urban streets of Liverpool, near the dock-yards, where she'd come to meet us after we'd disembarked from the Empress of England, and had a few hours to kill before reporting to the small, overnight ferry that would shuttle us across the way into Belfast Harbour after a week of adventure on the high seas, playing ping pong with a little British girl named Pippa. Why my mother and sister weren't with us I can't recall, but they were both prone to extreme seasickness, so maybe they were in recovery somewhere, but very vividly indeed do I remember this same old aunt turning me away (the better to protect my virgin eyes) from the sight of the brute, Liverpudlian teens and young adults bustling through the shop-lined avenues, sporting greasy, lanky hair, denim trousers and leather jackets, cigarettes drooping from their gobs with stylish, insouciant panache (emulating, though I didn't know it at the time, a young Marlon Brando and James Dean); rockers, in a world of rockers and mods as unfamiliar to me as the Forbidden City of China. Only many years afterwards did it occur to me that, if I was eight, the year was 1963, and somewhere (probably nearby) a local band called the Beatles were bestirring the lusts of these same rough-hewn kids, in a basement dive stinking of stale cigarette smoke and coffee called the Cavern Club, although of course from my perspective they may as well have been playing on Mars.

Not that life in Canada was made so unremarkable by comparison – far from it. It seems in hindsight I dragged hare-brained adventure along for the ride, regardless which side of the Atlantic I happened to be on (indeed, 'hare-brained adventure' might be the defining characteristic of *all* children's developmental years, from Alaska to Timbuktu) but Ireland, as my parents well understood, was that special thing in a world of special things, a jewel of unsurpassed beauty and uniqueness, whose authoritative stamp was to leave me for evermore thinking of myself as more Irish than Canadian.

When not yearning to be back home, my father had made it our family's summertime business to explore Canada, by car, which meant at least one long drive out to Nova Scotia, where we (fortuitously) witnessed a total eclipse of the sun (the same eclipse Carly Simon references in her song, *You're So Vain*) as well as innumerable camping trips up to Algonquin National

Park, where each year he secured the same, modest site on Pog Lake, and where inclement weather was certain to follow with uncanny predictability. There on Pog Lake (in the pouring rain) my dad would once again roll out the ancient army tent he refused to replace with anything better: a canvas-and-metal-tube *faux*-habitation, far from water-resistant. That stank of the wartime skirmishes it had been commissioned to officiate. One year, between the stretching and the assembling of this monster tent, the time honoured picking of the strawberries and wild blueberries (in the rain) and the hiking, canoeing and feeding of the deer, I was ambushed by a neighbouring camp's lunatic Alsatian, in furtherance of its plan to chew my face off – an incident that nearly brought that year's rain-clogged adventure to a halt, but (on the strength of my shaken reassurances that I was fine) didn't, though I've mistrusted dogs large and small ever since. Another year up on Pog Lake – on a dare – I bet my sister I could swim out to a small island in the middle of the lake, an act of foolhardiness my parents would never have condoned, so we set out in the early morning, with me in the spirit of the stupidly adventurous, and my level-headed sister, who knew full well how truly stupid my spirit of adventure could get, following in the canoe, for safety's sake. About three-quarters of the way to the island, my sister, who was no master seaman, clubbed me upside the head with her paddle (accidentally, right Shona? Hmmm?) Which nearly knocked me senseless and left me seeing stars, still, when I dragged myself ashore ten long minutes later.

Canada was a unique adventure, sure enough, at times painfully unique, but nothing could hold a candle to Ireland, land of my birth, rendered just exotic enough by virtue of its perennial novelty to glow with the romantic lustre of a mythical landscape come to life –

Shangri-La, Aladdin's (or Lawrence's) Arabia, Laputa, Atlantis, the strange dreamscapes of Edgar Rice Burroughs's Martian melodramas. Dreary and blustery though the weather often was, it was an Irish dreariness, an Irish bluster, each with its own special charm, an Irish scattering of weather that fell like fairy-dust from the clouds into my bedazzled eyes, which no amount of Canadian sunshine or cloudless, nondescript skies could render less bewitching. Not that I spent my time in Ireland dancing naked with the leprechauns on Slieve Donard (I didn't), but everywhere I turned seemed fecund with fresh evidence that this was a special place, a magical place, and I was made the more magical for being part of it. I recall family outings up the Antrim coast, with nothing to the west but the crashing waves of the Atlantic, rolling in from the horizon like bottle-green ranks of soldiers scattering in foamy thunder into the cliffs below; the same briny waters, trapped in a concrete harbour off Port Rush, to the South, where my sister and I (under the scrutiny of our family) paddled gleefully in circles in yellow-rubber dinghies you could rent from the harbour-master for five pence, and were guaranteed to return you to land soaked from head to foot. That same harbour inlet was crawling with marine life, and for an hour one morning I watched the ambulation of an enormous crab – a crab the width of a garbage-can lid – as it scuttled sideways across the shoals below, stopping here and there in the sand to investigate the seaweed waving in the tide, or explore the rocks for microorganisms. My homeland was all sunsets and sunrises, filled with wonder; rainbows so bright they brought the traffic to a halt, leprechauns frolicking in the mountains – it was the Emerald Isles – Shangri-La! Laputa! But I suppose of all my memories the one which will remain foremost in my mind will always be my memories of the five weeks I attended Orangefield Grammar school, in east Belfast. Yes. You read right – five weeks. After five weeks the powers-that-be at Orangefield expelled me. They kicked me out, with dark warnings that I was in dire need of psychiatric attention (at eight) and that I should never return to Orangefield Grammar again. Which (until now) I didn't.

An academic year in an Irish school had become a family tradition by the time I was sent to Orangefield. Two or three years earlier my sister had gone to the Methody School (also in Belfast – a school much-attended by the men and women in my family, including my uncle Conrad and my father) where my impression from my parents' conversations was she was not enjoying the experience. Ten months after her departure, she suddenly reappeared, with a residual Irish accent which quickly faded away, and a look in her eye that suggested she'd just stepped off a roller coaster she'd been assured would be great fun, but which had been no fun at all, and now that she was on solid ground again had the wherewithal to question not only her assumptions about the purpose of roller coasters, but the concept of 'fun' itself.

Orangefield Grammar had a similar effect on me. Many years after my brief tenure there, while working my way through Franz Kafka's The Castle, I paused at a telling scene and let out a startled breath – *whoa!* Orangefield! Not that I so much resembled the bewildered Land Surveyor K, who must report to the eponymous castle on the hill (and its officious representative, Herr Klamm) to carry out his orders, fulfil his duties (whatever they might have been) as recognized the same deep background of foreboding that hung over the place like a shroud – and neither did Orangefield particularly resemble Kafka's spooky, turreted fortress in the mountains – except insofar as its aloof presence darkened and disconnected every hint of routine human interaction, from a shared smile to the exchange of vital information, which otherwise might have been taken for granted, and without which we're left stranded with nothing to rely on but our own, isolated devices. I was ostracised and bullied at Orangefield, being a foreigner air-dropped out of the blue without explanation, which puzzled and alarmed me, and at risk for a bloody nose or two – but that wasn't what bothered me most. The worst of it was the sense that there was a hovering disconnect at Orangefield, that seemed to short circuit my every effort to bridge the gap between myself and – well- anyone with an Irish accent. Which is to say everyone. And unlike the Land Surveyor K, I got it. I got that I was now the one suffering the vertigo of the culturally disenfranchised, I was immobilized and isolated by forces beyond my control, and, incredibly, for the first time ever there was nothing I could do about it.

"You! You! You there! New boy!"

I wheeled around in the schoolyard – a little disconcerted to hear myself addressed by a teacher as something so easily dismissed as 'new boy'.

"Yes! Come here! What's this you're wearing? Where do you think you're going in those clothes?"

"Oh! Well, you know I'm –"

A condescending smile spread across this frumpy old woman's mug.

"Of course," she finally mused. "You're the Canadian boy."

"Ahh."

My experience with teachers was not vast in the early sixties, but even I knew teachers were nice people, decent souls, uniformly kind, empathetic, good natured to a fault and quick with a smile – here at Orangefield a new order of educator was being rolled out for my consideration. The default position here seemed to be frosty, ill-humoured condescension – why? As bad luck would have it, I was sitting in class on my first morning when, through his thick guttural accent, this new iteration of teacher asked what anyone could tell him about friction. His name was Mr. Gallon, and he bore a disturbing resemblance to Gomez Addams, but without the sense of humour. When called upon I demonstrated how heat was generated when your two hands are rubbed together. "That's friction, boy, friction!" Mr Gallon laughed, "I'm asking you about *fractions!*"

A chorus of callous laughter rang out, which seemed harsh even by the standards of schoolboys, but what surprised me most was how Mr. Gallon's non-reaction seemed to endorse my being laughed at by the others – childhood cruelty I understood (being a child myself) adult cruelty not so much; but teacher cruelty? That was something new. To my eight-year-old self that defied credulity – it was beyond the pale – and so dumbfounding it superseded any embarrassment I might have felt after my blunder over friction and fraction. In the Canada I had left behind such a reaction by a teacher would be unthinkable – grounds for censure – but at Orangefield it was just business as usual. How strange! Having a bit of fun at the expense of the Canadian boy, nothing more, which fit the profile of cultural disenfranchisement I was experiencing now myself, and added its weight to the burden of the experience. Like the Land Surveyor K, I was oblivious to the fact I was living in an enormous, fantastical bubble – a land of confusion – and was only too willing to shrug off the evidence I was in over my head – the squalor of the classrooms, the ink-wells and pen-nibs from when Dickens was teaching, the cobwebby windows and ancient benches where we all sat, lined up shoulder to shoulder like dominoes, a century of tough little schoolboys having carved their frustrations into the wood. In Canada kids weren't lined up behind rows of carved-up desks like galley slaves, and their teachers didn't treat them like the punchlines to a cruel joke.

"What are you looking at, wee man?"

"I'm not looking at anything."

"You're the Canadian boy."

By then I was sick of being called "the Canadian boy." I had a name. By then everyone should have known my goddamn name.

"I'm as Irish as you are."

"You should take that back, wee man – at the rate you're going you're headed for a proper cuffing."

"All I'm saying is I have a name."

It took a while for me to snap and finally do what I did. I still had two weeks of my normal self (though floating in an abnormal bubble) left in reserve, though like the hour-glass measuring Dorothy's allotted time the moment was inexorably approaching, the moment when everything was destined to change: not that things were so fraught with trouble as I feared when at their worse. Sure, I was bullied and terrorised by tough Irish kids, and condescended to by Irish teachers entrusted with my well-being, but for the most part the kids of Orangefield treated me as a curiosity and no more – an anomaly to be regarded as such. After all, I was a species whose existence had never been dreamed of, and treated as a welcome novelty. Only by my family and a clan of eight children – the Donnelley children – who lived in the house next door to my grandmother's in east Belfast, not ten minutes from Orangefield Grammar – was I regarded as anything more. Across the road from the house in that curiously zoned neighbourhood was an enormous building from which each morning an aroma of freshly baking bread spilled into the neighbourhood. What a great smell! I loved waking up to that smell – and I enjoyed the company of Danny Donnelley, whose sympathy for my unique plight I appreciated very much indeed. We were like two peas in a pod, Danny and I, for the brief time we were friends in Ireland, though since then Danny has become a highly regarded academic and mainstay in the Belfast Presbytery, one of Orangefield's most celebrated ex-students (second only to Van Morrison, the dreamy founder of Celtic mystic folk-rock, who wrote an eponymous song about his alma mater) while I was the Canadian juvenile delinquent who was expelled almost before he'd arrived.

"You think you're pretty tough, don't you, wee man?"

"Look – just leave me alone!"

"The wee man thinks he's brave!"

One time Danny and I threw a stink-bomb (glass-encased globules of sulpha, legally obtainable by children in Belfast, unheard-of in Canada) into that bakery, then ran like hell, to see what would happen next. (Nothing.) Behind the bakery, a filthy stream – partially clogged into a swamp of industrial effluvia – contained the remains of an ancient wooden boat, which we played pirates on without a second thought for the witch's brew of rotting flour and yeast that had been fomenting back there since time began. We went to the Queen's University's Museum of Ancient History, where within a box of glass the papery remains of a mummy grinned out at us – at me – as though in knowing anticipation of what was to come. In the soccer pitch behind my grandmother's house old Mrs. Grogan kept a goat on a chain, which we would play with on

Saturday mornings. But none of this took away from the drizzle of condescension from the teachers, the canings for the smallest infraction to the rules (capital punishment having been phased out of Canadian schools by that time, except for the most egregious infractions) and of course the bullying and threats from a small group of boys who seemed especially to have it in for me.

Then there was the knife. On Canadian television I had seen Tonto (of Lone Ranger fame) hurl a knife end over end at a tree, where it struck home and twanged with a satisfying *thunk!*, and I was hell-bent to learn the trick. I dug an old spring-loaded knife out of my father's tool-kit (later up-graded to a proper Bowie knife, with birthday money) and after a few thousand practice throws spaced over many months, I was able to torque the knife into a tree fifty percent of the time, then eighty, and then nearly every time. Not surprisingly, I brought this talent (along with the knife) with me to Ireland, so as to impress the kids in the neighbourhood.

"Ooch! It's the wee Canadian lad! Look lads! It's the—"

"Shut the fuck up! Shut up! Shut up! Shut up!"

On the playground the next morning a new attitude prevailed, not only amongst the children of Orangefield, but their teachers as well – their teachers especially – an attitude which pervaded every nook and cranny of the ancient brick buildings – the Dickensian classrooms, the foul-smelling cafeterias, and the corridors formerly bristling with the threat of imminent assault – the very places where Van Morrison had stocked up ten years earlier on everything he would need to spin his mystical, Irish blarney into popular song. Now I was no longer the 'wee lad', the 'new boy' or the 'Canadian boy' but the crazy savage from the wilds of the untamed Canadian west, who had threatened to saw the heads off a small group of innocent schoolboys, minding their own business on a sunny summer day, for no better reason than that they breathed the same air he breathed. After an unusually civilized lunch-period I was summoned to the principal's office, where my mother and grandmother both sat waiting, and was informed that perhaps Orangefield Grammar and I weren't such a good match, after all. The principal's manner was aloof and reserved of judgement (as opposed to the manner of sadistic glee I'd grown accustomed to, and which he barely suppressed while caning me for being two minutes late to elementary Maths) but that did little to mitigate my mother's undisguised scorn for a system that would allow her son to be harassed and bullied for weeks, then, when he finally reacted in kind, to suggest the problem lay with the boy, and perhaps psychiatric intervention might be in order.

In any event my life in Belfast was much improved after that, and I took to educating myself in Belfast's many public libraries, museums, art galleries and spacious botanical gardens, where during school hours I was free to roam at will, wherever my natural inquisitiveness might take me. There were four of them out on the soccer pitch that fateful weekend, the same four bullies who had been tormenting me for weeks, so why they didn't just take the knife from my hands and beat the shit out of me is a mystery – I'm guessing they saw something in my eyes that convinced them a hasty retreat was the wiser course of action. But my lesson had been learned as well. This odd life I was living, as a mechanical toy suspended on a wire between two disparate cultural environments – a boy in a bubble watching the world through a necessarily distorted field – was both a blessing and a curse: one which, for the thousandth time, I vowed to embrace with all the passion and fervour of my youthful heart, to be born again, to be born again.

Long Ride Up

"This is bad."

"That's enough, Winter."

That was my brother, Ben. The realist. The anchor.

"It's bad. it makes for bad fiction! It defies credulity!"

"Duly noted."

"That doesn't help us much," my sister Shona sighed.

"Or her," my brother muttered.

It wasn't much of an elevator – vertical transportation for hospital business only, not visitors. Industrial somehow, but intended for the dead and dying too, a steel car with wrap-around gun-metal handrails at hip level, utilitarian, grimy with ghostly handprints. The elevator was choking with ghosts. Everything was. Ghosts hovered over the corridors and nurse stations. Ghosts shadowed the orderlies. They lay dormant in supply closets, recumbent behind stacks of sterilized gauze, boxes of disposable plastic syringes, waiting, watching, drawing up their plans. Didn't they ever clean these things? If you woke from a nightmare in this anonymous box, you would intuit first that you were in a service elevator, and that the service elevator was in a hospital – along with library elevators the slowest rising objects ever to defy the law of gravity.

But not slow enough, as far as I was concerned. If the cable were to snap and we to plunge to our inglorious deaths, that would be just fine by me. Better that than what waited above.

The hospital had called me at home not an hour before.

"Mr. Crowley?"

"Yes – who is this please?"

"My name is Gabrielle. I'm calling from St. Joseph's. Are you Winston Crowley? Can you come over to the hospital, Winston?"

"Sure. Is my mother OK?"

"Your mom's OK, but we need to talk. Your sister's going to be here shortly."

"Shona's there?"

"She'll be here shortly."

"And Ben?"

"Your brother's here."

It was Sunday morning, a cold day in mid-February. By rights at this hour my brother ought to have been in church, with our father. My mom was finally scheduled to come home the next afternoon, and my first thought, after that call, had been *"Jesus! Now* what?"

What more could go wrong? It was a reasonable question. My mother had been entombed in St. Joseph's – five minutes from where I lived – for four long months. She had been admitted the previous October 31st, Halloween morning, for a hip replacement, her third, her first evidently having reached its best-before date. My sister Shona brought her down that Halloween morning, and I had agreed to meet them at the hospital main entrance, and help shepherd our frail, stoic, primly dressed mother through the routines of admittance, and preparation for what was to come.

That was seven-thirty All Hallows Eve morning. I remember my courageous mother, dressed as though for church at the crack of dawn, sitting in the waiting room in a stiff-backed chair, looking every bit the brave child awaiting harsh words from some scolding elder, while I went in search of Shona, still out parking her car. By eleven that night my sister, brother, father and I were pacing the post-op waiting room, nearly five hours past when her surgery should have concluded.

"Something's gone wrong."

"This is routine surgery," my optimistic father reminded us. "And your mother's now had three of them."

"I know, I know, dad. It's routine surgery. Nothing ever goes wrong, until something does."

"Let's try and stay hopeful, Winter," my sister added glumly.

"They stack these surgeries up back-to-back, and squeeze them into a day," added Ben. "Like an assembly line. Anything–"

The surgeon came in just then, dressed not in scrubs but a suit and tie, eager to take his leave. The long delay had been due to difficulty with our mother's previous artificial hip, which calcified bone had welded to the stump of her femur, creating "one hell of a problem" getting it out of there. I had visions of exhausted, frustrated mechanics yanking, pulling and banging away at a rusted-out bolt, with large monkey-wrenches and hammers, until finally it was time to break out the blow-torches.

"She'll be OK though, right?"

"Once we got the old one out, everything went perfectly," the weary doctor assured us. "She's going to be fine."

Except she wasn't.

As hours turned to days, then many days, a flurry of alarmed activity began swirling around my mother's semi-private room. Far from improving, she began exhibiting symptoms unrelated to her surgery. Her legs began swelling, and she was too weak to prop herself on an elbow, let alone crawl out of bed, assisted or not. Slowly but surely she was beginning to look like death. By the fourth or fifth day her nurses were no longer greeting us each evening with guarded, cheerful optimism. Her doctors' clinical officiousness was replaced with genuine puzzlement. New blood-work was ordered. Something disastrous was afoot. Her veins were swimming in clots (which explained the swollen legs) and she was put on ever-more potent blood thinners and 'clot busters,' to no obvious avail. Wall-to-wall X-rays and specimen samples were ordered and pored over. A week passed, then another, time spent to no avail treating my mother's blood clots. Their best efforts had failed to stem the clotting, and a full body EKG finally revealed what the X-rays had not. The discovery was an alarming one.

Undetected on her X-rays, my mother's pulmonary artery had been partially choked off by what her doctors described as, not so much a blood clot, as an 'enormous amorphous mass,' which had been building up, possibly, for years. This explained symptoms which had previously baffled her family doctor. Occasional trouble breathing (her lungs were tip-top); periodic weakness in her limbs and cold extremities (her blood pressure and blood sugar were fine), so that explained that. What to do about it was a grievously different question, and her status was downgraded from 'baffling' to 'life-threatening,' as the search for a solution quickly turned desperate.

The answer blessedly fell out of the sky from Ottawa, where an ambitious young surgeon named Fraser Rubens was spearheading a cutting-edge operating procedure, and my mother's predicament couldn't have fit his bill better. So the nurses wrapped my weary but ever-stoic mother warmly – after more than eight weeks her stoicism had become the stuff of legend – and arrangements were made to air-lift her, by helicopter, around mid-December, to the University of Ottawa Heart Institute, where the likelihood of her survival jumped from incalculably abysmal to fifty/fifty, which sounded pretty good to me.

Dr Rubin's procedure was a little tricky. Let me walk you through it.

The doctors were going to place the woman who gave me birth on a table, anaesthetise her, lower her body temperature, drain her blood and stop her heart, then saw her open down the centre of her chest. Then they were going to pry open her rib-cage, and remove (carefully! carefully!) her heart and lungs, so as to create a clean line to her pulmonary artery, harbourer of her 'amorphous mass.'

The next step – now that she was good and cold and split-open and (temporarily! temporarily!) dead, was simply to slice open the artery, scoop out the guck, flush her out like a carburettor, sew the artery closed, replace the heart and lungs, close up her rib-cage, sew up her chest, pump her blood (kept warm artificially all this time) back into her, restart her heart, then wheel her away to sleep it off.

"One of us should speak for us all," my sister suggested. "When we get up there. If we all walk in with this it'll be too much."

"I'll do it," my brother said, grimly.

"That's A-OK with me," I said.

"Me too," Shona said.

Incredibly, the operation was scheduled for midnight of December 31st. The last day of the year 2004. Perhaps Dr. Rubens had a sense of humour, or maybe he was just a busy guy. Victor Frankenstein with a humanitarian agenda. A brand new year was waiting in the wings, beckoning. Ben, Shona, my father, my aunt Kathleen – my mom's sister – and I had individually made our way up to Ottawa, to be there for her and to collectively worry and fret. The weather in Ottawa, as usual for December, was bitterly cold; lunar-like conditions, the whole city seemingly encased in a glittering exoskeleton of ice, as beautiful as any winter scene but brutally hard to walk through. We'd gotten rooms in a residence for med students that was attached to the Heart Institute, just around the corner. On a sunny summer day the two buildings were a five minute stroll apart. Getting from one to the other in December, it felt like you were taking your life in your hands.

My mom had arrived well before the scheduled surgery, for tests. She joked that here she was in the capital city of Canada, for the first time in decades, and she was stuck in yet another hospital. The next morning I braved the cold and bought a disposable camera at a pharmacy, and began taking pictures. For posterity. On the night of the surgery my sister and aunt and I were sitting around, just about as glum as three people could be, while my father and brother watched television in the next room, and we decided to taxi into town for a drink.

I didn't really feel like going but my aunt thought it would be a good idea, morale-wise. We found a pub which, at ten o'clock, wasn't yet too full of New Year's revellers, though it was still pretty busy. We drank our drinks and got party hats. I still have mine – it's signed and dated, and it's sitting on the television in my home office, like the jaunty little keepsake it is. I'm looking at it right now.

Happy New Year 2005

While my mom was at St. Joe's – both before and after the operation – I got to know my father very well. For the first time in our lives it seemed we had a compelling common concern. Every night during those long months I drove up to the family house to collect him, and bring us both down to the hospital. While my mom was sick he was living alone, probably for the first time in his life. That worried me. He seemed to be handling it well, however, except for one thing.

"You know, when mom finally gets home again, you're going to have to quit smoking in here."

"I know, son."

The air in the house had taken on a bluish tinge, from his incessant smoking.

On the trip down to the hospital we talked – not as father and son, but for the first time as two men with a shared fear, and a common hope. My father knew my belief in God was not as his own, and, diplomatically, over the years religion was a subject we left alone between us. One of many. It had snowed all day, but now the sky was clear, and electric with stars. A full moon hung low on the horizon, trembling in the sky like a tri-master billowed out under full sail, propelled on a cosmic wind.

"So beautiful," my father said quietly.

"Aye."

"The world has such a lovely order to it, don't you think?"

You could hear the worry in his voice.

"The Greeks had a word for it. Teleological," I said. "Purposeful from afar."

"Aye."

"She's going to be OK, Dad. Right?"

"Right."

Then something on the car radio caught my attention, and I turned up the volume. "Oh, listen to that! That's interesting."

"What is, Winter?"

"Beethoven's Violin Concerto in D. But listen! It's been scored for piano," I laughed in wonder. "That's weird. I must have listened to the violin version a hundred times."

"It's hard to believe, sometimes," said my dad, who also worshipped Beethoven, listening to the Concerto, "that such a man ever walked the earth as flesh and bone."

"Aye."

When finally we completed the long ride up, from St. Joe's morgue to the fourth floor, where my mother was looking forward after four months to returning to her normal life with her husband on the west mountain, my sister, brother and I paused and mentally caught our collective breath. Everyone dies. That's an inescapable fact. The human race has figured out the mysteries of space and time, the expanding universe, the genesis of self-awareness, the causes and cure of many diseases, but not death. One fine day my mother will die, I know that, as will I, as will Ben and Shona, and as will you. It should come as no surprise except when it does. Throughout the hospital ward where she slowly but surely got well again, after her surgery in Ottawa, my mother was known as the miracle patient. I don't think any of them thought she would survive her ordeal, and I confess I didn't think so either. It never occurred to me that of the two of them it would be my dad who would not survive. That he didn't still haunts me, to this very day, even while my mother (thank God!) continues to live and breathe, a miracle, a stoic, the woman who gave me life. I'm profoundly grateful for her continued existence, but I think about my father every day. I miss my dad, obnoxious and perplexing though he could be. I still find myself looking for him on every street. It's hard to believe that such a man had ever walked the earth, as flesh and bone.

Death Slips on a Banana Peel

Why am I alive? Why are *you* alive? I'm not complaining or anything. I firmly believe the world is a better place with me in it, especially for me. And neither, when I ask the question, am I necessarily speaking in an ontological, teleological or existential sense – more in a Curley, Larry and Moe sense. A Keystone Cops sense. Because when you think about it, few and far between are the adults walking amongst us who haven't defied, not just the cosmic, but the *comedic* odds – some of us on truly stooge-like orders of magnitude, rising to a whole new level of stupidity, surviving the random pratfalls and disasters of childhood. Probably that's why kids are born so resilient. When you finally get to be an adult, and intelligent and stuff, evolution reluctantly concedes you can afford to start getting fragile. But beware! You may not be out there looking for them, but you might yet slip on a banana peel, and not just in the metaphorical sense.

If children didn't come equipped with a built-in (and deeply flawed) sense of their own, indestructible natures, we'd have to conclude they were suicidal. Mercifully, just the opposite is true. Far from lusting for self-annihilation, what children seek is adventure, and in the pursuit of it willingly run face-first into telephone poles, drown in rivers, stick knives into electrical sockets, fall down stairs, drop into lidless storm-sewers, swagger out into traffic, jump from roof-tops, detonate fire-crackers in their hands, swan-dive into shallow water, and much more besides. By rights, the oldest person on earth should be fifteen. But miraculously, most of us dodge these childhood bullets, and as grown-ups, though we may still take reckless chances, we usually avoid suicidal ones. Sure, we play the Lottery and tune in to network TV. We jump from airplanes for thrills and voluntarily drink Jägermeister. Harmless risks all; timid risks, which we earn the right to experience only through a relinquishment of our sense of wonder. I could ask, "Is it worth it?" but since I'm still here, I guess it is.

I can't speak for the stupid things I did when too young to remember, obviously – you'd need to ask my mom about that, and she'd be delighted to tell you. The first thing I *do* remember, is shuffling sleepily towards the family bathroom, at five one memorable morning, and impaling the ball of my foot on a sewing needle. What such an object was doing in the carpet of our second-floor landing, I couldn't tell you. I'm guessing my mom wasn't booby-trapping the house against incontinent children. I trundled on, undeterred, to the bathroom, had my little bowel movement, delivering into the porcelain bowl a pellet such as a bunny might have pooped, and only then investigated the strange sensation emanating from the bottom of my foot. The needle going in had not been painful – but I remember vividly a sensation such as I had never experienced before, and even at the age of four, it felt – *incorrect*. So I took a look, and didn't like what I saw one bit – four inches of cotton thread curled out from between my wriggling toes – when I gave it a tug I could see the needle it was threaded through wasn't going anywhere. So huh. Imagine that. That's a sticky wicket. The obvious thing when you're such an age is to wipe your butt, wrap the errant thread around your toe, crawl back into bed, and suffer Mr. Sandman to escort you back to the land of pleasant dreams. But this was different, and not one bit of it did I like. Plus, my foot was starting to throb. The idea of awakening – and alarming – my mom and dad at such an hour seemed beyond the makings of slapstick comedy, as unthinkable as asking them to flood the basement for a fishing-hole, or borrowing the family car; but awaken them I did, and as you can imagine, mayhem ensued.

Speaking of threading needles, when I was twelve I began using our pool-time at Westmount High School to see how close to clusters of my fellow students, without killing anyone, I could get while needling into the water from the six-meter board; a height it had taken me months to master my fear of, and from which the pool could have been bone-dry, for all I could tell, myopic little existentialist that I was. Why so ill-considered, you wonder? Why so stupid? Good questions. The only answer I can credit has something to do with children's universal inability to foresee future consequences – the moment is now and the future non-existent, *ergo* inconsequential. It's sort of like Pascal's wager, in reverse. In the absence of a vengeful God there's no future, and salvation resides in worship of the forgiving now. It's not that kids are inherently stupid, it's just that their common sense buttons haven't been installed yet. So the Great Wager is won not when you die, and flutter off to heaven, but when you survive, and stagger into adulthood, which makes children both wise beyond their years, and susceptible to violent death. They dive from precarious perches, from one existence into another, with no thought to the possibility that their life (and someone else's) might be extinguished in an instant.

A yielding substance like water is of course as nothing compared to ice, when it comes to fulfilling the existential yearnings of the stupidly young. Have you ever tried to knock down a tree with your face? I have, and I can't say I can recommend it. For Christmas, 1965 – the year I was ten – my parents caved to my incessant whining and bought me a set of beginner skis and poles. Frothing with excitement, I trundled over to what the kids all called The Old Lady's Hill (more formally, the Idyllwild Manor retirement facility, on the west mountain) and with an unearned bravado I strapped these polished planks to my feet, only quickly to find on my very first run I was stuck in the ruts of a bobsled that had just finished crashing on the hill. What I remember of the next moment was an impact and a bright flash – a small dilation as of the eye of God momentarily opening upon the City of Gold – a blink followed by stars – billions and billions of stars; whole galaxies of traumatized unconsciousness packed into a moment. When I reopened my eyes, much to my amazement, I was still alive, and there I lay, crumpled and shivering in a mound of blood-splattered snow, with a circle of worried faces looking down, unblinking. In defiance of the general consensus, I struggled to my feet, touched a finger gingerly to my face, and determined from the results to walk directly home. My mom met me at our front door – she took one look at me standing there, a little sheepishly, and, yes, once again, ladies and gentlemen – mayhem. Our family doctor was called to our home (back then family doctors did that) and spent thirty long minutes plucking tree-bark and dirt out of my cheek with tweezers, muttering unhappily the whole while. I was but ten, and already Dr. Osbaldestine was getting fed-up with my adventurous predilections.

Many such hair-raisers and barn-burners were crunched (ahem) into those years, surrounding that mishap. Five anxiety-charged weeks at a public school in Belfast; playground encounters with hard objects and sharp projectiles; a most memorable circumcision – but they fell within the arena of God's decree (as opposed to Winston's divine fiat) where childhood experience tends towards self-inflicted disaster. We grew up – my sister and brother and I – on the lip of the Niagara escarpment – our little part known affectionately as 'Hamilton Mountain' – a terrain tailor-made for the carrying out of just such fiats, in spades. The escarpment, due to the drama of the swath it cuts, dividing Hamilton into a lower and upper-city, is assumed to be a fault-line, like the Marianas trench or the San Andreas fault in California – but it's not. It was brought into being some four-hundred million years ago by the slow build-up and compaction of silt, making it not a fault but a *cuesta*. You're welcome. Whatever you call it, that enormous crack in the geography was no mountain, yet to those living within trundling distance it was plenty formidable. It was our Himalaya, our Khumbu Icefall, our magnet, our playground, our scenery, our teacher, and our cautionate warning – not that we heeded it. The top of the senior hill at the Chedoke Ski Club began at the foot of the street I lived on, so during the winter months, often seven nights a week, I would trundle on over there, then ski down that shale-compacted *cuesta* to the clubhouse, where I bought a lift-ticket to further my self-destructive aspirations. The trail I needed to take to get to the clubhouse was marked NO SKIING, but such instructions were meant for the faint of heart, and routinely I skied it and many others until I was nineteen, at which point I finally learned the lesson I had failed to learn (see: *Wager, Pascal's*, above) nine long years before. "You know, Winter," sighed the much-put-upon Dr. Osbaldestine, "By some miracle this leg isn't broken.

But you jammed it good. In years to come, this injury is going to come back to haunt you."

Prophetic words, and not the first ringing out – like teleological bells – from the mysteries of childhood's end. I am the product of a deeply religious family – their fervour for the strict Irish-Protestant tradition probably dates back to the Norman conquest. Sadly, I was the exception to that tradition – to my younger self my family's devotion to Protestantism and its rituals registered as little more than an eccentricity, an aberration, like their adherence to the Irish culture or their lilting, lyrical accents. My stubborn unwillingness (as my family saw it) to buy into the orthodoxies of the faith distressed my father more than I'll ever know, although I know he feared the damnation of my soul; *that* I know with certainty. But as a child all I knew was I was expected to attend church, receive the blessings of the sacrament, sing the old hymns and bow my head in fervent prayer – but the requisite sincerity was beyond my ability to display. This God whom my family worshiped seemed as phantasmagorical as a voice from a burning bush, a chimera no mortal man could comprehend, let alone interpret. Or take seriously. So Pascal's Wager for me was a non-starter, not to be indulged. It also didn't hurt that, like children everywhere, I regarded myself as indestructible.

Having said that, let me now say this – even a non-existent God must necessarily be merciful. That's the *ontological* wager, in reverse, as devised for indestructible children; something so great nothing greater can be imagined can't be real – but since God *can* be imagined, God must be real. *Ipso facto* God is both real and not real at the same time. Perhaps that proof is the exclusive provenance of divinity – the *quid pro quo* to the miracle of existence. Only in adulthood do we begin to doubt our own imaginations. One bright, cold afternoon my sister and I took that wager – we were fourteen and eleven respectively – over by the craggy lip of the brow, where we often went to explore, scampering cheerfully up and down through the bracken and rough shale, delighting in our existence, and daring fate to prove our delight misplaced.

"Winter," my sister said. "I don't – We can't get up this way."

"No."

"It's slippery, too icy. We'll need to go back."

"OK." We turned to retrace our steps, only to find that how we'd arrived here in the first place somehow had been swallowed in a complex chaos of slippery slopes, impenetrable thickets, tall trees, and broken walls of jagged shale and limestone. Deep canyons of ice tilted towards the sky, so precipitously that just looking up at them made me dizzy. We were a good forty feet down the side of the escarpment – further down than we'd ever climbed before. So huh. That was a sticky-wicket. I sat down on an icy rock, and in doing so slid forward and nearly off the edge of a twenty-foot drop.

"Winston! No! Be careful!"

I squirmed a little, the better to secure my ass to the slope, only to find any such effort only served to reduce what little purchase my ass had even further. Shona plopped herself down to one side, in some snow, then put out a mitten.

"It's better here," she said. "Take my hand. I'll–"

Just then she slipped herself, laterally, and with a terrified squeak skidded right into me, knocking us both sideways into a small, icy crevasse formed by two slabs of snow-capped shale. We landed rough, then just sat there for a while, small and terrified, stunned into silence, no longer fierce explorers, hunters of the mighty polar bear, war-torn soldiers bloodied in the trenches or even that most recent of dazzling heroes, American astronauts – this all happened during the course of NASA's Gemini program – but two dirty, exhausted, thoroughly scuffed children, terrified and on the brink of panic. I looked up into my sister's beautiful eyes, and she looked at me. We were in trouble. That much was chiselled into our expressions. The only thing to be determined was, how insurmountable that trouble was going to be – and it occurred to me with maximum alarm that trouble might have *no upper limit;* that, not unlike with the astronauts, even the sky isn't the limit – but how could that be? Could disaster potentially be unlimited? Could disaster be like a balloon – which might expand tentatively to the size of a children's party decoration before popping comically, but also might expand exponentially, before exploding in a booming fireball that consumes us all? Shona sat there beside me, bug-eyed with fear; this charming, Irish muffin who had known me all my life – her dark hair blowing wildly around her face, her sparkling eyes darkened by a fear that froze her expression and swallowed her childish assumptions, as it had swallowed my own.

So huh.

"You remember Nana's book, Winter?" my sister asked me. "Nana's Jesus book?"

Nana's Jesus book. I remembered it. I'm remembering it now. Only the Christmas before, my mother's own mother – our nana – had visited from Ireland. Along with the toys, tweeds, scones, rashers and righteous indignation, to find herself in a land of banked snow and howling winds, she also brought a book for me, entitled *The Saving Power of Jesus*, a slender, beautifully-illustrated collection of anecdotes about the miraculous interventions of 'gentle Jesus,' who answered the prayers of children in distress. Nothing subtle there, but Irish Presbyterianism isn't a nuanced religion, and neither was our nana. So Shona and I prayed the recurring prayer of *The Saving Power of Jesus,* up there in the crags and crevasses, while a ferocious wind howled through our hair and clothing and death threatened to slip on a banana peel. We prayed fervently, she and I, with earnest conviction. The prayer goes as follows. Shona went first.

Gentle Jesus, are you there?
Hear you this my troubled prayer
Spare me from this dreadful plight
Even if just for one night.

Our parents were unhappy when finally we got home that night, thirty minutes late for dinner, a big breach of Presbyterian etiquette, until they saw the state we were in, at which point, alas, well, you can imagine. Mayhem. We were bedraggled and scratched from head to foot, caked in bloody mud and beyond exhausted. The details of how we arrived in that dire state got distorted in the explaining, I need hardly tell you, the better to spare our childish dignity from the consequence of our stunted decision-making skills. Indeed, until this very moment I have mentioned the 'Gentle Jesus' prayer my sister and I bowed our heads and sent up to heaven so fervently that day to no-one. It was our little secret, not for any good reason, other than an unspoken suspicion that to speak of it might compromise the great miracle it had somehow triggered. Because somehow we survived. Do children think that way? Does God *work* that way? Perhaps not in so many words; words, and their usefulness in further explicating our understanding of childhood, and of heaven and earth, are in the adult domain, as is adult doubt in an unimaginable god, both real and non-existent, which lose much in the translation.

Gentle Jesus, are you there?

My second big skiing accident – as foreseen, my hip has been bothering me five long years now – signalled the end of the disastrous close-encounters I could shrug off as the stuff of childhood. Not too much later came the alcohol and drug years – for a decade those years rolled out with a vengeance, descending on me like a blizzard. For the sake of those who know me and assume I was always the respectable educator and *auteur* I am today, I think I'll just skip those years. Massive ingestion of pot, acid, and cocaine chased down with a lake of whiskey neither add nor detract from the ontological wager, and had no obvious effect on the frequency (or severity) of my casual collisions with fate. Neither did they damage my stellar academic performance, or blunt my ambition, so I guess as a poster boy for the 'Just Say No!' movement, I make a poor candidate. I certainly didn't quit all that to safe-guard my respectability. I guess I just outgrew the bullshit. So I didn't die of an overdose – or in a fiery car crash – for the same reason I didn't crush my skull diving from the high-diving board – it wasn't God's decree but Winston's divine fiat. Which may be another way of saying I drew the luck of the draw. The luck of the Irish.

Hear you this my troubled prayer

Out in the wind-blasted fields of a little town called Hope there's a sprawling cemetery. This is where we buried my father. He won Pascal's wager. The stone that stands above his grave is actually a dual memorial marker – one day it will also commemorate my mother's existence, but the date of her death is missing as yet. My uncle Albert is buried out there, as well, as is my uncle James. Winners all. The markers have multiplied over and over again since the day we laid my father to rest. When we buried my uncle Albert there were only a small handful of them. Now there's no end to them. My cousin and her husband even have a grave on reserve, marked by a headstone with everything on it but their dates of death, which have yet to occur. *There's* forward thinking for you! They'll bury my sister and brother there, of that I'm sure – and no doubt one fine day that's where they'll bury me. That's OK. It's a very quiet place, filled with many people I know and love, with plenty yet to come. Winners all, of Pascal's wager. My headstone will read:

Here lie the mortal remains of
Winston James Colm Crowley
1955 06 10 – 2039 02 17
"I'M WITH THEM!"